Dragons Walk Among Us

A Novel

Jackson von Altek

in·tel·li·gent·ia

This first edition is published by
Intelligentia Entertainment Development Corp.
29 Whittier Ave.
Trenton, New Jersey
USA 08618

Library of Congress Cataloging-in-Publication data is available upon request.

ISBN-13: 978-0985411725
ISBN-10: 0985411724

For Timothy James

Dragons Walk Among Us

Preface

I can still recall the exact moment when I became interested in the genre of adventure fantasy. When I was in second grade I was visiting the library with my class one afternoon and I came across a book that featured the work of the artist Frank Frazetta. Frank created larger-than-life creatures based on brawny men often juxtaposed over busty females. His bold images immediately captivated me. Upon seeing these images, an intense sexual curiosity developed in my young mind. I remember catching myself after a moment of being lost in the fantasy and sexual energy of his work and quickly looking around the large room, which was filled with my classmates and teachers, to make sure I had not been discovered. While there is nothing obscene or pornographic about Frank's work, it created an immediate string of stories that ran through my mind surrounding his characters. It was a marvelous moment. My young mind, for the first time, began to explore the existence of fantastical stories that fueled sexuality. I closed the book and was completely surprised when I was able to check it out under the watchful eye of our strict, aging librarian. With the book under my arm, I ran almost a full mile to my home.

I have been a storyteller for as long as I can remember. I derive tremendous satisfaction in capturing the attention and imagination of an audience, whisking them away from daily life, and taking them on an unexpected adventure. For many years now, I have been encouraged by my audiences and my friends who have enjoyed my storytelling to write. I finally reached a point in my life where I could sit down and devote the necessary time to complete a proper piece of work. I will be the first to admit that it is far easier to tell a story to an audience than to put it down on paper. I will also confess that it is far easier to write when you have talented editors working along side of you.

At the beginning of this project, I had a large number of stories that I had developed over the years from which to choose. I chose this particular story because of my frustration with the treatment of fantasy in modern-day entertainment. Fantasy is in most instances always geared towards, or at least anchored in, a young audience. While I enjoy these works, they always feel incomplete to me as an adult. I always think back to the work of Frank Frazetta.

While working on this novel I came across the work of Hollywood photographer, Justin Monroe. Justin's vision as an artist is incredible. It is an intelligent blend of fantasy and eroticism. I was lucky enough to meet him and have his encouragement while working on the story.

I challenged myself in my first written work to craft a story in the framework of a fantasy trilogy, specifically written for adult gay men. I hesitate to call this an erotic novel as eroticism is not the main theme or ultimate goal of the work. There are erotic moments within the text but they are a necessity in telling the story of adult characters that are searching for and finding love. Were I not to include their sexuality, I would be robbing the characters of the element that truly makes them human.

It is my sincere hope that this book, and the trilogy's two remaining books, will take you on a fantastical adventure that leads you far away from our less-than-perfect everyday world.

Jackson von Altek
January 2012

A boy who is loved never grows old and never dies.

CHAPTER I

Perched high atop the only hill overlooking Paris, the neighborhood of Montmartre has a centuries-old reputation for being the home to the underbelly of Paris society. This is thanks to the many men and women who have successfully sought out the city's unique location in order to quench their thirst for the occasional or more frequent foray into debauchery. In modern times, some residents would argue that things have changed in Montmartre, and that perhaps its once well-earned reputation was, in fact, more myth and legend. Still, there are always those Parisians who disagree.

This was to be the night's planned destination for seventeen-year-old Jean Paul. Located in the 18th arrondissement, Montmartre was far from the boy's own neighborhood in the 6th, not only in distance, but also in personality. Jean Paul had suffered greatly throughout his childhood despite growing up in a wealthy family. He lived in the cold dark shadow of his father, one of France's wealthiest industrialists. He was starved for affection from his father while forbidden to see his mother. His father had filed for a divorce just five hours after Jean Paul was born and the boy had been immediately removed from her care. While Montmartre would seem an unlikely place for a young man of Jean Paul's age and family stature, he made the trip nightly, only to return home to his more prestigious address just before dawn. He had become expert at silently entering his father's apartment in the predawn hours without waking the servants and slipping into his bed undetected by anyone.

To compensate for the unresolved relationship with his father and loss of his mother, Jean Paul had developed a habit of using crystal meth to dampen his lingering pain. Two years of constant abuse of the substance had taken its toll on his face and body. A once handsome and youthful boy, he was becoming increasingly drawn in the face and hardened. While the unfortunate and frightening visible effects of crystal meth addiction would normally have alarmed any parent, his father did not view the visible changes in his son's appearance as negative. His father detested Jean Paul's mother, whom Jean Paul strongly resembled. When the addiction began to rob Jean Paul of his facial beauty and resemblance to his mother, Jean Paul's father was so pleased that the reason for the change was never even contemplated.

When Jean Paul had no cash, he would steal an antique book from his father's library to sell on the street. That evening, his father had an unexpected meeting with a business associate in the library after work, which was unusual as he normally kept his business away from his home. This unexpected delay caused Jean Paul to contemplate taking some silverware from the dining room, but he could think of no place to sell it at that late hour. He did know where he could sell a book. He sat on the corner of his bed, slowly running his hands back and forth over his thighs, and listened for the library door to open. After what seemed like an eternity, he finally heard the door, followed by voices and footsteps down the hall. Jean Paul slipped into the library, pulled a book from a high shelf, and left the apartment. This unanticipated delay would now cause him the misfortune of being late. As his addiction progressed, he had given up on any attempts of subscribing to fixed times or schedules. His only concern was that his meth dealer, Benoit, never liked to wait for him, and would surely demonstrate his anger.

Jean Paul was an addict, but he made every attempt to be responsible with his drug use as he was aware of the negative affect it could have on his father's reputation. He could have easily bought drugs in his own neighborhood, or better yet, have them delivered to his apartment; however, he purposely traveled to the other end of the city where he was less likely to be recognized or discovered. He never used his mobile phone to contact Benoit, thereby avoiding any possible digital trace of his activities. If discovered, his addiction would provide the French press with a sensational story about the son of one of its wealthiest citizens, which would deeply embarrass his father and reinforce the distance that lay between them.

Jean Paul took the Métro across the city, exited the train at Montmartre, and walked to the central square where the street artists gathered each day to sell their art. There, he located a young American man, Malcolm, sitting on the curb next to his giant white dog. Jean Paul could rely on Malcolm to give him immediate cash in exchange for his father's book.

"Bonsoir, Malcolm," Jean Paul called out to get Malcolm's attention.

"Bonsoir," Malcolm replied as he looked up from stroking the dog.

"I have a book to sell." Jean Paul held out the book for Malcolm's inspection.

Malcolm stood up and took the book to examine it. "I can't afford to pay you what it's really worth."

"Can you give me 40 euros for it?" Jean Paul asked impatiently.

"I can give you 40 euros, but you and I know it's worth much more."

"Tonight it's only worth 40 euros. So, I will take your offer."

Malcolm pulled 40 euros from his pants pocket and held it out. Jean Paul grabbed the money and dashed off into the crowd.

"Au revoir," Malcolm called out futilely, after the disappearing Jean Paul.

Jean Paul met Benoit every other night on one of Montmartre's hillside step paths. By evening the tourist traffic had died down and the ancient street lamps provided a low level of light, diminishing the chance that he might be recognized. Since these steps ran between two buildings, there was no way for a police vehicle to suddenly appear and apprehend him.

As he began to climb the steps, he took note of a young man leaning against a wall reading a newspaper. The man was too well dressed to be an undercover cop; he also didn't carry any kind of bag that would conceal a camera, so it was unlikely that he was a member of the press. Still, Jean Paul was careful to watch the man, but the man never looked up from his paper. Jean Paul climbed to the midpoint section where he could see the large, overweight figure of Benoit looking down at him, shaking his head in disgust, saying, "No, no, no."

Benoit flicked his burning cigarette directly at Jean Paul, hitting him in the chest as he approached. Jean Paul quickly brushed it away before it could burn his scarf. Knowing it was pointless, Jean Paul tried to diffuse the situation with a friendly greeting.

"Bonsoir."

"You're late, again," Benoit practically spat with disdain.

"You think I don't know that? I got here as fast as I could."

Benoit grabbed Jean Paul by his jacket collar and pulled him close enough that Jean Paul could smell the stench of Benoit's bad breath.

"Listen fuck face, I would rather be home screwing my dumb-ass girlfriend than waiting out here freezing my balls off."

Jean Paul pushed back hard and Benoit released him. He reached into his jacket pocket, pulled out a roll of tightly wound euros, and skillfully palmed it, and said in an angry tone, "Don't worry, I have your money."

Jean Paul swiftly glanced around to make sure no one was watching from the steps or a nearby window, and then at the man below who was still reading the paper. He slipped the money into the side pocket of Benoit's leather jacket.

Benoit pulled out a small bag of crystal meth and dangled it a few inches in front of Jean Paul's face. "Is this what you want? You little piece of shit!"

"I paid for it," Jean Paul asserted.

"How bad do you want this? Bad enough to suck me off?" Benoit asked in a mock-serious tone of concern.

"Don't be a dick, just give me my stuff," Jean Paul demanded.

Benoit dropped the bag on the ground at his feet. "While you're down there picking it up, you can make up for being late."

Jean Paul didn't move.

"Pick it up!" Benoit ordered.

Jean Paul saw that he had no choice but to play Benoit's little game. He held eye contact with Benoit as he bent down and picked up the bag. He stood back up, glared at Benoit, and left, quickly climbing the remaining stairs to the sidewalk above.

"Next time, don't make me wait or you'll pay triple!" Benoit called after him.

Benoit was left standing alone, and he removed the cash roll from his pocket, quickly counting it to confirm it was the correct amount. He started down the stairs, taking notice of the man loitering below. The man dropped the newspaper into the trashcan next to him and began to climb the stairs towards Benoit who immediately became suspicious of the approaching stranger and maintained a defensive position. As the stranger got closer, Benoit called out angrily to intimidate the approaching man, "Get the fuck out of my way!"

The man had to be deaf not to hear him. With his head down, the man continued to climb the stairs toward Benoit. As the man reached him, he looked up at Benoit with his dark eyes as a broad menacing smile grew across his face. He grabbed the front of Benoit's jacket and pulled him over his outstretched leg. Benoit went violently crashing down the stairs. The man stood and watched until Benoit hit the ground below. He then walked back down the stairs at a leisurely pace towards Benoit, who was lying with his back against the cobblestone, his hands and face wet with blood. A broken thighbone had pierced his skin and was bleeding profusely through his ripped jeans.

"What do you want from me?" Benoit cried out as the man approached.

The man silently looked down at Benoit's broken and bleeding leg. He appeared extremely pleased. With a demonic smile, he eyed the protruding white bone and, without ever acknowledging Benoit, he said aloud to himself, "That looks like it hurt."

Struggling with the pain, Benoit managed, "Of course it hurt, you stupid fuck!"

The man's smile widened and mused aloud only to himself, "What about this?"

He kicked the exposed bone.

Benoit screamed and rolled over onto his side, grabbing at his leg.

"Now that hurt," the stranger confirmed as he watched Benoit suffer. "But, not as much as this." He grabbed Benoit by the back of his pants and, with super-human strength, threw him twenty feet into the air, watching him flip over and then fall back to the ground onto his back. With a loud dull thud, Benoit's skull cracked and split open as it hit the cobblestone. A pool of red began to form as the blood streamed out from the back of his head. The man squatted down and appeared oddly fascinated and delighted by the growing pool of blood that now framed Benoit's lifeless face. He began to run two fingers through the pool as if he were finger painting on the cobblestone. He put the two fingers into his mouth to taste the blood. He searched the dead man's pockets and took his wallet and Jean Paul's cash before walking away.

The stranger continued to wind through the dark streets of Montmartre until he reached the top steps of the Basilica of Sacré Cœur, where he looked down upon the city and its many lights. The music of the carousel could be heard from several hundred feet below. He took a couple of deep breaths and exhaled as he concentrated. He carefully began to sniff the evening air and, following the scent, he turned to the left and walked into the darker area of the Basilica park below.

Farther down the hill, Jean Paul was huddled in a corner smoking the meth from a glass pipe, the euphoria starting to take him away. Reveling in his high after he had finished, he started down the steps toward the carousel below. He stopped at the railing directly above the carousel and watched the people wandering about like ants below him.

The stranger approached him from behind and put his arm around Jean Paul's shoulder. Jean Paul turned to look at him, a bit dazed as his mind adjusted to the high of the meth.

The stranger smiled. "That stuff you're smoking is shit."

Jean Paul yanked himself away from the man. "Go fuck yourself!"

"No offense, but it is shit. Complete shit. I want you to try this."

The stranger took Jean Paul's hand and placed a small plastic bag partially filled with iridescent metallic crystals in his palm, and with the utmost care he folded Jean Paul's fingers over the bag.

Jean Paul opened his fingers and looked down at the bag in his palm and then up at the man. "What is it?"

The stranger smiled back at him. "It is your future."

"Is it any good?"

"Best high you will ever have. You wound me by even asking the question."

"I don't have any money left," John Paul confessed.

"Today it's free. A little taste for my new friend."

"And the next time?" Jean Paul enquired.

"Next time, you pay me two hundred," the stranger replied, never dropping his friendly smile.

"That's a good amount of cash," Jean Paul replied, a bit surprised.

"A boy like you can afford the best."

"I'll try it. If I like it, maybe I'll come back for more tomorrow night," Jean Paul offered.

The stranger laughed confidently. "I know you'll come back to me." He began to walk away and, without turning back, he said, "They always do. My name is Kadar. I am at the carousel every night at this time when you want more."

Kadar continued on, passing the carousel and disappearing into the dark of the Paris night, leaving Jean Paul standing alone.

CHAPTER II

The next morning, the dawn's light served as an unofficial herald at the ancient cemetery in Montmartre, as life returned in the form of a handful of old French widows dressed in black. Each morning they entered the cobblestone walkways, making their daily visits to the graves of loved ones past. All of this activity was being quietly monitored by Malcolm's snowy white Great Pyrenees, whose large brown eyes had remained vigilant throughout the night and into the early morning. As an old groundskeeper walked by, the dog let out a low growl, warning anyone within ten feet that a stranger was passing. Chevalier, as the dog was known, had been guarding Malcolm as he slept in the part of the cemetery that was covered by the overpass bridge. The two of them often slept there at night to take shelter from the rain.

As Chevalier surveyed the morning activity, Malcolm slept soundly despite the damp ground and cold gravestones. Since coming to France in early summer, Malcolm had begun to sleep through the night. This was not something he had been able to do in recent years. It wasn't the sleeping conditions, which were a challenge; it was the presence of Chevalier watching over him. The young man's thin body twitched and stirred slightly as he lay between the graves, entering in and out of dreams. This morning, Malcolm was dreaming about being home in Vermont years earlier. It was a recurring dream that took him back to a defining moment in his life that he had yet to fully understand:

As he trudges through a late afternoon snowstorm on a remote country road, he rounds a bend and discovers the beginnings of a snowy field filled with debris. It starts with a couple of random and broken Christmas cookies then continues with some smashed presents, an overturned holiday turkey, a boy's Timex watch, more presents, and finally an overturned minivan with the headlights still on. As he gets closer to the car, he sees a fourteen-year-old boy who has been thrown from the car, lying in the snow. He lies face up and spread out like a snow angel with his clothes torn and face bloodied beyond recognition. His body is convulsing from the pain of the impact. Malcolm runs toward the boy but when he reaches him, everything goes black . . .

Malcolm awoke gasping for a single breath of air. Opening his eyes, he looked into Chevalier's large brown eyes staring down at him. Still half asleep and relieved to have woken up, he mumbled, "I hate when I dream."

He scratched Chevalier's right ear for a moment and then looked at his watch, which was a well-worn version of the one in his dream. He exhaled hard, sat up, stretched and yawned and slowly made it to his feet. He looked down at Chevalier as he ran his fingers through his own thick, tousled, black hair.

"You seem like you could use some coffee. You'll be pleased. We made enough money yesterday to buy you some almond croissants for breakfast."

He rolled up his sleeping bag and a wool blanket that he laid out for Chevalier. He affixed them both to his backpack. He lifted the pack onto his shoulders and picked up the fabric drawstring bag that contained his small inventory of the books that he sold each day. Taking Chevalier by a makeshift rope leash, he and the dog headed out of the cemetery, walking amongst the graves.

"We're going to have to put some serious effort into finding an apartment that will take us both before the temperature drops any lower. I was really cold last night and I just don't think I can keep sleeping outside for much longer."

The two continued to walk until they reached one grave in particular that had a bronze life-sized statue of a seated woman with her eyes closed, her arms outstretched, and a soulful suffering look on her face.

"I wish you had met my mother," Malcolm said to Chevalier as he appeared to lose himself in the face of the statue. "This statue reminds me so much of her."

He stood staring at the statue for a moment before saying in a low voice, "We should go now—the boulangerie calls."

Malcolm and Chevalier left the cemetery and walked across to the bakery.

He was greeted by a young woman at the counter as he entered. "Bonjour, Malcolm."

"Bonjour, Celine. Three almond croissants, please."

She took a bag from the shelf, placed three croissants inside, and handed it to Malcolm, commenting, "No regular croissants for Chevalier today? Business must be good."

He took the bag from the woman and paid her. He took note of the bold headline on the front page of a newspaper lying on the counter in front of him which when translated read: "Over 30 Parisian Men Have Vanished!"

Observing Malcolm reading the headline prompted Celine to say, "Imagine, all these man are missing. Did you hear? They found a body of a drug dealer late last night only three blocks from here. His skull had been cracked open."

"No, I hadn't heard," Malcolm replied.

"You should be careful," she cautioned.

"Chevalier watches out for me. À demain," he replied, as he headed toward the door.

"À demain," she called back after him.

Malcolm left the shop with Chevalier and walked several blocks to the central artist's square in Montmartre where he had met Jean Paul the night before. The artists and a few street musicians were busy setting up for the morning, drinking coffee and smoking cigarettes. He headed towards his usual spot next to Charlotte, an aging French pastel artist. Despite her skin and hands being weathered and worn from forty years of working outdoors as a portrait street artist, she still retained an exceptional beauty that wonderfully transcended her age. She was smoking a cigarette as he approached. Malcolm did not care for cigarettes, but he did admire her feminine smoking style that was reminiscent of a 1950s Hollywood actress.

Charlotte called out and waved, "Bonjour, Malcolm!"

He stopped to kiss her on both of her cheeks. "Bonjour, Charlotte."

"Have you seen this?" she asked as she held the newspaper up directly in front of his face. "You should read this right away. You aren't safe sleeping in that cemetery at night."

"I've been hearing about the missing men for the last week," he assured her.

"Half of Paris will go missing before the Police Nationale will come up with a lead. I know what these men are like. Where will we be if Paris has no men?" she asked, as she took another long drag from her cigarette.

Malcolm had no answer.

"I think this is terrorism," Charlotte said. "The terrorists are stealing France's most important commodity."

Malcolm went about preparing his small area and untied the wool blanket and sleeping bag from his backpack. He folded the sleeping bag several times to create a makeshift dog bed for Chevalier and used the wool blanket to display the books he offered for sale.

Charlotte continued. "The Ministry of the Interior has to be under heavy political pressure to provide answers. The public is panicking, and when they do that here, politicians will find themselves retired in Corsica. The Police Nationale are not really the ones to blame as they are completely underfunded by the ministry. Anyone with half a brain in Paris knows that!"

Malcolm posted a sign that read, "Don't be afraid, I speak English!"—and below it: "My Dog, Your Camera, One Euro." People continued to pass by as he completed his meager setup.

Charlotte pressed on, regardless of Malcolm's silence. "Well, at least you'll be safe from the drug dealers. The gangs are killing each other off. We finally get all the drugs off the streets and now we have no men."

She poked Malcolm with her finger to get his attention. "You need to be aware of all of this if you're going to be French!"

Out of politeness he looked up at Charlotte. She said in a more serious tone, "The world is just not a safe place anymore, everything is changing. At least someone has the good sense to start killing all the drug dealers. I never liked them much anyway."

Charlotte's attention then immediately shifted to a female American tourist who seemed interested in having a portrait done. Malcolm knew that once Charlotte started her work, she would remain distracted for the period of time it took her to create the portrait. Charlotte loved to talk and her subjects unknowingly became her captive audience once she started to draw them.

CHAPTER III

Professor Trechus was a popular young professor at the Sorbonne. His energetic and impassioned lectures on the science of geology captivated his students and reinforced his reputation at the university. Even those students with no interest in the planet Earth or its history were known to take his class just based on his looks alone. His strong jaw line and chiseled features were reminiscent of those carved into great Roman statues. He was undeniably, very handsome. He was an impeccable dresser who, despite the season, always dressed in black and the darkest shades of charcoal and purple. He did not own a single white or light colored shirt. Unbeknownst to the people around him, he was in mourning and had been for quite some time.

He stood at the lectern in the antique wood-paneled lecture hall, looking up at the twenty-two students who sat in the seats that rose before him. Their sleepy faces were illuminated by the morning sunlight streaming in from the windows above. He stopped for a moment to clean his glasses, and then placed them back on his head. It was a curious thing that he did not need prescription glasses, but he was slow to age and felt that they provided him with a more mature presence among his students and the other faculty.

He continued now in a more serious tone. "So far this semester we have focused on understanding the world through order. That is, each event follows fixed rules and has a defined outcome."

He raised his voice to again make his point. "A defined outcome!"

He looked around the room to ensure he had everyone's attention, and when he was satisfied, he relaxed his tone. "Think about it, in nature it's the abnormal occurrences that make for the most fascinating moments. Psychology is interesting but abnormal psychology is fascinating. It's the same for geology."

He walked over to the board where there was a large diagram of the earth's geologic time scale. He ran back and forth along the scale with a laser pointer as he continued. "If we believe the English, and their 'Mr. Arthur Holmes,' then we know the earth was created 4.6 billion years ago. Is it enough to say 'poof,' there it was?"

He stopped to see if his students were contemplating his question, and then continued, "NO! There was some cosmic abnormality that created the world and the universe that we know today. It was in a swamp mix of goo that the first proteins came together under random conditions to form the first living organisms."

He walked forward and sat on the edge of his desk. "So is it the rules or the exceptions that are more important in the development of geology? We go from the Paleozoic period—when fish, amphibians, and land plants become the dominate species—and hopscotch right across the Mesozoic Era and head into 183 million years which gives us the Triassic, Jurassic, and Cretaceous periods. Now the earth is swarming with the largest and fiercest predators the world has ever known. And then what happens?"

He looked down at a young woman sitting directly in front of him.

She smiled. "They all die?"

"Yes!" he laughed. "Like the famous 'Ring Around the Rosie' song says—they all fall down."

He took a step toward the students. "Was it a normal day when they just fell over? No! It was something strange and unique that brought down Earth's mightiest predators. I am not here to debate what the actual cause was—but did it kill everything? No, it spared the meek, the insects, the smaller fish, and the plants. If we believe the K-T extinction theory, then we believe in a general rule of extinction, and not extinction by exception. Why is this?"

He looked into the group for an answer, and a young man in the back responded, "Certain complete and entire species died out while others remained seemingly intact."

Trechus took another step forward, leaving some of the students behind him as he spoke with growing enthusiasm. "Precisely! A meteor hits the earth and every single Tyrannosaurus rex falls over dead. The point here is that they did not all die in an afternoon. Considering the global distribution of species, we have to assume that some creatures within a species were actually smarter than others, like humans. You would think that some survived, at least beyond the Mesozoic Era, and made their way into the Cenozoic period. Therefore, we should see later examples, or at least genetic derivations, of the species."

A young man interjected. "So if we believe the current theory which is based on 'all fall down' extinction, then should we consider the theory to be inaccurate?"

Trechus stepped right in front of the student as he answered him. "If you take only one thing from my course, understand that in a dynamic environment such as nature, every species has a survival instinct that would potentially drive it to overcome extinction. Considering the odds alone, certainly several out of millions of creatures should have survived their race's extinction."

"So why don't we see a Tyrannosaurus rex on the Champs Elysees if, in theory, several managed to survive and go on to flourish?" the student asked.

The professor turned and started to walk down the steps. "Good question! Consider the science of Cryptozoology. A science dedicated to uncovering creatures thought to be extinct or, in some cases, based on myth or legend."

He sat back down on the edge of his desk. "Every couple of years we pull a fish out of the ocean that we believed to have been extinct. What's swimming in the bottom of the lake in Lochness, Scotland?

Perhaps these creatures don't want to be found. Perhaps they are just smarter than we are. I know it may be a blow to mankind's ego, but these creatures may not have an interest in interacting with us."

A young woman in front of him asked, "So you believe there are dinosaurs somewhere in Scotland with enough mental consciousness to know that they should hide from human beings?"

Trechus quickly went to the board, using his hands to emphasize his point. "Look at these lines on the time scale. Strong, bold, and exacting. I want you to look at these lines as fuzzy and broken and leave your minds open to the high probabilities of alternative outcomes among the species."

He walked back and stood in front of the class. "Considering what we have discussed here today, I would like you to apply what you have learned from your study of evolution and cryptozoology and select a mythical or legendary creature. For our next class, trace a possible evolutionary tract that would go from prehistoric to modern time and theorize how your creature might exist undiscovered in the world today."

A student from the back called out, "How many pages?"

"I think five to seven pages is fair for a weekend assignment, but still allow you to do the topic justice. I assure you I have no interest in reading any more student papers on the topic of 'Bigfoot' so please be more creative when selecting your subjects. Does anyone have any questions? I have no office hours today so speak now."

After hearing no response, Trechus smiled and said, "That's all for today; I know many of you are eager to go and celebrate the Beaujolais Nouveau with your friends so I will let you go a few minutes early."

The noise in the lecture hall grew louder as the students started to collect their things and exit the hall. Trechus collected his class notes from the lectern and put them into his briefcase. Before closing it, he removed a leather-bound, first-edition copy of Camus' *The Plague* to read on the Métro ride home.

CHAPTER IV

The morning was busy for Malcolm. He sold two books before one of his regular customers came by and bought the book that Malcolm had acquired from Jean Paul the night before. Malcolm was still chilled from the previous night's cold air. This left him feeling more pressure to find a suitable apartment for the winter. While Paris was friendly to dogs, landlords that he had visited were not impressed with a young American without solid employment and a dog that could bark loud enough to rattle the glass in the windows.

Few people stopped that morning to show any interest in Chevalier, so the dog became bored and began nudging Malcolm's hand for attention. Malcolm responded by crossing the street and entering the café he frequented during the workday. He returned to Chevalier moments later with a café au lait in a ceramic cup. Malcolm opened the paper bag from the boulangerie and removed the last almond croissant. He tore off a sizable piece and fed it to Chevalier. He gave him another piece and then held the coffee cup at a slight angle so the dog could easily lick the coffee out of the cup.

Trechus exited the Montmartre Métro station on his way home. He continued reading his book as he walked along the sidewalk. He looked up briefly to check for oncoming cars as he crossed the street. His attention was diverted by the odd sight of a dog drinking a café au lait from a ceramic cup on the other side of the street. He looked to see what dog owner would allow such ill-advised behavior, and spotted

Malcolm as the culprit. Trechus might have been immediately angry with Malcolm had he not been struck by the beauty of the young man. He crossed the street and stood in front of Malcolm and Chevalier, watching for a couple of seconds before he commented in French, "I suppose it's OK to give a dog coffee as long as he's a French breed and you're serving French coffee."

Malcolm did not look up at Trechus, but continued the task at hand while he responded in French. "He's a bear in the morning if he doesn't get his coffee."

Truly concerned for Chevalier, Trechus tried a more politically correct approach. "Forgive me, I don't wish to be too personal, but are you really sure coffee is good for him?"

Malcolm continued feeding Chevalier, and, without making eye contact with Trechus, said in all seriousness, "Trust me. When you've been abandoned on the street, chocolate and caffeine are the least of your worries."

Trechus smiled, now picking up on Malcolm's accent. Switching to English, he said, "You're American."

Malcolm now stopped feeding Chevalier and looked up with suspicion at Trechus. "Did my cruelty to animals give me away?" he asked in English.

"It was your accent," Trechus confirmed.

Malcolm sighed. "Yes, I was American. Now, I just am."

He hoped that ignoring Trechus would make him go away, so he turned his attention back to Chevalier, showing no further interest in a discussion.

Trechus remained gently persistent. "And you have a dog, a French dog."

Again, without looking up at Trechus, Malcolm continued to allow Chevalier to drink from the cup and answered, "He's from Paris—he prefers to be called a Parisian dog."

"Of course, my mistake. How long have you owned him?"

Malcolm took the cup away from Chevalier and again looked up at Trechus, deciding to move to the offensive. "I don't consider myself his owner. It sounds too much like slavery, don't you think?"

"I would agree. So how would you define your relationship then?"

"He's a friend," Malcolm said nonchalantly.

Trechus smiled at Malcolm. "The French make loyal friends."

"In this case you mean that Parisians make loyal friends."

Trechus laughed in surrender to Malcolm's wit. "I stand corrected. You're right; he is a Parisian dog and a Parisian friend."

Malcolm relaxed a bit, sensing that Trechus was harmless. "It's a sore subject with Chevalier, and many other Parisians."

Trechus motioned toward Chevalier. "May I approach him?"

"Only if he'll let you," Malcolm cautioned.

Trechus got down on one knee and let Chevalier approach and sniff him. Chevalier was very interested in his scent and continued to sniff around his body with great interest.

"He smells something good. Do you have cats? He really likes the smell of felines."

"No, no cats." Trechus looked into Chevalier's big brown eyes. "You're a beauty. How old is he?"

"I honestly don't know," Malcolm replied.

"Where did you find him?"

Malcolm grinned. "I didn't find Chevalier. He found me."

"These dogs are known for protecting herds of goats in the Pyrenees Mountains. I believe I am at least correct on that point?"

"Yeah, you are. I'm not much of a goat herd, but being that Chevalier has commitment issues, I wouldn't expect him to start with a large herd."

Trechus laughed. He stood up and took out his mobile phone. "Can I take a picture?"

Malcolm pointed to his posted sign. "My Dog, Your Camera, One Euro."

"Why does it feel like I'm being hustled here?" Trechus asked.

"Before I started charging, I was wasting too much time with all the American tourists stopping to take a picture of the giant white dog. Hey, since models get paid, why not Chevalier? Before this gig, he had no source of income. At least now he's responsible and supporting himself without the need of government aid."

Trechus reached into his wallet and handed Malcolm ten euros. "I still feel like I'm only feeding into Chevalier's caffeine addiction. How can I be sure he'll buy food with the money?"

"It is a good thing you're speaking English. If he knew you were questioning his integrity, things would get ugly."

"No, I want to stay on the good side of a dog that size. How about five pictures for ten euros?"

Malcolm corrected him. "Its only five euros for five pictures of Chevalier."

"How about five pictures of both of you together for ten euros?"

Malcolm paused to consider the proposition. "I'm cool with that."

Trechus took the photographs of Chevalier and Malcolm together, counting them as he went. As he finished, he caught a whiff of an odd scent and held his nose skyward and began to sniff the surrounding air. At that moment, Chevalier started to bark. Charlotte, who had just finished her client's portrait, got up from her stool to see what was going on.

Trechus quickly turned to scan the crowd of people who had just passed behind him. He was not sure who was carrying the strange odor that his highly acute sense of smell had detected. The scent reminded him of one that he had known a long time ago; one that he, with his past experience, associated with extreme danger. As his eyes scanned the farthest edges of the crowd, Belazare, who had also picked up Trechus' scent, now turned and looked back at Trechus. The two men locked eyes for a split second, and then Belazare turned and began to move quickly away through the crowd, pushing people out of his way.

Trechus dropped his book on the ground in front of Malcolm and took off, sprinting after Belazare through the crowded sidewalk, and then into the street. Belazare turned to realize that Trechus was in pursuit and began to run, violently pushing people aside, their groceries and personal belongings spilling onto the ground. Belazare rounded the first corner, and as Trechus reached that corner, Belazare was rounding the second corner. As Trechus turned the second corner, there was no sign of Belazare. He stopped for a moment and realized that he had lost him. He turned to walk back to Malcolm.

When he got back, Malcolm and Charlotte were both curious and concerned. Trechus smiled at the two of them to diffuse the situation as Malcolm inquired, "Is everything all right?"

Trechus tried his best to appear indifferent. "Yes, I thought I recognized someone. It was not the person I thought."

Charlotte lit a cigarette and gave Trechus a long stare as she said in an accusing tone, "He seemed to be afraid of you!"

"It's probably nothing—but if he does comes around again, just stay clear of him," Trechus replied.

Charlotte eyed Trechus carefully and then asked, "Are you a cop?"

Trechus looked surprised. "No, I'm a university professor."

Malcolm's interest was suddenly peaked. "At the Sorbonne?"

"Yes, at the Sorbonne."

"Very cool," he said, almost forgetting what had just happened.

"It is not very cool to me," Charlotte interjected. "I still wish you were a cop. I know the guy you were chasing is a not a good guy. Students run after their university professors, not the other way around."

Trechus was not sure how to respond, so he opted to distance himself from Charlotte.

"Well, I really should be on my way. My book?"

Trechus motioned toward the book he had dropped, which was now sitting on top of Malcolm's backpack. Malcolm picked it up and handed it back to him.

"It's a very nice book. I can sell it for you when you're finished reading it."

"My books are like pets to me," Trechus said. "I would have a hard time parting with them."

Malcolm, not wanting to let a sale walk away, asked, "Any interest in my books? Surely a well-paid professor like yourself has a couple of euros to spend on some books."

Trechus smiled at Malcolm. "I'll have to come back when I have more time."

"Please, come back and buy something. If you want more photographs of Chevalier, you know where to find us. Charlotte can even sketch you if you like, with or without Chevalier."

"I will," Trechus promised.

He petted Chevalier before leaving. "Au revoir, Monsieur Chevalier." He turned to Malcolm. "Take care of yourselves, and make sure Chevalier cuts back on the coffee." Turning to Charlotte he said with a slight gentlemanly bow reminiscent of an earlier age, "Au revoir, madame."

"Au revoir, monsieur," she replied in a befittingly formal tone.

Trechus walked away and resumed reading his book as he headed up the street. Before he rounded the corner he stopped reading and turned around and looked back at Malcolm. He smiled to himself and then went on his way.

Charlotte thought it best to appear ignorant of the brief encounter between Malcolm and Trechus, but she had followed every word closely. With Trechus gone, she took the opportunity to speak to Malcolm about him, sketching while she spoke, pretending to be more interested in her work than the conversation. "The professor, he is a handsome man."

"I suppose so," Malcolm said, dryly.

"He seemed to like you."

Malcolm looked over at her and said, "I think he liked Chevalier. He is most likely reporting me to the French authorities right now for animal cruelty."

Charlotte continued to appear engrossed in her work. "You know he'll be back. Probably, tomorrow."

"I am sure he walks by this place every day," Malcolm responded shortly.

She turned to look at Malcolm. "You should be kind to him. Who knows? You may want to go to university someday."

"Charlotte, it is a nice thought, but I've already realized it is not going to happen for me."

"Here!" Charlotte said, as she took the drawing she had just completed and handed it to Malcolm. "It's a sketch of the man the professor thinks is dangerous. Just in case he comes back. You should remember what he looks like."

Malcolm studied the sketch of the strange man for a moment and then folded it up and put it into the pocket of his backpack.

CHAPTER V

To the outside world, anyone who looked at Trechus' life would observe that it appeared to be quite ordinary. He was a stickler for simplistic repetitive detail. At the Sorbonne he was regarded by his colleagues as a pleasant enough fellow, but decidedly French. In other words, he respectfully kept to himself and never mixed socially with the other faculty, and certainly never with any of the students. Trechus, by his own choice, subscribed to a life that could best be described as elegant yet monastic.

Trechus had no friends in Paris to speak of. When he was not lecturing at the Sorbonne, he was at home reading classic and ancient novels. His hobby was reading classic novels in different languages. He had not only read Moby Dick nineteen times in English and seven times in French, but he had also read it in nine other languages.

His passion was French wine. He had an extensive cellar that held just short of 20,000 bottles. While this might qualify him as a collector or at least a dedicated hobbyist, he had no airs about the size or exceptional quality of his wine inventory; he simply viewed it as a chef would view a well-stocked pantry. His cellar was a necessity.

What would, however, be considered odd about Trechus was his home. As a simple professor with seemingly no friends or family, he lived not in an apartment, but in a large mansion in the middle of Montmartre. The mansion took up half a city block, and the size of its rooms for a residence in Paris would be considered, by any Parisian standards, to be enormous.

The house was not only impressive in its size, but also in its condition. The house retained its original furnishings and paint colors from the time of its construction. With little wear over the years, it was not much different from the day it had first been built during the reign of Louis XIV.

While Trechus was currently subscribing to a life of solitude, he did employ a full-time housekeeper named Monique Montplaisir who lived well out of his way in the attic space of his home. The French Creole housekeeper, who was originally from New Orleans, was a deeply superstitious woman whose religious practices originated from the traditions of Louisiana Voodoo. While Trechus would have preferred the dedicated housekeeper live in more comfortable accommodations on a lower floor, she insisted on the attic space after first coming to the house and walking through all the rooms before making her selection. She never gave a reason for her choice and Trechus never asked for one.

Trechus had two friends, one who lived in the Loire Valley and the second who lived in Siberia. He visited them infrequently and he invited them to visit him even less. It had been more than five years since he had hosted either one of them at his home in Paris.

His isolation was of his own choice based on his interest. He had no psychiatric condition or phobias that imprisoned him at home; he just did and behaved as he pleased with no one to answer to. It was not that he did not take pleasure in people or the act of socializing, he just had not met anyone in a long time who piqued his interest. He had no cause to give up the guarded private life he had created for himself or receive visitors, of any kind, at his home. He was a man who was extremely comfortable with himself, and he enjoyed his time alone with his books.

Trechus arrived home just before noon and immediately made a phone call. When he got a message that the caller was unavailable he left a message, "Valerian, it's Trechus. I think I just saw a Black Dragon here in Paris. Call me when you get this message."

He hung up the phone and went into the large opulent dining room and sat down at one end of the long table where a place was set for him and the afternoon wine set out. He poured himself some wine and started to read from the book he brought along with him. Monique entered the room from the service door carrying Trechus' lunch plate. Upon seeing that he had laid his book out directly in front of him on the table, she reminded him in a low voice, "Bonjour monsieur. If you wish to eat you are going to have to move your book or would you prefer I come back?"

Looking up with a smile he replied, "Bonjour Monique. No, I will move my book."

As he lifted his book from the table, she placed an extremely large plate of steak tartare in front of him and poured him more wine. Trechus began to eat and continued his reading by holding the book up with his left hand and resting his elbow on the table. Monique returned to the kitchen and he would not see her again until the dinner hour.

When Trechus had finished his lunch, he went into the grand salon where he sat in a sunny spot and read until he had finished *The Plague* at around six in the evening. He returned the book to its place on the bookshelf before going down to his wine cellar. He selected two bottles of wine for the evening meal, as well as a bottle of armagnac that was covered in a thick coating of dust from its near hundred years in the cellar.

At seven the butcher arrived, as he did every night of the week, with an order of meat. The delivery always came in generic cardboard boxes, each weighing approximately ten to twelve pounds. Four boxes were delivered to the front steps of his home and Trechus never allowed them to be taken any further than the front porch. He always carried them into the house himself. The process was so routine and automatic that the butcher, who delivered them on his way home from work, often did not even have to ring the bell as Trechus would be there waiting for him. The butcher knew nothing about Trechus other than he was his best customer and paid top dollar for the best forty pounds of meat the butcher could bring in from around the world. His butcher shop on the Left Bank had become famous due to Trechus' demand for beef from Japan, Brazil, and the United States—a demand that allowed him to stock the beef for other customers. It was no coincidence that Trechus had chosen a supplier who was not located in the vicinity of his immediate neighborhood. As an older French gentleman who respected another man's privacy, the butcher never once questioned what Trechus did with all the meat, and Trechus appreciated and retained him for that very reason.

Trechus would drink the first bottle of wine while he read before dinner. He would sit alone and read in the dining room during dinner where he would consume a second bottle of wine. After dinner, he would retire to the salon to read for the rest of the evening. At midnight he would go upstairs to bed and wake on his own accord at six in the morning.

That evening he was chilled enough to light a fire in the fireplace. He usually kept the house at 58 degrees Fahrenheit which suited his constitution, but that evening the temperature in the house was barely 50 degrees. Winter had arrived early in France, but the cold weather was no matter, sitting and reading by the fire now provided him his happiest moments.

Following dinner that evening, he poured himself a glass of armagnac, sat on the sofa in front of the roaring fire, and thought about his meeting with Malcolm earlier in the day. He pulled his mobile phone from his pocket and began scrolling through the pictures of Malcolm and Chevalier. As he scrolled through the pictures, the phone rang. He answered it and, after listening to the voice on the other end, he said, "Valerian! Hello! Thanks for calling me back."

"It is good to hear your voice," Valerian replied with a heavy Russian accent. "It must be important since you're horrible about keeping in contact with your friends. Paris must be burning if you're reaching out to me!"

"As I said in my message earlier, I believe I saw a Black Dragon today."

"A Black Dragon in Paris? I guess it's time for them to return. Were you able to follow him?"

"No, he sensed me and then disappeared too quickly."

"If you're right, and I know you well enough to know that you are, you're facing quite a serious problem my friend."

"I do need your expertise here."

"Did you just ask me to come and see you in Paris? Are you actually asking me to visit?" Valerian teased Trechus, breaking the serious tone.

"Yes, I am inviting you here to Paris," Trechus replied, opting to maintain a serious tone.

"I'm completely surprised by your invitation."

"Don't be so surprised. I'm asking for help, not company. However, I do admit, it would be good to see you."

"I shouldn't leave you alone so much."

"Listen, there are some other alarming statistics here of which you should be aware. There are many abductions each day now."

"I have been reading about this in the Russian newspapers. How many men do they estimate go missing each day?"

"The police aren't sure how many occur daily, but they estimate that about thirty men are missing in total."

"If they say thirty, then it is probably more like forty or fifty."

"I agree. I'm sure their numbers are low."

"You detected one dragon, but he won't be alone. You know there will be more."

"Valerian, I don't know if this is related, but Paris has been struck recently by a radical increase in gang-related murders of drug dealers."

"Sounds like your dragons are taking over the drug trade."

"Why do you think the dragons are entering the drug business now?"

"In the modern world, you can't do much without cash flow. It's likely become their way of financing their activities. Have you spoken to Rodin about this yet?"

"No, dealing with Rodin is your job. I thought you would want to come to Paris first and get a better understanding of the threat before going to Rodin with this."

"I agree, I will come right away and then we can go and see Rodin together. If I fly myself and leave now, I can be there by early morning."

"No, I don't think you should fly yourself. Wait until tomorrow and take a commercial flight. They have those now."

"I will gladly get on an airplane if it means an opportunity to visit with you."

"It's been too long," Trechus acknowledged.

"It's sad that I only get a call when you find a Black Dragon," Valerian lamented.

"Yes, you can thank the Black Dragons for finally getting us together again."

"Tell me, do you still employ that witch?"

"Monique is not a witch."

"The last time I visited I developed three boils on my ass after I left. I could not sit down for a month. I am certain she was behind it. I am not the type who could develop boils on my own."

"Perhaps you might start by keeping some of your thoughts inside your head instead of allowing them to escape through your lips."

"Are you implying that I am overly harsh with the woman?"

"I am merely suggesting that you show her a little more respect."

"For the sake of a peaceful visit, I will try."

"I would appreciate it Valerian. I would hate to think of you standing for a month again when you return home."

"If you won't sympathize with my terrible suffering after my last visit I have no other choice than to bid you good night."

"Good night," Trechus said as he hung up the phone and smiled at the exchange he just had with Valerian. He was a crazy, wild Russian but then that was his appeal. Trechus went back to scrolling through the pictures of Malcolm.

CHAPTER VI

Trechus returned to the artist's area the next afternoon in search of Malcolm. It was easy to find him as he was next to Charlotte in his usual spot. As Trechus approached Malcolm, he stopped and watched him sell an antique copy of Grimms' Fairy Tales to an elderly woman. She was thin and frail, and Malcolm held her hand and spoke to her with a gentleness in his eyes that was incredibly beautiful.

"Bonjour, monsieur," a melodious female voice called out.

Trechus turned to see Charlotte standing close by.

He bowed slightly and replied, "Bonjour, madame."

Charlotte came forward and was now observing Malcolm from the same vantage point as Trechus. She turned to Trechus and said in a low voice, "He has an exquisite gentleness about him, a unique trait for a young man. Especially in today's world."

Trechus continued to watch Malcolm and, without looking at Charlotte, replied, "I see that."

He paused for a moment and then asked her, "You're a friend of his?"

She smiled. "As much as an old woman like me can be."

Trechus was momentarily captivated by Malcolm, who the older woman thanked warmly. She then slowly began to walk away, leaning on her cane.

Trechus smiled as he approached Malcolm, and called out, "I hope I'm not interrupting you, but I've brought some lunch for Chevalier."

Malcolm looked up and grinned at Trechus. "I hope it's chocolate mousse. That's his favorite!"

Trechus eyed him skeptically. "I hope you're kidding about the chocolate mousse. I brought him some plain beef and rice that I prepared myself."

"Everything is Chevalier's choice, but don't feel bad if he doesn't eat it."

Trechus pulled a large foil package out of his briefcase. He opened up the top and placed it on the ground in front of Chevalier who immediately rose to investigate and, with little hesitation, began eating the rice and beef. Trechus took a seat next to Chevalier on the ground as he ate. He started a conversation with the dog. "So, Chevalier, does your friend have a name?"

Chevalier continued to eat as Trechus smiled and looked up at Malcolm, who was standing above him with his arms crossed. Malcolm smiled. "My name is Malcolm Quinn."

Trechus extended his hand upward and replied, "Well, Malcolm Quinn, friend of Chevalier, it's a pleasure to finally meet you by name."

Malcolm shook Trechus' hand.

"I am Trechus," he said, as he stood up and continued. "I wasn't sure if you had a picture of Chevalier so I brought you this."

Trechus reached into his coat pocket and pulled out a small gift box and offered it to Malcolm. Malcolm stood up to accept the gift. As Malcolm stood up, Trechus saw that Malcolm's pants had a large tear down the back side of his right leg. The tear was large enough that it exposed the lower portion of Malcolm's well worn boxer shorts. Trechus did not comment on the obvious tear so as not to embarrass Malcolm and handed him the box. Malcolm opened the box and removed a small pocket-sized men's locket. He opened the locket and there were two pictures on each side of the locket of him with Chevalier from the day before. Malcolm looked down at the pictures for a couple seconds, and then he looked up at Trechus with a profound expression on his face.

"Thanks, Trechus," he said in a voice just louder than a whisper.

Not expecting such an intense response, Trechus asked, "Is something wrong?"

"No," Malcolm replied as he stared down at the picture. "Really, it's nothing."

Trechus hadn't meant to upset Malcolm with the gift, so he tried to change the subject. "May I look at your books?"

It worked, and Malcolm looked up and said in a more matter-of-fact tone, "Any of my books can be yours for a few euros."

Trechus started to survey the small collection of books that was laid out on the blanket in front of him. He began to examine the quality of each of the books by looking at the cover and thumbing through the pages. He avoided direct eye contact with Malcolm by keeping his nose buried in the pages as he spoke. "How long have you been in Paris?"

"For five months now."

"How long have you been together with Chevalier?"

"From the first week."

Trechus picked up another book and began the same examination process, still avoiding direct eye contact as he said, "You're lucky to have him."

"Do you live in Paris?" Malcolm asked.

Trechus looked up from the book as Malcolm's new interest in him caught his attention. "Yes, I was born in Greece, but now I live her. What made you want to move to Paris?"

"When I was a boy my mother used to tell me wonderful stories about living in Paris when she was a student at the Sorbonne. Her stories made me want live here."

"So you're a student at the Sorbonne?" Trechus asked.

"No, I was never able to finish high school."

"Has your mother come to visit you?"

"No, my mother and father died when I was fourteen."

"That's terrible! I am so very sorry," Trechus replied.

"Me too. I think she would be happy to know that I made it to Paris."

"Do you have other family?"

"No. I am, as they say, alone in the world."

"So, it's Malcolm against the world."

"I guess you could say that."

Trechus hesitated, and then asked, "Would it be too forward of me to ask who raised you after your parents died?"

"No. I was in the foster care system for three years."

"How old are you now?" Trechus asked.

"I turned nineteen yesterday."

"Joyeux anniversaire! Happy birthday."

"Thanks, but it's just another day to me. I really don't even think about it anymore."

"I can understand that," Trechus said, and then he held up two books and said, "I'm interested in these two."

"Those two will cost you 80 euros."

"Sold," Trechus confirmed.

"I have some paper. Do you want me to wrap them for you?"

"Here's 80 euros, and yes, please wrap them. Can you hold onto the books for me until I return later?"

"Certainly, we'll be here until 10 tonight—or you can always pick them up tomorrow."

"No, I'll be back for them tonight just after 7 o'clock."

"Chevalier and I will be here."

Trechus went over to Chevalier and bent down and scratched him behind the ear. "See you later, boy."

Trechus walked away as Malcolm watched him with curiosity. Charlotte was in the middle of sketching a young girl but noticed Malcolm watching Trechus walk away. She commented, "Your friend came back."

Still watching Trechus and without turning to look at her he replied, "I have no idea what to make of this guy."

She continued to work. "He's fascinated by you."

Malcolm looked at her directly and said, "I'm sorry. I'm just not fascinating so I don't know what that means."

Charlotte stopped working and put her chalk down. She now spoke to him with a deliberate tone. "You're too hard on yourself and you demand too much meaning from things. A young man like you should be open to just letting the world unfold around him."

CHAPTER VII

At 7:15 that evening, Trechus returned to the square that was now bustling with activity as people stopped by the square before going on to dinner. He saw that Malcolm's books were still laid out, but there was no sign of him or Chevalier. Upon seeing Trechus, Charlotte called out from behind her easel, "Malcolm is away for a few minutes walking Chevalier."

"Thank you. I'll wait for him," he replied.

"It's kind that you've returned to see him. He needs a friend."

"I'd like to do what I can for him," he confided.

"I believe you do," Charlotte said before returning to her drawing.

Trechus began to scan Malcolm's books. As he was examining the spine of a book, Malcolm returned with Chevalier. Unaware of their return, Trechus continued to look at the books. Malcolm interrupted Trechus' attention by handing him the wrapped package of books he had bought earlier that day and saying, "I took the books with me so no one would take them while I was gone."

Trechus looked up and smiled at the sight of Malcolm's handsome face. The young man's sapphire blue eyes sparkled brightly in the evening light. Trechus was temporarily mesmerized by what he saw. Catching himself, he said quickly, "I appreciate that."

"I hope you don't find my collection of books too basic for the academic tastes of a university professor."

"No, not at all," Trechus confirmed. "I am impressed by the quality. Do you ever have the chance to read any of them?"

"When I have time. It helps me with my French."

"Whose work do you admire?"

"Sartre, Victor Hugo, and André Gide."

"I like your collection. It's impressive to find such quality on the street here in Montmartre. I should like to buy them all."

"You want all of them?" Malcolm was surprised.

"Yes, all of them," Trechus confirmed.

"You don't have to buy all of them."

"You said they're for sale?" Trechus pressed.

"Yes, they're for sale, but it will cost a good deal of money. I really don't expect you to buy all of them."

"How much?"

"I don't know."

"Really, how much," Trechus insisted.

"1200 euros."

"I'm good with that price." Trechus took out his wallet and handed Malcolm 1200 euros.

"Why are you being so generous to me?" Malcolm asked.

"Have you had dinner yet?" Trechus replied, ignoring the question.

"You didn't answer my question."

"You didn't answer mine."

"No, I haven't had dinner," Malcolm said, remaining serious.

"Good, let's go to dinner now."

"I can't go to dinner now, I'm working," Malcolm protested.

"There's no work left, you've sold all your books," Trechus said, with a smile.

"I still can't have dinner with you."

"Why not?"

"It would be too strange. I don't know you."

"It's just dinner. You're hungry right?"

"Yes, I could use some dinner, but I'm more than capable of getting it on my own. I don't need you to feed me."

"Do you not like me? Would you prefer I just go away?"

"No, I like you," Malcolm said, and then paused briefly. "I just don't know you."

"So how do you know you like me?" Trechus teased.

Charlotte was busy sketching another client, but stopped and put down her chalk. She looked at Malcolm for a second before she turned to her client with a smile, and asked, "If you please, one moment."

She turned back towards Malcolm and called to get his attention, "Malcolm!"

He turned and looked at her.

She continued gently. "Dear boy. An adventure awaits. Now is not the time to hesitate. You can do this." She nodded her head in encouragement.

He looked at her and heard her voice of reason, but became embarrassed that she had overheard the entire conversation. He felt trapped. He looked at Trechus. "I guess you're right. I don't know you but I should get to know you. But, why does it have to be dinner? Can't we just talk or have a drink together?"

"Why not dinner?" Trechus remained insistent.

"I can't leave Chevalier alone on the sidewalk while we're in a restaurant. He won't like being left behind and he'll bark up a storm."

"We can eat at a cafe that's friendly to dogs. This is Paris."

"I haven't showered in a couple of days and I'm quite sure I don't smell too good."

Trechus laughed and said, "Yes, I did notice that earlier—you're a bit aromatic."

Malcolm said in a mild panic, "See, then people are going to be looking at me in the cafe. My stink will ruin their dinner and probably yours."

"Do you deliver?" Trechus inquired.

"What?" Malcolm was confused.

Trechus' tone became serious. "I just bought a pile of heavy books that I can't carry on my own. Can you deliver them to my home as an added service?"

"What do you mean—you can't carry them? You're twice my size!"

"OK, I bought them but I don't want to bother carrying them. So I would like you to deliver them."

"When?" Malcolm asked.

"Right now is perfect for me. I live less than a five minute walk from here."

"OK, I can bring them now. I'll have dinner with you some other time."

"I don't think your business offers good customer service," Trechus advised.

"Are you making fun of me?"

"No, I take you very seriously."

"OK," Malcolm said, now completely frustrated. "Then, what's the catch?"

"Catch? What are you talking about? What catch?"

"Where I come from, if it sounds too good to be true then there's always a catch. You bought all of my books and now you want to have dinner with someone you don't know? Not very French of you."

"Spoken like a true American, always looking for the catch. You're forgetting that I'm Greek. The Greek game is far different from the French game."

"How is it different?" Malcolm asked.

"That, you'll have to discover for yourself," Trechus assured him.

Malcolm stood in front of Trechus, frozen and speechless.

"Let's go have some fun. You do know how to have fun?" Trechus asked.

"I know how to have fun."

"Prove it. Collect your things and let's go."

"OK, I surrender."

Malcolm collected the books and put them in his bag.

"Got everything?" Trechus asked.

Malcolm nodded.

"Good, let's go."

Charlotte, who was obviously listening, stood up from her stool as they walked away together and said, "I wish you both a pleasant evening. Bonne soirée!" She smiled at Malcolm's good fortune.

CHAPTER VIII

Trechus and Malcolm walked the four blocks to Trechus' house with Chevalier in tow. When they arrived at the house and entered, Trechus said, "You can leave your stuff here by the door and you can take his leash off so he can become familiar with the place."

Malcolm took Chevalier's leash off so he could roam free. Chevalier took advantage of his new-found freedom and went about sniffing the corners of the large hallway, but stayed within eyesight of Malcolm.

"Are you sure it is safe to leave my stuff here? Someone won't come along and take it?" Malcolm asked.

"No," Trechus chuckled. "Your things will be quite safe here."

"If you don't mind, I would prefer to leave them in your apartment," Malcolm insisted.

"You don't understand. I don't have an apartment in this building. This building is my home. All of it is my home."

"The whole thing?"

"Yes, the whole building."

"And you live here alone?" Malcolm asked as he looked around the large hallway.

"Yes, I live here alone. Well, not entirely alone. I have a housekeeper, Monique, who lives in the attic."

"You know you're strange, right?"

Trechus laughed. "Yes, I am very, very different."

Malcolm began walking down the hall surveying the palatial entry hall. He stopped and looked back at Trechus confessing, "I can't believe this place. I have never seen anything like it."

"Malcolm, it's just a home," Trechus humbly assured him as he followed behind him.

"This is not 'just a home'; this is more like a hotel."

"Really, it is just a home."

Malcolm started to shyly wander into the oversized dining room that held the large dining table that could easily seat twenty people. He marveled at the two great crystal chandeliers and fine wall paneling. As he entered, he noticed that one end of the long table was decorated with birthday decorations and that there was a beautiful cake on the table.

Malcolm turned to Trechus who stood behind him in the doorway. "Whose birthday is it?"

Trechus looked at Malcolm. "I hope you're not mad but I have a confession to make."

"What?" Malcolm laughed. "This really isn't your house?"

"Seriously, I didn't feel right about you missing your birthday, so I arranged a little birthday party for you."

"Trechus. Please tell me you're kidding me."

"No, I'm serious."

"No, you're kidding. I know you're kidding."

"Why would I kid you about a cake? Look for yourself."

Still believing it was a joke, Malcolm approached the cake until he was close enough to read the inscription:

"HAPPY BIRTHDAY MALCOLM!
JOYEUX ANNIVERSAIRE!"

Malcolm couldn't control the emotion as his eyes welled up. He began to wipe away the tears.

"I'm sorry. I hope this isn't too much. I thought it would be nice if Chevalier and I threw you a small birthday party."

"I haven't had a birthday cake since my parents died," Malcolm admitted.

"It's probably time to change that."

"This is really kind of you. I can't even remember the last time I ate cake. I've never even seen a cake like this."

"Here, give me your coat," Trechus said.

"I'm dirty and I smell and now I'm crying. How can I stay?" Malcolm asked as he wiped the tears from his eyes.

"Relax, there's time before dinner. You can take a bath and clean up."

"Are you sure?"

"It's your birthday party. You have to stay."

"A bath does sound good."

"The bathroom is up the stairs and down the hall."

"Do you have bubbles?" Malcolm asked sheepishly.

"You mean champagne? Yes, of course. I will bring you some."

"No, I meant for a bubble bath."

"Oh, a bubble bath! Yes, of course."

While his eyes were still teary, Malcolm grinned at the prospect of a bubble bath.

"Funny thing, I've been dreaming about a bubble bath ever since the weather got cold."

"Then allow me at to make at least one of your dreams come true."

Trechus lead Malcolm back out into the hall where there were a collection of shopping bags. Trechus picked up the bags and handed them to Malcolm and said apologetically, "I hope you don't mind but I noticed you have quite a tear in your jeans so I got another pair for you and a couple of other things. I hope it is not too much. I started shopping for a pair of jeans for you this afternoon and got a little carried away."

"I will pay you for them," Malcolm offered.

"Let's just consider the clothes a birthday present."

"The tear in my pants is really bad isn't it?"

"It's time for a new pair. Come, let's go upstairs."

Trechus led Malcolm up the staircase to the second floor and down the hall to a bathroom. The bathroom was consistent with every other room in the house. It was a large, formal room with high ceilings. It was decorated in an older classic style with a large reading chair next to an antique claw-foot tub. The room was no less impressive to Malcolm who had never seen a personal bathroom this size. Trechus turned on the water in the tub and poured some lavender-colored liquid into the water; bubbles started to foam in the bottom of the tub.

"I'll go and get you some champagne while you start your bath," Trechus offered as he left the room, closing the door behind him.

Malcolm began to strip down and took off his watch as the tub was filling. He noticed that his body odor was worse than he had thought. He got into the tub and sat down. The warm water was so inviting but his body odor was so bad that, out of shame, he immediately began to scrub his body hard. He couldn't imagine how people could bear to be around him.

After scrubbing himself completely from head to toe three times, he slipped his whole body and head below the surface. He remained underwater with his eyes closed. The warm water felt comforting against his skin and he lost himself for a moment in the silence of his submersion. This was his momentary heaven. Outside, the everyday cold had begun to get to him. He did his best to remain tough when it came to bad weather, since he had no other option. This ordinary luxury reminded him of how hard his life had been. He was not feeling sorry for himself, but was simply enjoying the experience for what it was. He came up only for a breath and then submerged himself again, fixating on the feeling of warmth, weightlessness, and silence. As he came to the surface and sat up, a pile of soap bubbles collected on top of his head, covering most of his dark hair. He leaned back against the side of the tub, feeling as though he had crossed into another existence. Trechus knocked on the door and opened it a bit.

"Can I come in?" Trechus asked.

"Of course. It's OK, I'm in the tub," Malcolm replied with glee.

Trechus entered the bathroom, carrying two flutes of champagne. He smiled as he saw the large pile of soap piled on Malcolm's head. "You look adorable," he commented as he handed him the flute of champagne.

Trechus sat in the armchair next to the tub. He raised his glass and toasted Malcolm, "Happy Birthday, Malcolm. To your new life in Paris."

They both drank.

"Finish your bath and I'll go check with Monique on dinner. I'll take your clothes downstairs and have her wash them for you."

"Be careful, they smell horrible," Malcolm advised.

"Let's hope I can get Monique to wash them, she might be more inclined to burn them," Trechus teased as he collected the clothes from the floor and started to clean out the pockets of Malcolm's pants removing his wallet and silver locket and placing them on the table next to the tub with Malcolm's watch.

"Can you bring me my backpack? I have a change of clothes that are almost clean."

"Why don't you try on some of the clothes I bought for you today? We should make sure I got the right sizes. You can at least wear them to dinner while your clothes are being cleaned."

Malcolm was skeptical as he glanced over at the shopping bags.

Trechus sensed he was uncomfortable and did his best to encourage him. "They're only clothes. If you don't like them, I can always take them back."

"It just feels weird that you would buy me clothes. I guess I can put them on without underwear."

"I bought you underwear."

"You bought me underwear??"

"Malcolm, you are in Paris. Here, underwear for men and women has the highest regard. It is the foundation of your wardrobe. How can you feel good in your clothes if you don't feel sexy in your underwear? At least let me teach you some basic Parisian fashion principles. I am a little disappointed in Charlotte that she has not been a better instructor in the ways of fashion."

Trechus held up the thread bare flannel boxer shorts by the waistband as an example and continued, "These have seen much better days. These should be burned."

"Don't!" Malcolm cautioned. "My mother gave those to me. I keep everything she gave me."

Trechus could see from the expression on Malcolm's face that this was a sensitive issue and smiled sympathetically. "OK, we will wash them and get them back to you tonight."

"I would appreciate it."

Trechus left the room leaving Malcolm sitting in the tub. Malcolm drank the rest of his champagne and carefully placed the flute on the small table next to the tub. He stood up and began to dry himself off before getting out of the tub. Malcolm looked over at the bags as his skepticism turned into curiosity. He began to look through the first bag and pulled out three pairs of different style and colored briefs. They were of exceptional quality and unlike anything he had ever seen before, but what was more meaningful to him was that they were new. Everything he had been given while in foster care had come from either The Goodwill Store or was a well worn hand-me-down.

With his back to the door, he put on the first pair, dancing around a little—the champagne was starting to go to his head. Trechus appeared in the open doorway with the half-empty bottle of champagne and stopped and watched him. Malcolm took off the first pair and stood there naked for a moment as he held up the second pair to examine the elaborate waistband. Trechus was stunned by the young man's beauty. Malcolm's naked body looked to Trechus as if it had just been pulled from a Caravaggio painting. As Malcolm finished his examination of the waistband, he turned and saw Trechus watching him. Startled and embarrassed, he instinctively covered himself with the briefs. Trechus did not mean to appear invasive.

"I'm sorry. I did not mean to stare. I was just bringing you some more champagne."

Malcolm reached for his towel and struggled a bit to hold the briefs in place as he wrapped the towel around himself.

"I really should just go. I never should have come."

"Don't go, your clothes are in the washer and dinner is ready."

"I need to go. I'm not sure what I am doing here."

"Please, Malcolm, you don't have to go."

"Trechus, just bring my clothes back and let me leave."

"Malcolm, they're being washed, by now they are wet and full of soap."

"What am I supposed to do?"

Trechus said calmly. "Finish dressing. I bought you a new pair of jeans, two shirts and some socks. They are all there in the bags. Dress and come downstairs when you're ready. I really would like you to stay."

Malcolm wanted to leave but could not bring himself to say he would go. He replied, "OK, I'll stay for dinner. I really do want a piece of that cake."

"Thanks. I'll leave you to finish getting dressed," Trechus said as he left the room, closing the door behind him.

Malcolm finished dressing while he talked to himself out loud. "What the fuck am I doing here? I'm going to be found dead, floating in the Seine. Who is this guy?"

He looked down at the items Trechus had removed from his pockets and picked up the small pocket frame. He looked at the picture of Chevalier and him and sat down in the chair next to the tub. Again he spoke to himself. "Breathe Malcolm, just breathe. He's a good guy. He's got to be a good guy."

Ten minutes later, Malcolm appeared at the door to the dining room wearing his new clothes. Trechus was waiting for him.

"You look very handsome." Trechus offered.

"Thank you for the clothes. They feel a bit weird."

"How so?"

"I just have not had new clothes in a very long time. They even smell new."

Malcolm looked down at the long table, which had been exquisitely set for two people on the far end. A row of six impressive silver candelabras were lit and covered the length of the table, casting a warm glow throughout the room. Malcolm hesitated for a moment; it all didn't seem real to him.

"Sit here." Trechus pulled out the chair for Malcolm at the head of the table.

"I really don't know what to say about all this. I've never eaten at a table this size before."

Behind Malcolm the service door to the dining room opened a few inches and Monique looked into the dining room and studied Malcolm for couple of seconds with a critical eye before silently closing the door.

Malcolm looked down at the magnificent china and crystal and gently touched the Christofle silver forks as if to confirm they were real.

"I know it's all a bit much, but a large room like this requires an equally large table."

In front of Malcolm was a lobster soufflé on a fine silver tray decorated with fresh thyme and rosemary. The smell from the soufflé reminded Malcolm of how hungry he was. Malcolm looked up at Trechus and asked, "How often do you eat here?"

"I eat here every night."

"All by yourself?" Malcolm was surprised.

"Yes, I eat here alone."

"But I mean, how often do you have company?"

"I never have company. Well . . . not never—but not for a very long time."

Trechus uncorked a bottle and poured some white wine into the two wine glasses.

"What changed, why did you stop having company?" Malcolm was becoming very curious about Trechus' rather odd behavior.

"I lost someone close to me and just became more interested in books. Here, try this Vouvray," Trechus said, attempting to change the subject. "It's considered by many to be the most exquisite white wine ever produced."

Malcolm picked up the glass and took a good size gulp of wine.

"You don't drink wine often, do you?" Trechus asked.

"Why? Did I do it wrong?" Malcolm said innocently. "I've never had wine before."

"Here, let me show you."

Trechus took Malcolm's napkin and folded it a couple of times, and then attempted to blindfold Malcolm. Malcolm pulled back.

"Do you trust me?" Trechus asked.

"Not entirely," Malcolm replied cautiously.

"It's just a blindfold."

"Why do I have to be blindfolded to drink wine? What are you going to give me instead?"

"You really don't trust anyone," Trechus insisted.

"I meet you. I don't know you. You keep giving me things. Now you want to blindfold me. It's all too weird."

"Do you think I mean to harm you?"

"No, not really," Malcolm admitted.

"Well, then humor me and let me be weird."

"OK, but only for a minute," Malcolm conceded.

Malcolm sat still while Trechus tied the napkin around his head. Trechus began by picking up the glass, expertly swirling the wine as he tilted the glass, and held it just below Malcolm's nose.

"Inhale through your nose slowly and allow the aroma of the wine to stir your senses."

Malcolm repeatedly inhaled the aroma of the wine.

"Are you getting it?" Trechus asked.

"That is amazing," Malcolm confirmed.

"What do you smell?"

"I smell apples . . . and I smell mushrooms."

"Now take a sip, and hold it in your mouth as you breathe."

Trechus gave Malcolm a sip.

"Hold it in your mouth for a couple of seconds, breathing through your nose. Now swallow. What do you taste?"

"I taste apples. Lemons and . . . grapefruit," Malcolm replied.

"Impressive for a young man with little experience."

"How old is this wine?" Malcolm asked.

"Be fair to me. In Greece we never ask a woman her age or the price of her dress. In France it is the same, but with wine as well. If you wish to know the age of the wine, you can be discrete and ask to look at the label if your host does not offer the information."

"May I see the label?"

"You may see the label, but not until I tell you to remove the blindfold."

"I think you enjoy having control over young men too much."

Trechus laughed. "Only when I am teaching them something."

"I'd prefer if I could see you."

"I don't want you to focus on me but concentrate on the wine—which I assure you is much more interesting."

With a serving spoon, Trechus cut into the soufflé and placed a helping onto the center of Malcolm's plate and then his own. He picked up Malcolm's fork and instructed him. "Now, I am going to introduce you to the subtle flavors of this soufflé with the wine. Open your mouth."

Trechus took a fork and filled it with a piece of the lobster soufflé from Malcolm's plate. "Open wider, this is a little bigger than I thought."

Malcolm obliged and began to blush in the process.

"That's good. Now, I am going to put a fork full of lobster soufflé in your mouth and I want you to experience the taste of the different flavors."

Trechus placed the fork into Malcolm's mouth and slowly pulled it back out.

Malcolm smiled as he began to chew.

"Stop for a moment," Trechus instructed. "Let the food sit on your tongue as you breathe."

Malcolm obeyed.

"Now I am going to give you some more wine so you can see how the wine and food mix together in your mouth and how it heightens the experience."

Malcolm obliged again, and chewed and swallowed with childlike delight.

"OK, that was magical! Do it again!"

"You're becoming a demanding little bird," Trechus teased.

"I want more," Malcolm replied, in a playful demanding tone.

"Tell me again, but this time in French," Trechus requested.

"Je veux plus, s'il vous plait, monsieur," Malcolm replied.

"Open wide," Trechus directed.

Malcolm obeyed, obviously enjoying Trechus' game.

"I think this piece is too big for you," Trechus teased Malcolm.

"No, give it to me. I want it, sir!"

"Get ready, here it comes."

Trechus placed the fork full of soufflé into Malcolm's mouth. The wine was relaxing Malcolm, and the blindfold now titillated him. The sound of Trechus' deep seductive voice taking control of him as they played the game aroused him so that he had to shift in the chair as his cock strained against his new tight fitting jeans. Malcolm discretely reached under the table and pulled the front of his jeans to provide some additional room and relief for himself.

Trechus thought Malcolm looked more beautiful than ever in the candlelight. The warm colors illuminated his beautiful face and pale skin as his youthful personality only made him more endearing. Trechus wanted to see Malcolm's sapphire eyes again, so he said, "I think it is only fair that I remove this."

Trechus took off the blindfold, and Malcolm's blue eyes immediately flashed brilliantly in the candlelight.

"Thanks! That was an incredible experience—but I was sort of hoping you were going to tie my hands up next," Malcolm said, grinning.

"Next time. I promise," Trechus assured him.

Malcolm now had the opportunity to examine the label on the bottle that was sitting in front of him.

"This wine was made in 1919?" he asked.

"Yes, the Vouvray Haut-Lieu Moelleux Domaine Huet."

"I won't even ask how much that costs."

"I don't have an answer," Trechus replied. "I bought it along with fifty other cases from a neighbor's estate after he had passed away. They told me that he had been saving these four cases to enjoy during his retirement. Sadly, he died before he had the chance to retire and drink the forty-eight magnificent bottles."

"That's a sad story," Malcolm agreed.

"Yes. He was never able to enjoy the wine. Now, if you will excuse me for a moment I'm going to get a second bottle of wine for you to try."

Trechus stood up and cleared the two plates from the table, taking them into the kitchen. As the service door swung shut he could overhear Trechus talking to someone but could not hear the reply.

Malcolm took the serving dish that held the remaining lobster soufflé and placed it on the floor for Chevalier.

"It's good stuff," he told Chevalier, as the dog happily ate from the dish.

Trechus returned to the room with a decanter containing a new bottle of wine.

"Is someone else here?" Malcolm asked.

"Yes, Monique had a question for me. She went back to the attic. So, onto the next wine. I decanted this wine thirty minutes ago. It's a 1928 Chateau Latour Pauillac—my personal favorite. Some people think the '29 is better than the '28, but I prefer the '28."

"I mean this with all sincerity: who are you?" Malcolm asked.

Trechus stopped pouring the wine into Malcolm's glass and considered the question. "Difficult to answer," he replied.

"Now you're avoiding the question."

"You wouldn't believe me if I told you. Here, allow me to distract you with some wine."

"Okay. If I love the wine you don't have to answer the question."

Trechus poured Malcolm a glass of the bordeaux and watched as the young man took the time to swirl the glass and then place it under his nose and inhale. Finally, he tasted the wine.

Malcolm smiled and said, "Just keep pouring that wine and you don't have to answer any more questions tonight. I have a new love!"

"It's hard not to love Latour. Are you familiar with steak tartare?"

"I've never had it but I'll try anything."

"Most Americans don't like the way it looks," Trechus warned.

"No problem, I've a blindfold here if I need it," Malcolm replied.

CHAPTER IX

After dinner, Trechus sat on the Louis XIV embroidered white silk-covered settee in the salon in front of a roaring fire, cradling a glass of armagnac in his hand. Malcolm came into the room with a large plateful of birthday cake and sat down next to him on the settee. He started to eat the cake, totally focused on the process and clearly enjoying himself.

"Slow down, that's your fifth piece," Trechus cautioned Malcolm.

"Truthfully," Malcolm proudly admitted, "it's my sixth piece. I just ate a piece in the dining room before I came back. I forgot how much I like cake."

"Let me know when you want to go back to your apartment and I'll call a car service. It's starting to rain."

"Trechus, Chevalier and I don't need a car service. We can walk."

"Don't be ridiculous. How far do you live from here?"

"That depends."

"Depends on what?"

"Where we decide to stay. Tonight we'll stay in the cemetery where the road crosses over. The underpass is useful when it rains."

"Are you serious?" Trechus asked.

"We have no problem living outside," Malcolm said, assuring Trechus his condition was not dire.

"But . . . you're homeless!" Trechus protested.

"You make it sound like a bad thing. Like I should be apologizing for it."

"No. I'm not asking you to apologize. Being homeless isn't a good thing for anyone."

Malcolm became defensive. "Whether it's good or bad is a stupid argument because for many people it's an inescapable reality. It's been fine for us."

"Well, you're not going there tonight. It's raining out and it's not summer anymore."

"We live fine in the rain," Malcolm said defiantly.

"I'm sorry, but there is no way I am going to send Chevalier out in the rain tonight. He's staying here. If you want to sleep in the cemetery then you can come back for him in the morning."

"You'd take my dog away from me?" Malcolm asked.

"You told me you had no ownership over him."

"I suppose Chevalier would be happier sleeping by the fire."

"You can both sleep here by the fire, or in a bedroom upstairs if you prefer."

"Okay. But I'm only staying because I want to finish the rest of the cake in the morning."

Within ten minutes, Malcolm was peacefully asleep on the settee. Trechus stayed up for another half hour drinking armagnac and watching Malcolm sleep as the fire slowly died down. He then got up, covered Malcolm with a blanket, and blew out the candles that illuminated the room. He looked at the clock on the mantel. Valerian was not due for another hour, so he went upstairs to his bedroom to read until Valerian arrived.

Forty minutes later, in the darkness of the salon, Chevalier awoke first with a growl and then began to bark loudly. He stood up and charged out of the salon toward the front door, barking and whining urgently. Malcolm awoke and started chasing after him. As he reached the front door, Malcolm was able to grab Chevalier by the collar. Holding him back, Malcolm managed to get to the door just as it opened.

In the doorway stood a tall muscular figure in an exquisite red wool coat. It was difficult to make out his features in the low light of the hallway against the brighter street lights that backlit him. Malcolm continued struggling with Chevalier.

"Who are you?" Malcolm demanded in English.

The figure proudly proclaimed in a heavy Russian accent, "I am the great Valerian."

Despite the commotion, Malcolm was still half asleep and did not immediately understand so he asked, "What's a Valerian?"

The man started to laugh heartily and said, "You're very funny. I like you."

"I don't care if you like me! My dog doesn't like you."

Valerian maintained his bold and friendly manner. "This dog could kill a Russian bear. I respect that and so should you."

Trechus, now wearing only a T-shirt and briefs, came running down the stairs in an effort to resolve the commotion.

"Trechus!" Valerian called out. He stepped in from the street to reveal his handsome face and short cropped blond hair. He looked to be in his mid-thirties. "It's not everyday that I am received by you with such an impressive show of force. I see you have hired a small army to protect yourself."

Trechus put his hand on Malcolm's shoulder, "It's OK, Malcolm, Valerian is my friend." He turned to Valerian. "Valerian, I want to introduce you to Malcolm, and this is Chevalier."

"Good evening," Valerian said to Malcolm, with a slight bow.

"Valerian is my oldest friend," Trechus told Malcolm.

Valerian got down on one knee while still standing in the doorway, and directed Malcolm, "Go ahead, release your mighty beast."

Malcolm released Chevalier who, at first, charged Valerian but then stopped short. The dog carefully studied Valerian's scent with his sharp inquisitive nose. Upon completion of the examination, his tail began to wag.

Valerian marveled as he stroked the dog's head. "What an outstanding creature. I miss the days when dogs were mighty among men. They tell me that American women carry their dogs in their handbags. Is this true? Can you imagine this dog in a handbag? Ridiculous!"

Valerian stood up and embraced Trechus warmly.

"How are you my old friend?" Trechus asked.

"Things go well these days. Now tell me about this young man!" Valerian enthusiastically took Malcolm's hand between both of his and gave him a strong handshake.

"You're a good man," he told Malcolm. "I can tell that about you already."

Valerian switched his attention back to Trechus. "Trechus, you have decided to interact with people again. How surprising! This is a cause for celebration."

Trechus replied, "Well, I couldn't very well sit in my house all alone reading old books forever."

"Oh yes! You could," Valerian laughed. He turned back to Malcolm. "But now I see a bright light that will finally lead you out of your self-imposed seclusion—or do you prefer the word 'exile'? The English language has too many words that don't always mean the same thing."

Trechus cut him off. "I'm afraid your enthusiasm will keep us awake all night. Malcolm does have to work in the morning. I'll warn you now that he is an antique book seller and responsible for selling me another ten books today."

"I can see your attraction." Valerian smiled and then paused to consider the hour before he continued. "No, no, a young man like Malcolm should get his rest. Our discussion can wait until the morning when we are all fresh and have the light of day to elucidate things. There is no cause for an inquisition tonight!"

Trechus smiled at Malcolm. "Valerian is like a giant boulder rolling down the side of a mountain. It's best just to get out of the way."

"He does mean that in good way," Valerian noted.

Trechus smiled. "Sometimes, I mean it in a good way."

"And the witch? I mean Monique," Valerian inquired.

"So you have returned," Monique called out to Valerian as she walked barefoot down the stairs from the second floor into the main hall.

Malcolm's attention quickly shifted to Monique who he was curious to meet. He was immediately taken by her mysterious dark eyes and was surprised by her beauty. She wore a flowing skirt of exquisite fabric and a Creole headdress with oversized gold hoop earrings. Chevalier who otherwise would have been confrontational to a stranger under the circumstances, uncharacteristically, sat down and did not move as she approached.

"Yes, Valerian. The witch still dwells in the House of Trechus," Monique proclaimed. She walked directly up to Malcolm and looked into his eyes. She gently brushed his hair out of his eyes with her fingertips. She looked deep into his eyes and then said approvingly, "I like you."

She turned to Valerian and said scornfully, "But the witch does not like you."

CHAPTER X

The next morning, the sun streamed into the great dining room where Valerian and Malcolm sat talking over breakfast. Malcolm was forking down the last third of his birthday cake directly from the cake stand. Valerian picked up a silver bell from the edge of table and rang it. There was no immediate response so he rang it harder a second time and for a longer period. Monique emerged from the servant's door carrying a silver tray with glass of milk and a cup of tea.

Valerian protested, "If we are to get along, you must provide the guests of this home with an adequate level of service."

She put the tray down on the edge of the table. She put the glass of milk down in front of Malcolm and said, "Here my angel, you should not be eating all that cake without a glass of goats milk."

She looked disapprovingly at Valerian. "If I am tardy it is because I took extra time to brew you this special cup of tea this morning."

Valerian picked it up and smelled the tea. "It smells like dried bat wings."

"Don't worry," she retorted. "I would not waist such a precious commodity on the likes of you."

Monique picked up the tray and left the room. Valerian and Malcolm sat looking at their drinks. Malcolm picked his glass up and took a sip. He liked the way it tasted and after drinking from the glass confirmed, "It actually tastes just like cows milk."

Valerian picked up the cup of tea and smelled it again.

"Are you afraid to drink it?" Malcolm asked.

"Afraid," Valerian scoffed. "The first thing you should know about me is I fear nothing."

Trechus entered the room, reading from a novel.

"You're too late, Trechus," Valerian informed him and diverting Malcolm's attention away from the untried cup of tea. "I have decided that I will keep Malcolm for myself. He will look stunning against the backdrop of the Siberian forest in winter."

"You insist that I need to make friends and now you're stealing them away from me?" Trechus protested, putting down his book.

"You know how much I covet beautiful things. I absolutely must be allowed to take him home," Valerian said with a big smile.

"Remind me again, Valerian, why I invited you here?"

"You called me to ask for my help—and I am helping you."

Trechus looked at Malcolm. "No one is safe in the path of the oncoming boulder."

Valerian became more animated. "Admit it, you love me!"

"I appreciate you greatly," Trechus said, pausing for the effect. "In extremely small doses."

"See, you do love me!"

"Malcolm, please don't wind him up in the morning. If you let him out of his cage before noon, he is incorrigible for the rest of the day."

"He's fine," Malcolm told Trechus. "We had a good long talk this morning."

Trechus looked down at the cup of tea and asked, "Did you try the tea Valerian? Monique made it for you special. She only makes it on special occasions so consider it a peace offering. Try it. It's quite wonderful."

Valerian hesitated. Trechus took the cup and took a sip and handed the cup to Valerian saying, "Its fine Valerian. She would not poison you."

Valerian picked up the cup and drank from it. "You know, it is actually quite good."

"What are your plans for today?" Trechus asked Malcolm.

"Back to work. I need to go to the flea market this morning and buy some more books, or I'll have nothing to sell today," Malcolm replied, getting up from the table.

"Can we meet later?" Trechus asked.

Before Malcolm could answer, Valerian cried out, "YES! We must definitely meet up. I will teach you how to drink vodka and eat caviar like a good Russian."

Malcolm smiled and said, "Trechus knows where to find us." Turning to Valerian he asked, "Can I look for some books for you?"

"Please do! There are many old Russian books in private collections here in Paris. When the Tsar fell, many of Russia's grandest treasures made it here to France by way of Monaco."

"Malcolm, make sure the books have pictures. He likes pictures," Trechus joked.

"Trechus, you're a hopeless academic snob," Valerian said, but went on to explain to Malcolm. "What he means to say is that besides fine examples of Russian literature, I absolutely adore Russian comic books!"

Malcolm smiled. "I've seen them around! I'll look for you today in the flea markets."

Malcolm walked out of the dining room and into the entry room where he began to collect his belongings. Trechus followed him and opened the front door. Malcolm started to head out with Chevalier in tow.

"Can you come back for the evening?" Trechus asked.

Malcolm looked uneasy. "Trechus, I'm not comfortable being your charity case."

Putting as much sympathy into his voice as he could muster, Trechus said, "I was only thinking of Chevalier."

Malcolm smiled. "You know that's only going to work for so long."

"Yes, I know. I'm working on alternative manipulation techniques, but they're still under development and not fully tested."

Malcolm responded with mock caution, "Many have tried and all have failed."

"Failure for me is not an option. You're going to be late for the flea market."

"Now you're trying to get rid of me?" Malcolm asked.

"No, I'm forcing you to maintain your independence," Trechus replied.

"À bientôt, Trechus," Malcolm said, as he walked out the door. He then stopped dead in his tracks and turned to look back at Trechus. "Thanks again, for the cake. It really meant a lot to me."

"I'll have a cake for you next year," Trechus confirmed. "I promise."

He waved goodbye as Malcolm and Chevalier headed down the front stairs and up the block. Trechus closed the door behind him. As he turned, Valerian was standing against the wall with his arms and legs crossed, sporting a fierce grin as he commented, "Why do you look taller when you are in love?"

"Who said anything about love? He's just a kid."

"You don't need to say a single word. You always forget I know you better than you know yourself."

"I assure you, Valerian, I am not in love."

"Why? Why? Why must you always make it so difficult? Look at yourself. You always wear these somber dark colors when you are in mourning. It is time to start living again. Mourning does not become you."

"I am content. I do not wish to fall in love."

"It appears to me that it is too late for that. Surely, Trechus, there are another two thousand books you can read this year. So explain to me why an enchanting young man is sleeping in your salon?"

"He's a young man who needs some help. I am only offering my help."

"And not your heart?"

"Valerian, I know you have a fine talent to make things out to be more than they are, but in this case I feel nothing but a mild friendship for the man."

"I don't care if you want to lie to me. I am just your oldest friend in the world. But please, do not be dishonest with yourself."

"My plan is help him Valerian, that is all."

"You're correct as usual. Malcolm does need your help. He is alone in the world and unloved. I hope you will help him find his way."

"Not to change the subject, but I thought you came to track the dragons."

Valerian looked at Trechus sternly as he said, "I came to help you in whatever capacity I can."

"We really need to focus on dragons right now. The news in the morning papers is not good. More drug dealers dead, and many more men are missing."

"A good friend can take a moment to be concerned about you and help you to understand your feelings."

"And right now, Valerian, my feelings tell me that we need to focus on the Black Dragons before the situation worsens."

CHAPTER XI

Christian exited the restaurant following a long business lunch and walked out onto the sidewalk. He stood facing the sun to warm his body. After spending too much of his time indoors, the heat on his face felt foreign to him. He had disregarded his body for so long in pursuit of this business deal that he had grown numb to the outside world. With the contracts finally signed that morning, he felt optimistic that the overwhelming sense of pressure he felt would give way to a more familiar personal feeling. He had just concluded a monumental sale for his company: an enormous contract that would include over one billion euros worth of concrete for the national construction projects of the Nigerian government. The pressure that came with the closing of such a transaction was mind numbing, and he was now feeling like an emotional casualty of the deal. He felt no desire for ecstatic celebration. He just stood in the sunlight as a sense of relief overcame him as he searched for some part of his former self that he had left behind many months ago. He was temporarily free from his demanding boss, the hundreds of hours of sitting on planes and in airports, and, for the moment, the dangers of traveling in Nigeria.

He felt the need to do something to make him forget about his career for the afternoon. He started to walk west on rue de Rivoli, past the Louvre, and headed toward Le Marais with no exact goal or plan in mind. What sort of reward should he give himself? Some clothes shopping? A ridiculously expensive bottle of wine? A sauna at the gym?

A feeling stirred inside him and his decision was made without his brain. He immediately changed direction and headed north, turning onto the street where his favorite sauna was located.

When he arrived at the sauna, he showed his membership card to the desk manager and was given a towel. He pushed hard against the heavy door to enter. The air in the gym rushed out, dense from humidity and the unmistaken odor of men. It was not a single scent but a mélange of scents. The smell was raw—a complex mix of musty gym clothes, day-old sweat, chlorine, and a faint hint of semen. It was not a smell he could describe or readily recall, but one with which he was familiar. To Christian, this was the scent of possibilities.

The excitement of being back after a six-month hiatus from the sauna began to grow and he quickly located his locker and opened the combination lock. He got undressed and stood for a moment before putting on his jock, shorts, sneakers, and muscle shirt that he kept stored in his locker. Two guys next to him, who just finished dressing, were leaving. A shame, he thought, as they were definite possibilities. Another guy was suiting up for a workout next to him, but Christian wasn't interested in someone who was that young and thin.

He walked out of the locker room into the adjoining weight room. He was encouraged to see that there was some activity going on there, as the afternoon attendance at Parisian men's saunas could be unpredictable. He immediately heard the deep-toned grunts of a man.

"Uugh . . . uuugh . . . . . . uuuugh!"

This was followed by a singular loud crash as the man dropped the heavy curling bar down on the steel rests of the preacher bench. These noises alone were a big turn-on for Christian. As he rounded the corner, seeking a glimpse of the man who was making these beckoning sounds, he came upon a deeply tanned, muscular guy in his mid-thirties, wearing a black tank top that accentuated his large biceps and extremely muscular shoulders.

The man started another set, purposefully pushing himself to the edge of his impressive physical strength. He was breathing heavily, and, as he strained against the weight, he eyed himself intensely in the mirrored wall directly in front of him. His biceps bulged throughout the set until he again dropped the bar onto the rest with a large crash. As he stared in the mirror at his handsome face, dripping with sweat, he noticed Christian's reflection looking at him from behind. He flashed Christian a quick grin and then stood up and walked away.

Christian had to exercise some self-control to resist following the man like a lost puppy. He distracted himself by focusing on getting his own routine started. He grabbed two forty-pound dumbbells, sat down on a recline bench, and started his first set of eight shoulder presses. As he finished his first set of eight, he dropped the dumbbells to the floor and looked up into the mirror that was on the wall in front of him. To his surprise, he could see the man's reflection in the mirror now standing several feet behind him. The man had removed his tank top and was going through a series of poses, admiring his stunning physique in the mirror. He appeared very consumed with himself as he posed. Christian watched for a couple of seconds, just long enough so that his embarrassing over-interest was not detected. He took a deep breath and exhaled, trying to stay focused on himself, and prepared for the next set. He began his second set of eight reps, and as he reached seven, the handsome stranger stepped forward and gently pushed his elbows up, saying softly into his left ear, "I'll help you get to ten."

Christian completed the two additional reps with the help of the stranger, dropped the weights onto the floor, looked up, and said, "Thanks for the help."

The man remained silent, standing behind him, and then he stepped forward, putting his hand on Christian's left shoulder as he got down on one knee. He looked at Christian in the mirror and then began to whisper into his ear. Christian could feel his steamy breath against his neck.

"My name is Drakas. I am going downstairs to shower now. Just in case you were wondering what I look like without these shorts on."

The man stood up, flexed his bicep in the mirror and gave it a slow seductive lick as Christian watched. Then, without a word, he turned and walked out of the weight area as Christian caught a glimpse of his ass in the mirror's reflection. Christian's mind was immediately made up to follow him, but he resisted and waited a minute so as not to appear too eager or sadly desperate.

Christian completed one more set of reps, but this time he put all of his might into it, loudly grunting out each number and then dropping the dumbbells on the rubber floor causing an extra loud bang as they bounced. He stood up and headed to the locker room, removing his muscle shirt on the way. There was a single thought in his mind, and he became completely focused on his mission. He quickly stripped down and hastily threw his muscle shirt, jock, shorts, and sneakers into the locker, and pulled out his towel from the locker and wrapped it around his waist. He took the back staircase down to the area where the showers, steam room, and cabins were located.

Christian entered the dimly lit communal shower room where Drakas was standing in the far back corner under a showerhead. Drakas was seductively running his hands over his wet naked body as he watched Christian enter the room. Christian stood and watched as Drakas performed for him. He then removed his own towel, hung it on a hook on the wall, and walked over to turn on the shower across from Drakas. As the water started to flow, Christian put his head under the water stream to wet down his hair. He turned around and looked at Drakas who was now covered in soap, his hands seductively moving over his body in rhythmic motions. Christian took some soap from the dispenser and started to wash under his arms and quickly cleaned the sweat from his body. Drakas took some more soap from the wall dispenser and began to soap up his cock and balls. Christian watched as Drakas' cock begin to get hard and grow to a size that hardly seemed human. Drakas flashed a wild grin, took another handful of soap, and began to rhythmically stroke his enormous erect shaft. Christian was so engrossed in Drakas' performance that he was unaware of his own erection. Drakas took note of Christian's erection and motioned toward Christian's cock by nodding his head and giving him a playful grin.

Drakas walked toward Christian and took some soap from the wall dispenser. He ran his soapy hands slowly across Christian's chest making his way up to his muscular shoulders. He reached around Christian's neck and pulled his mouth toward his and they began to kiss. Drakas skillfully slid his tongue into Christian's mouth and Christian went weak at the knees as his blood rushed through his body.

Kadar entered the shower room and observed the scene between Christian and Drakas. He stood and watched in the doorway with a towel wrapped around his waist, and then he lowered his hand and began to stroke the front of his towel. He removed the towel and hung it on the hook and leaned over to turn on the showerhead closest to the door. He began to let the steaming water flow over his body while never looking away from Christian and Drakas. Christian became aware of the new stranger and looked over at Kadar, who was slowly stroking his growing cock as he watched Christian. Kadar kissed the air, teasing Christian.

In a low voice, Drakas spoke into Christian's ear.

"That guy has a smoking-hot body. I think we should get something going with him?"

Christian was so wrapped up in watching Kadar now that all he could do was nod.

Drakas continued. "What about a little three-way action? I think he'd really be into it. Go over and ask him."

Christian could hardly believe his luck and quickly looked at Drakas to make sure he was serious. Drakas smiled confidently and nodded. Christian walked over to Kadar, who was watching him as he stroked his chest with one hand and his cock with his other hand.

Kadar spoke to Christian in a low tone. "The boys in the shower are never as sexy as you."

Christian was so seduced by his deep, masculine voice that he could barely form a sentence and only managed to say, "Would you, a three-way . . . all of us?"

Kadar looked over Christian's shoulder at Drakas, who continued his playful erotic show, putting his hand behind him and soaping his ass.

Kadar put his hand on Christian's shoulder and looked down at his ass and smiled. "You have a beautiful ass. I bet you love to get pounded."

Drakas walked over and asked, "Are we good for some three-way action?"

Kadar looked at Drakas. "No, count me out. I'm not comfortable here."

"You're not into us?" Drakas asked with disappointment.

"I'm into you. You're both dirty hot. Public sex in a place like this is just not my thing," Kadar replied.

"How about we go outside to a private place I know?" Drakas proposed.

"I'd be up for that. Is it close by?" Kadar asked.

"It's a ten minute walk from here," Drakas confirmed.

"Are you coming?" Kadar asked Christian.

Christian spoke up, "I'm coming."

"Excellent," Kadar replied as he reached down and wrapped his hand around Christian's erect shaft and squeezed. "I really want to feast on your whole body."

Christian could barely contain himself as Kadar grabbed him by the back of the neck and gave him a deep warm kiss.

"Let's get out of here," Drakas urged.

He handed Christian and Kadar their towels. They wrapped them around their waists and Drakas motioned with his hand for Christian to go first, saying, "After you."

Christian followed his lead as Drakas said, "Let's all meet out front in ten minutes."

Ten minutes later, Drakas stood with Kadar on the sidewalk in front of the sauna dressed in their street clothes, each carrying their own gym bags.

Kadar asked, "How many does this one make?"

"Am I supposed to be keeping track?" Drakas replied.

"You always keep track. That's why I never do."

"Does it matter how many?"

"Only to bolster my ego," Kadar said, smiling.

"This one makes sixty-nine."

"My favorite number," Kadar said, with an even bigger smile.

He reached into his bag and removed a bottle of water, which he handed to Drakas.

"Here. You better give it to him this time. He'll trust it more if it comes from you.

Drakas took the bottle from Kadar, opened it, and poured half the water out on the sidewalk. He then took a couple of small white pills from his pocket and dropped them into the bottle. He screwed the cap back on the bottle and shook it several times until the pills dissolved. Just then, Christian joined them.

"Are we ready?" Christian asked with a grin.

"Yeah, let's go," Kadar replied.

Drakas started to lead the way as he said, "Follow me."

The three men began walking down the street together. Drakas handed the bottle of

water to Christian. "Here, have some of my water. You must be thirsty."

Christian took the bottle from Drakas and drank from it. He went to hand it back to Drakas.

"Hold onto it for a while, too much water and I'll be pissing nonstop for the next two hours."

They passed a newsstand that held stacks of different newspapers with headlines that read, "OVER 50 Men Now Missing!" and "Is This The Work of Terrorists?"

The three men continued down the street together. Within minutes Drakas lead them into a very old apartment building and down to the cellar. In the back of the cellar was a heavy old, rusted iron door that Drakas pulled open to reveal a set of stairs cut directly into the chalky bedrock under the apartment building. Drakas pulled a high-powered flashlight from his gym bag, illuminating the way for the others as he continued to lead the way. As they walked down the ancient stairs and into the system of tunnels below, Christian marveled at the strange underground world of Paris' forgotten past. They passed through a short section of the catacombs where thousands of human bones were intricately and artistically stacked centuries ago when the cemeteries of Paris had been emptied and moved under the city.

"I've heard about these places, but I never thought to come here. I wouldn't even know how to get here," Christian admitted.

After several minutes, Christian began to stumble slightly as he walked down the tunnel following Drakas. At first, Kadar began gently pushing him along from behind, but as it became more difficult for Christian to walk and keep pace, Kadar began violently thrusting him forward as he called out, "Keep going, boy! A little farther then you can sit down."

Drakas lead them down another tunnel and stopped at the end.

"Sit down, here on the ground," he ordered Christian.

Christian was now visibly sweating, and he was relieved to finally sit as his head was spinning and it was becoming increasing difficult for him to breath. He was now so incoherent that he didn't even notice that he'd just pissed himself.

As he sat down, he said with slurred speech, "I don't feel well at all."

He leaned back against the wall, which was oddly blackened by soot, and found that he was sitting in the midst of a pile of ash. Kadar and Drakas took a couple steps back from him.

Christian felt extremely light headed, and looked up at them and noticed that there was something strange about their eyes. The whites had taken on a chrome-like metallic appearance.

"What's happening to your eyes?" he mumbled as he strained to keep his eyesight focused.

Without either one saying a word, Drakas spewed a red gelatinous fireball out of his mouth. The flames struck Christian like blazing slime, and completely engulfed him. His body thrashed violently on the ground, slowing until it went limp as he burned to death.

CHAPTER XII

Trechus was reading a book in his salon when Valerian returned shortly after dusk from spending the day tracking the Black Dragons through the city. Valerian entered the salon in such haste that he did not even bother to remove his coat. Trechus put his book down on the table to hear the news.

"Black Dragons have indeed come to Paris," Valerian reported. "Their foul stench is all over this city."

"As much as I am prepared to hear this, it still causes a knot in my stomach. How long have they been here?" Trechus asked.

"The faintest stench is about two weeks old, so maybe a little longer."

"How many do you think there are?"

"I have been able to track four different ones."

"I never picked up any scent until this week."

"You never picked up a scent as they were smart enough to avoid you. They know you're here. They're very clever this time. They're using the old underground network of tunnels beneath the city—except this section of Montmartre, your Métro line, and the Sorbonne. Clearly they collected a great deal of intelligence on you and your habits."

"What do you propose we do?"

"Right now, we should do nothing. They won't come after us unless we provoke them. We are at a disadvantage, as they know where you live and work. I do not believe it was a chance meeting the other day. The dragon you saw clearly intended to get a look at you."

"I'm sorry I missed this. I should have picked up on it sooner."

"You never had the opportunity to discover them. They came here, and the first thing they did was track and find you. Then they organized their movements to avoid detection. Tomorrow, we must go to see Rodin. He will have to decide how he wants us to deal with them."

"So you must believe they are getting ready to attack the city?" Trechus asked cautiously.

"We are a long way from their last attack in 1346—but then we are only in the early stages. There are a handful here now, but there is no indication of how many more may still be out there. Men are disappearing, but there are no signs of sickness yet."

The two men looked at each other in silence as they both considered the full magnitude of the situation.

"I am not suggesting that you're in immediate danger, but, nonetheless, your safety has become a concern. You also need to consider Malcolm. Anyone who is associated with you could easily fall into harm's way."

"I'm supposed to meet him now and bring him back here."

"I do think that after tonight you need to distance yourself from Malcolm for his own safety. Perhaps even consider sending him away. This will relieve you from having to tell him who you really are at a time when he is clearly not ready to understand."

"I agree," Trechus replied.

"When the danger has passed, you can resume your friendship with him. But, of course, you know I believe 'friendship' is the wrong word."

"The word 'friendship' bothers you?"

"You allow no visitors to your house. You live for years, locked away in your own private world, and suddenly there is a young stranger in your home with no explanation. You refer to him only as a friend and nothing more."

"Would you at least give me an opportunity to get to know him? Not to mention, see if he has any interest in me at all as a friend or otherwise."

"Trechus, affection is all in the eyes. It is in his eyes and it is surely in your eyes, clear as day."

"Why are you pushing this so hard?"

"Because I miss you, the real you. I miss the Trechus who is wild with passion and embracing life. What you have created here with these books is not worthy of you or your great talents."

"Does it matter that I am happy the way I am?"

Valerian looked him in the eye as he said with caution, "Every minute you spend protecting yourself from sorrow is indeed, another minute stolen away from your happiness."

Trechus paused to consider Valerian's words. He replied in a tone of regret, "There is truth to what you say."

"Trechus, I am not in the habit of being dishonest with you and I am prepared to give you a good thrashing if you dare to imply otherwise."

"Taking myself out of the equation for a moment, there is Malcolm to consider. He comes with a good deal of . . . I guess it is best to say, emotional baggage."

"Perfect! See, you both have something in common. I consider you're both well-balanced in the baggage department."

Trechus smiled dearly at his old friend but was careful not to laugh, as he knew Valerian was expecting him to take his words seriously.

Valerian became louder and more animated. "You're lost in books, living the lives of others. In case you forgot, these characters that you spend your life with are not even real. Paper and ink, that is all they really are. No heart, no soul, just black stuff on wood pulp."

"You know why I do this."

"Fuck the loss. Everyday we lose something. Just because Malcolm may one day walk out on you—or worse, die—is no reason not to make the most of your time together now."

Valerian picked up the book Trechus had been reading and asked, "Who are the characters in this novel?"

"Charles Ryder and Sebastian Flyte."

"Are they dear friends of yours?"

"Now you're being ridiculous."

"How did you feel when Peter died?"

"You know how much pain I suffered after his death."

Valerian tossed the book into the burning fire in the fireplace. "You just lost your friends Charles and Sebastian. Does it feel like you really lost anything of importance with these fictional characters."

Trechus smiled and asked politely of Valerian, "If I agree with you right here and now do you promise not to burn any more of my first editions?"

Valerian ignored the comment and shot back, "What is life? It is triumph intertwined with the tragic. Without one the other cannot exist. The greatest crime you can commit is to ignore life—and that, my friend, is your biggest sin. Do you know what will happen next? I don't! Tonight could be the last time you see Malcolm. Don't spend all your time hiding in books, go live your life."

"Are you finished?"

"Yes, I have run out of things to say," Valerian concluded.

"That is a first for you."

"You know something, you're right. I never have before."

"Are you hungry?"

"No, I am going back out to track those nasty sons-of-bitches. The night is young and I am in the mood to hunt."

CHAPTER XIII

Trechus stepped out of his house into the cold night air with a medium-sized white box tied with a red satin bow tucked under his arm. He walked briskly toward the square to meet Malcolm and Chevalier. The crowd was thin that evening when he arrived, so Malcolm could see him coming from a distance. Malcolm was talking with a customer to whom he was showing a book.

As he got closer, Malcolm called out, "That better not be a present."

Trechus called back, "Don't flatter yourself, it's not for you."

Charlotte, who was sitting next to Malcolm, stood up to greet Trechus.

"Bonsoir, monsieur," she said, kissing him on both cheeks.

"Bonsoir, madame," he replied, as he then greeted Malcolm. "Bonsoir, Malcolm."

"Bonsoir." Malcolm eyed the package with suspicion.

Trechus paid no attention to Malcolm and got down on one knee in front of Chevalier, opening the box to reveal a new black leather collar and matching leash. He put the collar on the dog and took off the makeshift one that Malcolm had fashioned for him out of old rope he had found in the park.

He stood up and admired his work. "Your leash was beautiful because you had made it with your own hands, but he needs something a little stronger for his own safety."

Malcolm smiled and put Trechus at ease. "I like it! Finally, he has a proper Parisian collar and leash set." He then looked at Trechus sternly. "I am still trying to understand why you're being so generous with us?"

"You and Chevalier deserve some kindness. You two have been through a great deal for being so young. I have the means to make things a little easier for you both."

"It's just that I'm having a hard time comprehending all of this. I don't want to appear ungrateful but I don't know how to respond or how I can repay you."

"Malcolm, the kindness I show you does not put you in debt to me," Trechus assured him.

"Well, in a way it does. I don't expect you or anyone else to do something for nothing."

"Why do you believe the world is void of random acts of kindness?" Trechus asked.

"Random acts of kindness don't exist for me," Malcolm replied.

"You're feeding and caring for a dog that was alone and starving on the street. How do you rationalize your kindness?"

"Trechus, look at my life. There is no kindness. You have been extremely generous, and I thank you. You just need to understand that no one has given me anything without taking from me. The foster parents I had gave me a home and in exchange took the money they got paid by the state and bought beer, cigarettes, and lottery tickets. That was my value to them. Beer, cigarettes, and lottery tickets that never paid shit. That is my reality."

Charlotte took a drag from her cigarette and exhaled. "The boy is right. People aren't kind anymore or even interested in being caring. The world has sadly changed. It's no wonder he feels this way. Certainly, it's not like the old days."

"So no one is kind anymore and I should follow that example?" Trechus asked.

"Of course the boy would be suspect of you," Charlotte chimed in. "He's never met anyone like you. What could you expect? Your behavior is so alien to him that you might as well be from a different planet."

She took another drag from her cigarette. "He is buried and trapped under his own emotions. If you truly care about him, you'll be patient with him and take the time to help him free himself."

She turned and eyed Malcolm. "You need to appreciate the hard work this man is investing in trying to find a lost human being. You may not understand him, but too bad. That's your problem. Don't make it his. Be thankful that someone is even bothering to try to discover you. You can be angry, mad, and furious with all the people who've done you wrong in your life, but it's not Trechus' responsibility to do penance for them."

Malcolm swallowed hard.

Charlotte smiled at him. "One thing I learned a long time ago is that when it comes to fixing the emotional state of men, there is nothing better than a good swift kick in the derrière."

Malcolm started laughing. "I feel better already! But I honestly think Trechus would benefit from another swift kick or two."

Trechus smiled at Charlotte's wisdom and candor.

"I do hate the world today," she continued. "It's made up of shortsighted people who only respond to instantaneous gratification. Everything is digital now, and therefore nothing physically exists anywhere. A flash of electricity and then it's gone, forever! No one wants to grow up to be happy anymore; everyone wants to grow up to be rich so they can buy lots of stuff! When I was a girl, I wanted to grow up not to have a great career but to have incredible love affairs. The world is wrongly fixated on the next email and text message. All digital shit! Not me! I am fixated on my next kiss, my next great love affair."

She shook her head. "I wish everyone would flush their mobile phones down the toilet. The sewer is where they belong. Our world has been robbed of the simple love letter poetically written on fine stationery and gently scented. Those were the days! How can anyone be seduced by an email? It's just appalling and sad. You can send Malcolm a hundred emails and it will never have the same effect of one handwritten letter. The love letters I have received in my years! I've saved every single one of them. I may not have much now as an old woman, but I have my memories."

She stopped, and looked politely at Trechus and Malcolm.

"Where are my manners? I should let you two young men get on with your evening. Destiny beckons and the night is young."

Malcolm leaned over and hugged Charlotte. "Thanks so much for kicking Trechus in the derrière. He really needed it."

Malcolm looked back and grinned at Trechus, and then started to collect and pack up his things.

Trechus said to Charlotte, "You really are a special lady."

"Thank you," she replied, "but I am really nothing more than a simple, old French woman, and I am comfortable with that."

"I will accept your modesty."

"Thank you. Sometimes I feel that it is all I have left," she replied.

"I won't believe that you don't still have your fair share of gentlemen callers."

"As a proper Parisian woman I would never imply or comment on such a thing."

"I promise, I will take your secret to the grave," Trechus said, holding up his right hand.

"Just until I die, then I want it spread all over France and into Italy and Spain. I want people to be talking about me for at least two or three generations!"

Trechus smiled. "I am so happy we met. I hope we become friends."

"I would like that," Charlotte said, kissing Trechus on both cheeks. "Bonne soirée."

"Bonne soirée."

Malcolm was just finishing packing up his things.

"Are you ready?" Trechus asked him.

"Yes, I have all my things."

Malcolm kissed Charlotte goodnight on both cheeks. He and Trechus began to walk away with Chevalier following behind them.

As they headed toward Trechus' house, Malcolm said, "I would like to be friends someday."

Trechus seemed puzzled. "Are we not friends now?"

"I think we are becoming friends," Malcolm confirmed.

Trechus smiled. "I think Chevalier's commitment issues are rubbing off on you.

CHAPTER XIV

After a long day out in the cold weather, Malcolm was eager to arrive at Trechus' house where he could warm himself in front of the fire. The damp weather of Paris was not agreeing with his health. He was feeling more pressure than ever to find an inexpensive apartment that would take him and his giant dog. Small dogs were usually acceptable, but when he showed up with Chevalier, most landlords would not even open the door. His promise not to abandon Chevalier was keeping him out on the street.

Malcolm and Chevalier followed Trechus into the house. Upon hearing them arrive home, Monique came from the kitchen to greet them. She had a warm smile on her face as she entered the hall, but her smile quickly diminished after she saw the condition Malcolm was in.

"The cold is ravaging you child. This is not good for you," she said as she bypassed Trechus and went straight to Malcolm.

Malcolm could only offer, "It was a long day."

"Go make yourself warm by the fire," she advised as she helped him take off his jacket. "I will go brew a special tea for you that will draw the cold from your body."

He found his way into the salon and made himself comfortable on the settee in front of the burning fire. As he lay back, he pushed one side of his face into the pillows of the settee, and for a brief moment could recall the warmth he felt when he had been in his childhood bed. He was relaxing now and felt himself drifting off to sleep, and he allowed himself to do so. There were no worries about Chevalier tonight. The dog seemed more at home in the house than he did on the street. If the winter got really cold and business didn't remain solid, he might try to find a farm in the country that could give Chevalier the home that he was failing to provide. He remained hopeful that Trechus could help him if it came to that.

He drifted off to sleep quickly. He awoke to the sight of Trechus' muscular forearm which was now less than an inch from his nose. Trechus was sitting next to him drinking a glass of wine and watching the fire burn.

"You've returned," Trechus said, smiling down at him.

Malcolm squinted and rubbed his face with his hand. "How long have I been out?"

"Maybe half an hour."

"This is so nice, waking up here—but I'm afraid I am getting spoiled."

"Malcolm, there is something I need to tell you. I'll be going away tomorrow with Valerian for an indefinite period of time. I am not sure how long I'll be gone."

"I think it's a good idea for Chevalier and me to go back and stay at the cemetery. You have been very generous, but we can't rely on you for a place to stay."

"Malcolm, I don't want you living on the street. I want to arrange for a small apartment for you and Chevalier before I leave tomorrow."

"You can't be the one who is always giving. I can't be the one constantly taking from you! It makes me feel pathetic."

"Malcolm, trust me—you're far from pathetic. I just want to make things easier for you."

"Can you see why I don't want your help? Please understand, Trechus. I need to do this on my own."

"You know I'm not comfortable with you sleeping in the cemetery at night with all that's going on right now. You really need to be in an apartment. It's about your safety."

"With Chevalier at my side, who would dare attack me?"

"Malcolm, don't joke. These days the danger in Paris is very real."

"OK, I won't joke. Are you angry with me?"

"No, why would you think that?" Trechus looked confused.

"I keep waiting for you to realize how messed up I am." Malcolm looked down. "When you do, I expect you won't want to have anything to do with me."

"I believe I am a good judge of character. I think you're perfect just the way you are."

"See, I get upset when you say things like that. I'm not perfect! When you say that, I feel like you're making fun of me. I live on the streets, most days I smell putrid, I'm not educated and there's little hope I will ever amount to anything."

"Don't speak like that. You are so much more than you think."

"As long as I'm a simple guy with few ambitions, I'll never be a disappointment to anyone."

"What if I told you that education, ambition, and being sophisticated were not important to me?"

"I would say you're lying." Malcolm looked him dead in the eye.

"Why?"

"You're all of those things! Of course they're important to you, they're what shaped you!"

"Malcolm, when you get older you'll realize that those things that you think are the most important things rarely have any meaning later in life. You have one wonderful quality that I have seldom seen in an individual. You're completely honest about yourself. You're not hiding behind some fabrication of a person you think you should be. When I look at you, I see Malcolm. I see the real Malcolm. Even now, you stand before me with all your imperfections and all your flaws making no attempt to mask yourself. I honestly love that about you."

"You don't really know me. I fear that one day when you do get to know me you'll be sadly disappointed."

"Malcolm, I like what I see. I like you because you're not perfect and because you don't try to hide it. Tomorrow, before I leave, I am going to arrange for an apartment for you and Chevalier. I insist, and if you refuse me I will be angry because I will have to go away and worry about you freezing to death in the cemetery or worse."

"I am not worried about myself but I do want to provide a home for Chevalier. If you could help us this one time, it would help. If I can't get a place to take us both I have to give him up and I just can't do that."

Malcolm laid his head against Trechus' shoulder and watched the flames dance across the burning logs. He felt more exhausted than usual. The cold weather of the day really beat him down. He felt as if a huge weight had been lifted now that Trechus would help him, and he would not have to give up Chevalier. He was able to relax now in a way that he had not known as an adult or could barely remember as a child. Sleep quickly overtook him and he breathed sweetly as he lay against Trechus' arm.

Trechus watched the fire burn as Malcolm slept. There was still a small portion of the cover of his book that had not completely burned in the fireplace. This caused him to reflect on his earlier conversation with Valerian. He had to admit to himself that he cared for Malcolm more than he was ready to admit to Valerian.

As Malcolm slept, he snuggled gently against Trechus' arm. Malcolm's face came in direct contact with Trechus' skin. Trechus could feel streams of Malcolm's warm breath as it traveled in waves down his forearm. Trechus leaned in and touched his nose to Malcolm's forehead as he took in the sweet smell of Malcolm's hair. He admired how beautiful a young man Malcolm was as he slept.

Malcolm shifted in his sleep and moved his arm across Trechus' chest until it came to rest on his pectoral muscle. This action aroused Trechus, who closed his eyes and imagined waking Malcolm, gently pulling off his clothes, and laying with him on the floor in front of the fire as he slowly explored every inch of Malcolm's beautiful body. The more he imagined it, the more it felt real to him. Malcolm's warm breath continued to stream down his arm in a way that continued to stir Trechus' desire for Malcolm.

Trechus' fantasy and physical proximity to Malcolm became too much for him to bear. He now admitted to himself that he wanted Malcolm, and probably had since the first moment he saw him on the street. He did not know how much longer he could remain next to him and hold himself back. Staying with Malcolm on the settee was no longer an option in his mind so he gently moved Malcolm off of him, taking care not to wake him.

Trechus decided it would be best to leave the room and go upstairs, away from any further temptation. He was breathing heavily now, signaling that he had taken this further than was prudent. He went out into the hall and sprinted up the stairs to his bathroom. He turned on the cold water in the shower and went over to the mirror. He looked at himself in the mirror and saw that his eyes had changed completely. It was no surprise to him that they now looked like two large gold metallic marbles with curious black slits running down through the center. He admired his reflection for a moment. Pulling his T-shirt off over his head, he exposed a curious V-shaped spine that was clearly not of a human kind. It consisted of two spines that protruded from his back and were scalloped, with bones running along the edges. He reached over his shoulder with his hand and rubbed the upper portion of his spine that connected to his shoulder. He then ran his hand down across his pecs as he continued to admire himself in the mirror.

He removed the rest of his clothes and stepped into the shower, letting the water flow over his body. He stood there as the cold water lowered his body temperature before he started to lather his body with soap.

Malcolm remained sleeping on the settee downstairs and entered another dreamscape:

He was walking down the same deserted road in Vermont as the snow fell. As he walked, a police car passed him with its sirens yelling. A brief moment later it was followed by an ambulance. As he arrived at the scene of the accident there was a flurry of activity. He watched as the EMTs picked his bloodied body up out of the snow and placed it onto a stretcher. As the stretcher was loaded into the ambulance, a police officer on the scene indicated to the other EMTs that there were no other survivors.

Malcolm awoke with a start, gasping for a single breath of air. It took a moment for him to recall where he was. Realizing Trechus was gone, he got up from the settee and went out into the dark hall. He continued down the hallway in search of Trechus, climbing the stairs to the second floor. As he walked down the hall he heard the noise of the running shower. He walked toward the noise in the dark hall and opened the door to Trechus' bathroom. The light from the bathroom streamed out into the hall. Trechus, who was still showering, turned to see Malcolm standing there in a state of terror. He was frozen by the sight of Trechus' golden eyes and the altered form of his double-back spine. Malcolm turned in horror and ran blindly down the hall toward the staircase, racing toward the front door. Still covered in lather, Trechus leapt from the shower and tore after Malcolm, jumping off the upper railing of the stairway and tackling Malcolm to the ground as he reached the ground floor. Malcolm tried to cry out for help, but Trechus covered his mouth with his hand. Fearing for his life, Malcolm desperately tried to struggle and get free from Trechus. He thrashed and twisted violently but Trechus' strength and body weight rendered him helpless. He tried again to call for help, but his cries were only muffled by Trechus' large hand.

"Stop it! Stop fighting me!" Trechus ordered Malcolm.

Chevalier charged into the hall barking and whining as he paced at the site of the two struggling. Malcolm began to relent, exhausted from the intense struggle. Completely helpless, he began to cry as fear for his life consumed him. The large tears rolled over Trechus' hand, which remained covering Malcolm's mouth.

"Trechus! Let him up!" Valerian shouted from the top of the stairs.

Malcolm looked up to see Valerian running down the stairs toward them and felt a momentary sense of relief that he was no longer alone with this creature. Valerian took Malcolm by his hand and Trechus released him. Valerian pulled Malcolm to his feet.

"What the fuck are you?!!" Malcolm was still shaking and crying, looking down at Trechus, who was still prone.

Trechus stared back at Malcolm in silence.

"I don't know what the fuck is going on here but I'm getting out of here, now!!" Malcolm said as he moved toward the door.

Valerian quickly grabbed Malcolm's arm. "You can't leave."

Malcolm violently tried to pull away from him. "Let me go!!" he yelled. "LET ME GO!!"

Valerian grabbed Malcolm by the back of his neck, pulling the young man's face close to his own as Malcolm did his best to resist. Valerian grabbed Malcolm's cheeks forcing his lips to part with one hand and blew a purple-colored smoke from his own lips into Malcolm's mouth. Shocked and resisting heavily, Malcolm had no choice but to gulp down the smoke. He began to choke excessively and fell to the floor, gasping for air as his body went limp. Trechus got up from the floor and he and Valerian stood over Malcolm's lifeless body.

Monique came rushing down the stairs into the hall and upon seeing Malcolm on the floor cried out in anger, "What have you done?"

CHAPTER XV

As the dawn approached, a Porsche Panamera sped down a French country road in the Loire Valley. The car entered through massive iron gates that guarded a magnificent limestone French chateau and raced up the long driveway toward the imposing 17th century structure, coming to an abrupt halt at the front steps. The front door immediately opened and a trim middle aged butler and two younger identical twin footmen immediately exited the house and quickly descending the steps to meet the arriving car.

The butler opened the passenger side door and said in a proper tone, "Bonjour, monsieur."

Valerian exited the car. "Jean-Yves, I assure you, there is nothing good about this morning."

The two athletic looking footmen went immediately to the rear of the car and opened the trunk to remove the luggage.

Trechus jumped out of the driver's seat. "Be careful!" He called out. "That dog will rip your throat out if you cross him." He went around to the back of the car to help the footmen with Chevalier.

Jean-Yves opened the passenger side door and looked down to see Malcolm unconscious, yellow foam spewing from his mouth with each breath.

"Help me get him out of the car," Valerian directed Jean-Yves.

As they pulled Malcolm from the car, Valerian easily threw him over his shoulder and carried him into the house. Malcolm gave a few low moans as Valerian climbed the stairs.

"I am going to need a bedroom and some rope to tie him down," Valerian directed Jean-Yves, who was now holding the front door open for him.

Valerian took Malcolm to a bedroom on the second floor and, with the help of Jean-Yves, stripped Malcolm down and secured him to the bed with rope. There, Malcolm spent the better part of the day floating back and forth between states of consciousness and unconsciousness. It was just after sundown when he was finally conscious enough to take note of his new surroundings. The room was dark but he could make out the details and splendor of the grand bedroom. He attempted to move slightly and quickly realized that his hands and feet were securely tied to the bed. He was covered in his own sweat and the sheet covering him was soaked with sweat and slightly stained along the top edge by the yellow foam emanating from his mouth. He had a pounding headache. He tried to call out for someone, but his attempts were futile as he could barely muster any sound from his aching vocal cords.

He lay there for a while before he heard footsteps coming down the hallway approaching the bedroom. The door opened and Jean-Yves entered the room followed by the two footman Janos and Milos. Janos was carrying a silver tray with a crystal decanter filled with a green liquid and a crystal glass. Milos followed carrying a silver tray with a crystal bowl half filled with soapy water and several towels draped over his arm. Jean-Yves observed that Malcolm was awake and directed Janos to put the tray down on the nightstand.

Looking up at the three men, Malcolm tried to speak.

"Don't try to speak yet," Jean-Yves instructed him as he stepped forward. "My name is Jean-Yves. I am the Estate Manager here at the chateau. While you are here, I will be responsible for looking after you."

With the kind of precision that only comes from years of practice, Janos and Milos pulled back the sweat soaked top sheet and discarded it. Malcolm now lay on the bed naked and restrained before the three men.

Milos took a small towel and dipped it into the crystal bowl and began to wash the dried yellow foam that was covering most of Malcolm's face, neck, and part of his chest. It did not easily wash away so Milos had to work at it. After he finished, he dried Malcolm with the second towel. Janos replaced the single soiled pillow that supported Malcolm's head with two larger ones that allowed him to see better into the room. Janos then joined Milos at the foot of the bed where they expertly unfolded a new top sheet and draped it on top of Malcolm. After they completed the task, the two footman went and stood side by side by the door to the room. Focusing in on them a bit better, Malcolm at first thought he was seeing double before he realized they were twin brothers.

Jean-Yves reached for the crystal decanter on the bedside table and poured some green liquid in the small crystal glass.

"Drink this, monsieur," he instructed Malcolm. "It will make you feel better and help to restore your voice."

He helped Malcolm to drink from the glass. After swallowing the contents of the glass, Malcolm began to attempt to clear his throat and found he could speak in a soft voice.

"That's the worst stuff I've ever tasted," he said with complete disgust.

"I wouldn't know, monsieur. I've have never had it," Jean-Yves replied dryly.

"What is it?"

"It is a mixture of herbs to help counteract the toxins you ingested."

"What toxins?" Malcolm asked, slightly alarmed.

"Monsieur, the toxins that were used to subdue you last night."

Malcolm paused and searched his memory. "It's all coming back to me now. I have this pounding headache."

"That is to be expected, monsieur. It usually takes twenty-four hours to clear the toxins out of the body. You should begin to feel like yourself again by morning."

"Where am I?" Malcolm asked in a low voice.

"I am not at liberty to say."

"Who brought me here?"

"Valerian and Trechus brought you here very early this morning from Paris."

"Do you restrain all your guests?"

"No, of course not, monsieur."

"Can you untie me?"

"No, monsieur. Only Rodin can do that."

"Who is Rodin?"

"I am not at liberty to say. Really, monsieur, you should get some rest."

"You're aware that this is kidnapping and you are now an accomplice."

"If you say so, monsieur," Jean-Yves said remaining professional and dry as any proper butler should.

"If you don't untie me I'm going to start screaming."

"Please don't do that, monsieur. Your vocal cords are not fully recovered and you may permanently damage your voice. I would not recommend it."

Jean-Yves turned and headed for the door.

"Hey, hey, where are you going?"

Jean-Yves ignored Malcolm and exited the room followed by Milos and Janos. Janos turned off the light and closed the door behind him. Some time passed before the door opened again and a large towering figure stood in the shadows of the doorway. The man had an incredibly large muscular build that almost seemed unreal for a man.

"Do you wish to speak in French or English?" the man asked in French with a gruff authoritative tone.

"English," Malcolm softly replied.

The man stepped forward, turned on the light, and said, "I am Rodin and I understand that you are Malcolm Quinn."

"What are you planning to do with me?" Malcolm demanded in a weak voice.

"I really don't know yet. What happens to you next will depend on what kind of man you are."

"What kind of man do I need to be to stay alive?"

"An honest and loyal man would be a good start."

"So while you decide my fate, I'm to be a prisoner here?"

"Let us both try to stay on the pleasant side of this unfortunate situation. For the time being, you're to be my permanent guest."

"Yeah, well I just met your man servant and can't say I was too impressed."

"You will show Jean-Yves the respect he is entitled to. He is a retired commander from the French Foreign Legion. I don't expect that you possess the intelligence to understand what that implies but I don't think you ever want to make the mistake of underestimating him. He can and will be lethal if necessary. If you are to stay on the right side of Jean-Yves, you must remain a gracious guest."

"You may call me a guest, but I am still here against my will. The French authorities would classify this as kidnapping."

"Fair enough, you have been kidnapped and your release is uncertain, maybe even unlikely. However, I assure you, the laws of men do not apply here and you should not insult me with your adolescent bravado. This is my domain and that makes me your Lord and Master. I will decide what is appropriate. Are we clear on this point?"

"Yes, we are clear," Malcolm replied, softly, but eyed him with an adolescent rage.

"Your friends Valerian and Trechus speak highly of you."

"I am not sure I can call two guys who poisoned and kidnapped me my friends!"

"I would suggest this: between now and the time you wake up tomorrow, you should seriously change your attitude. Your life now depends on it."

Malcolm looked up at Rodin, his eyes burning with contempt. Rodin grabbed the pillows from under Malcolm's head and pulled them hard, causing his head to fall back onto the mattress. He then pulled the top sheet away, leaving Malcolm naked and exposed.

"You're under my jurisdiction now and I will do with you as I wish."

"Go fuck yourself!" Malcolm fired back softly but in a determined voice.

Rodin pulled out his pocket watch as he walked to the middle of the room and looked down at the time as he said calmly, "You have every reason to be afraid of me."

After studying the time, Rodin returned the watch to his pocket and looked back up at Malcolm. "You just do not possess the intelligence yet to know why."

Rodin leaped from the center of the room, ten feet into the air toward Malcolm, and landed squarely on top of him. With a single rapid action, he grabbed Malcolm by the throat and squeezed tightly just to the point of choking him. Malcolm's eyes rapidly drained of rage and filled with fear and tears as he looked at Rodin and realized his mistake.

"If I wanted you dead I could easily detach your head from your body right now. I think you understand that, for me, it would be an easy task."

Malcolm was unable to speak as Rodin kept just enough precise pressure on his throat so the blood flow to his brain was being restricted, making him light headed. Rodin looked deep into Malcolm's eyes and then released his grip as he said, "Deep inside you there is a perfect being. I can see it in your eyes. You're trapped and suffocating under tons of your own emotional shit. The question remains, do I bother to heal you or do I just let you fester and rot?"

As Rodin eyed him, Malcolm understood that his situation was dire and he swallowed hard before he strained to get the words out.

"I want your help."

"I did not hear you," Rodin replied.

"I want your help," Malcolm said in a louder voice.

Rodin looked down at Malcolm and said, "So be it." He went to the door and opened it, speaking to Jean-Yves in the outer hall. "Jean-Yves come in here and clean up this mess."

"Yes, monsieur," Jean-Yves replied as Rodin left the room. Jean-Yves entered the room and picked up the sheet and pillows from the floor.

"Can you help me?" Malcolm asked.

"Only Rodin can do that," Jean-Yves replied.

Jean-Yves restored the pillows under Malcolm's head and covered him with the sheet. Jean-Yves left the room and turned off the light, leaving Malcolm alone in the near darkness of the room. The only light in the room came from the outdoor spotlights that illuminated the exterior of the chateau at night. Malcolm drifted in and out of sleep. He was unsure of how much time had passed when he was startled by the door being thrown open.

Rodin entered the room turning on the light and, without saying a word, ripped the top sheet off the bed. He unbuttoned and removed his waistcoat and cuff links and placed them on a side table. He pulled his suspenders off his shoulders. Malcolm watched as he unbuttoned his shirt and removed it to expose the tank top he wore underneath. As Rodin undressed, Malcolm was certain that Rodin meant to rape him. Rodin replaced his suspenders on his shoulders and removed a pair of fine black leather gloves from his back pocket and expertly slid his hand into each glove. Rodin untied the ropes restraining Malcolm to the bed, but left the individual ropes tied to his arms and legs. He remained silent and deliberate in his actions.

"What are you planning to do with me?" Malcolm asked anxiously.

Rodin did not respond and picked up Malcolm like a rag doll, threw him over his massive muscular shoulder, and carried him out of the room with the ropes tied to his hands and feet dangling from his naked body.

"What are you doing?!"

Rodin remained silent as he left the bedroom.

"Where are we going?" Malcolm was starting to panic.

Rodin, still silent, charged through the chateau as Malcolm flopped around on his shoulder feeling off balanced and completely powerless.

"I'll do whatever you want!! Just please, don't hurt me!!"

"Jean-Yves! Rodin shouted as he started down the stairs, but there was no answer. "Jean-Yves!" Rodin roared.

Jean-Yves appeared out of nowhere and met Rodin at the bottom of the stairs.

"Yes, monsieur?"

"Do you have everything ready outside?" Rodin asked.

"Yes, monsieur. We are ready for you."

"Get the door," Rodin ordered.

Jean-Yves rushed to get ahead of Rodin and open the front door.

Malcolm was too weak to fight back as Rodin carried him out into the frigid night air. Rodin carted him across the lawn to the side of the chateau where there were two large ancient stone pillars set in the center of three rings of burning fire. At the opening of the rings there was a leather wing chair with an ornate side table that contained a cigar box, a crystal decanter set, and an old-fashioned hand-cranked Victrola.

Milos and Janos stood waiting and ready as Rodin approached. Rodin lifted Malcolm off his shoulder and threw him at the two footmen, who struggled to catch Malcolm without falling over themselves.

"String him up!" Rodin roared.

As Rodin sat in the chair, Jean-Yves placed the needle of the Victrola on the record and Mozart's "Requiem Lacrimosa" began to play, filling the frigid night air with music. Jean-Yves opened the cigar box, selected a cigar, neatly trimmed the end, and handed it to Rodin. Rodin took the cigar and, with his own breath, blew a stream of purple fire from his lips, lighting the cigar. He began to smoke as Jean-Yves poured him a cognac.

Milos and Janos led Malcolm through the fire rings to the base of the pillars. Using the ropes tied to each of Malcolm's wrists, they expertly attached him to the pillars and pulled the ropes taut, spreading his arms away from his body. Malcolm was beginning to freeze in the cold, but he was more fixated on the shame of his exposed naked body displayed in such a manner in front of the other men. He wished dearly that he could tear the ropes off so he could use his hands to cover himself.

Next, the footmen took the leg ropes and threaded them through the iron rings at the base of each pillar and proceeded to pull them taut, spreading Malcolm's legs farther and farther apart. His body temperature was dropping, but the cold air subdued his pounding headache and soothed the ache in his throat. Within several minutes he was shivering uncontrollably. Malcolm heard several of the windows of the chateau open behind him, and then he faintly heard male voices speaking above him over the music. He was now even more self-conscious of his nudity, but worst of all, he did not know who, or how many people were watching him.

Malcolm had a clear view of Rodin, who sat in the chair twenty feet in front of him. Rodin drank his cognac and smoked his cigar and watched as Malcolm's lips began to turn blue from the cold.

Rodin turned to Jean-Yves and said, "I think our boy is ready."

Jean-Yves stepped forward with an elegant wooden box that he opened to reveal a stunning black leather cat-o-nine tails whip with an intricate handle. Rodin removed the whip from its box and examined it. Malcolm's eyes widened as he watched.

Rodin walked towards Malcolm and, as he reached him, Malcolm asked through chattering teeth, "What are you going to do?"

"You told me you needed my help," Rodin replied.

He walked around Malcolm, studying him as if he were a piece of art up for auction. He stopped for a moment when he was at Malcolm's backside and said, "I am going to help you. While you may question my method, I assure you it will be effective."

Rodin continued to walk around to Malcolm's front side, stopping as he took a moment to study the detail of the whip. "Now, I am going to determine who you really are."

Rodin's expression turned dark as he looked Malcolm squarely in the face. "Why don't we start with you telling me again to go fuck myself?"

"I won't do it," Malcolm replied, his teeth wildly chattering from the cold.

Rodin wound up and hit Malcolm hard across the chest with the whip. Malcolm's body wildly lunged back from the pain.

Malcolm screamed out, "Go fuck yourself."

As soon as he finished saying the words, the whip fell again on his chest. Malcolm screamed out again. Next, Rodin slowly walked behind Malcolm and stopped to speak directly into his ear. "Again. Tell me again."

Malcolm said in a low voice, breathing heavily, "Go fuck yourself."

The whip fell squarely on the center of his back.

"Again! Tell me again!" Rodin roared.

This time Malcolm hesitated, but called out, "Go fuck yourself!"

Rodin wound up and with all his strength hit Malcolm again.

"AGAIN!" Rodin roared.

Malcolm was breathing to the point of hyperventilating and remained silent.

"Again!" Rodin demanded.

Malcolm said nothing.

"Good, I am glad we got that out of your system," Rodin said, pausing for a moment. "Now. I want you to declare me, for all time, your Lord and Master."

Malcolm managed to speak just above a whisper, "You are my Lord and Master."

The whip fell hard, this time on his buttocks.

"I want to hear you when you speak to me," Rodin insisted as he brought the whip down on Malcolm again.

Malcolm cried out, "You are my Lord and Master!"

"Again" Rodin demanded as the whip fell on Malcolm.

"You are my Lord and Master!!" Malcolm cried out louder.

"I am indeed your Lord and Master." Rodin returned to sit in his chair. He picked up his burning cigar as Jean-Yves poured him a second glass of cognac. He eyed Malcolm and called out to him, "Now that I am your Lord and Master and I desire for you to take five lashes. How do you respond?"

Malcolm looked at him in a trusting manner. "I will take five lashes for you, sir."

"Jean-Yves, take my whip and administer the five lashes."

Jean-Yves took the whip from Rodin and walked toward Malcolm.

"Land each one squarely on his chest," Rodin called out to Jean-Yves.

When Jean-Yves reached Malcolm, he said quietly, "Malcolm, after each strike, you're required to call out the number followed by 'Sir.' So, after my first strike you say 'One, sir.' After the second, 'Two, sir.' Understand?"

Malcolm looked Jean-Yves in the eye and nodded.

Jean-Yves turned to Rodin. "Shall I commence, monsieur?"

Rodin sat back and nodded.

Jean-Yves wound up and he landed the first hit on Malcolm's chest.

Malcolm called out, "One, sir!"

"Keep your eyes on mine," Rodin corrected Malcolm.

Jean-Yves administered the second hit.

"Two, sir!"

The third lash hit and Malcolm struggled out, "Three, sir!"

"Louder boy! Show me how fucking tough you can be!" Rodin stood up and strode toward Jean-Yves, grabbed the whip, and administered a fierce fourth lash to Malcolm's chest.

"Four, sir!" Malcolm screamed out, his face flushed red and breathing hard.

"Good boy. Now let me see your eyes!"

Rodin looked into Malcolm's eyes that had welled up, but no tears fell.

"You're with me now, you're right here. The shit is all going away. Do you feel it?"

Malcolm did feel it. Despite his fear and the intense pain of the flogging, his mind was, for the first time that he could recall, entirely focused in the moment. There were no thoughts of anything before or after this exact moment. He now understood that Rodin was wiser and knew more about his own mind and troubles than even he could comprehend.

"Yes, sir! You're right. I do feel it," Malcolm said, as his body struggled against the pain and cold night air.

He was relieved. His psyche was clear with no competing thoughts or anxieties. His mind was in a state that was so foreign to him that he did not even feel like himself. His body hurt badly, but he felt this incredible connection to Rodin. He no longer cared that he was naked and exposed to the others.

"Are you ready for the final one?" Rodin asked.

"Yes, sir," Malcolm yelled out confidently.

Rodin walked behind Malcolm and ordered him, "Start breathing hard."

Malcolm began breathing hard, and on the third exhale, Rodin brought the whip down as hard as he could squarely on the center of his back down to his ass. Malcolm's body lurched forward.

Rodin walked around and looked directly into Malcolm's eyes. Malcolm could no longer hold back. He had made it through the intense pain of Rodin's flogging and his mind had let go. Rodin watched the tears flow from Malcolm's eyes, washing away all his years of pain.

"Now, we both know who you are," Rodin said compassionately as he used his thumbs to gently wipe the tears away from Malcolm's cheeks.

Rodin wrapped his giant arms around Malcolm's body and Malcolm's head fell into his huge shoulder. Malcolm breathed heavily, and with each breath he became more inebriated with the smell of Rodin's body. The intoxication and warmth of Rodin's body eased the pain. The footmen quickly untied the restraints and Rodin picked Malcolm up, cradling him as he carried him back to the chateau.

Rodin returned Malcolm to his bedroom where the footmen under the direction of Jean-Yves were busy changing out the sheets and making the bed with new pillows, blankets, and an exquisite feather duvet. Rodin put Malcolm down on the freshly made bed and skillfully untied the leg and arm restraints. Janos and Milos covered Malcolm with the sheet, blankets, and duvet. Rodin sat down on the edge of bed and brushed aside the hair from Malcolm's eyes as he said in a calming voice, "Close your eyes and sleep now. You are safe."

Malcolm closed his eyes as everyone left the room. His body quickly warmed under the bedding, and he felt a gentle wave of sleep take him over.

CHAPTER XVI

Malcolm awoke the next morning to the familiar comforting nudge of Chevalier's muzzle against his hand. He had never spent a night in luxury linens and his entire body enjoyed being wrapped in the warmth and new feel of the Egyptian cotton sheets. He moved to the edge of the bed so he could be closer to Chevalier, and he gently stroked the dog's head. The morning light and a clear mind allowed him to take in the full splendor of the bedroom.

"This beats waking up in the cemetery," he said to Chevalier.

Malcolm got up from the bed, still naked from the night before. He went over and looked out of the window to try to determine his whereabouts. The view was beautiful, even though summer had long passed, but it gave him no clue as to where he might be. He went to the bathroom and stood in front of the mirror, observing Rodin's handy work on his body. He traced the red lash marks across his chest with his fingers and studied them curiously. To his surprise, the lashes administered the night before were done so expertly that the resulting welts formed a deliberate and complex pattern across his body. The individual welts hurt a little, and more so when he touched and applied pressure to them. Feeling the pain and remembering the night before oddly invigorated him. He took a minute and posed in the mirror, wearing the marks like badges of honor. It surprised him, but he felt very proud of himself and comfortable with his body as it was.

Looking around the bathroom, and then the bedroom, he was unable to find his clothes, or any clothes for that matter. He went back into the bathroom and wrapped a large towel around his waist. He ventured out into the hall with Chevalier following behind him. There was no one in sight. Somewhere in the far distance, within the interior of the chateau, he could hear the sounds of swords clashing together as if a great battle were being fought. He and Chevalier walked together in the direction of the noise. At the far end of the long hall, he entered a large room where Rodin, Valerian, and Trechus were engaged in a sword and shield fight. They wore nothing and fought in their bare feet. The battle appeared fierce, and Rodin demonstrated his excellent sword skill as he fended off Valerian and Trechus and moved them into a defensive position. Rodin saw Malcolm enter the room and stopped fighting. All three were completely covered in sweat, but they were hardly out of breath, despite the intensity of their physical exertion.

"I'm sorry," Malcolm said, shyly. "I didn't mean to interrupt."

"Valerian and Trechus should be grateful for your interruption. You spared them from losing the fourth round."

Rodin handed his shield to Janos as Milos collected the swords and shields from Valerian and Trechus. Rodin approached Malcolm, still carrying his sword.

"Did you sleep?" he asked with interest.

"I slept very soundly, sir."

Rodin walked around Malcolm and used the tip of his sword to remove the towel from around Malcolm's waist, allowing it to drop to the floor. Malcolm did not flinch. Rodin looked into Malcolm's eyes.

"What a profound difference I see in you this morning," Rodin said proudly.

Rodin carefully studied the results of his flogging. He circled Malcolm, continuing his inspection. He carefully ran the blade of his sword over the population of red welts on Malcolm's shoulders, and continued downward to the few welts on the left cheek of his ass.

"Do they hurt?" Rodin asked.

"They sting a bit, but not in a bad way," Malcolm admitted.

"By now you should realize that we are not like the other boys," Rodin said, and he smiled at Malcolm for the first time.

He turned his attention back to Trechus and Valerian. "Trechus, front and center."

Trechus took his place, standing at attention in front of Rodin, his eyes forward and hands locked together behind his back, military style.

Rodin walked around Trechus, inspecting his muscles.

"He is impressive as a man, wouldn't you agree Malcolm?"

"Yes, he is," Malcolm replied as he could not help but stare at Trechus' exquisite body.

"But you know he is something far greater than a man."

"Yes, I know," Malcolm replied never diverting his gaze from Trechus.

Trechus, show Malcolm the part of you that is dragon," Rodin ordered.

Trechus began to breath deeply and then more rapidly and his eyes began to change. The round black pupils elongated into almond-shaped slits as the green iris color shifted to metallic gold and spread across the entire surface of his eyes.

As he continued to focus and breathe heavily, the spine on his back began to protrude, and then the single spine started to split into two parts, starting just below his neck. As the single spine formed two new spines running from his outer shoulder down to the small of his back, a striated plate formed between the two spines, supported by a new muscle mass that formed around the structure.

While Malcolm had seen Trechus in this state two nights ago, he was captivated to see his body make the extraordinary transformation. Malcolm did not expect the conversion to continue, but the bone structures on Trechus' back kept on growing and expanding outward, and a small set of wings began to form. The wings continued to grow and morph until they reached a wingspan that was close to twelve feet.

His entire transformation was spectacular. Malcolm could hardly believe his eyes.

"That's incredible," Malcolm said, in total awe.

Rodin agreed. "He can fly faster than any bird in the sky and dive for prey at speeds greater than any falcon."

Rodin looked down at Malcolm. "Is he not the most exquisite creature you have ever seen?"

"He is the most beautiful thing I have ever seen," Malcolm replied.

"I think you're getting a little excited there, Malcolm," Valerian interrupted with a grin.

Malcolm quickly looked down and realized that he was no longer flaccid, and moved to cover himself with his hands.

Trechus leaned down and picked up the towel that was next to Malcolm.

"Here, use this," Trechus said, as he handed the towel to Malcolm.

Malcolm looked into Trechus' altered eyes, and while they appeared alien to him, he could recognize the same gentleness he had grown to know in his human eyes.

"Thank you," Malcolm said, without turning away as he wrapped the towel back around his waist.

"I wasn't sure you would speak to me again," Trechus confessed.

"There's so much here that I can't even begin to comprehend. I need some time to adjust to all of this."

"I understand," Trechus replied in a solemn tone.

"Malcolm," Valerian piped in, "you must be famished. Can we get you some food?"

"I am hungry and some food would be great, but I came looking for my clothes."

"Jean-Yves!" Rodin called out.

"Oui, monsieur." Jean-Yves appeared immediately at the door to the room as if he were waiting outside in contemplation of the household's next demand.

"Young Malcolm's clothes have gone missing."

"Oui, some items were in need of repair so I sent all his clothes out yesterday to be mended and cleaned. They will be delivered here shortly. I will provide Malcolm with a robe until they are returned."

"Very well. See to it that Malcolm gets some food sent to his room."

"A tray is being prepared in the kitchen for him now, monsieur," Jean-Yves replied. "I will bring it up to him right away."

"Well, you seem to have the matter of our accidental guest well under control."

"Oui, monsieur."

"That will be all for now. Merci Jean-Yves."

"Oui, monsieur," Jean-Yves said before he left the room.

Malcolm was again in awe as he watched Trechus shift back into his human form and still could not take his eyes off of him.

"Now Malcolm, if you wouldn't mind excusing us," Rodin said to get his attention. "I have a hundred Spanish Doubloons riding on this match. I think it is only fair that we allow Valerian and Trechus to retain their dignity by losing to me without an audience." Rodin offered Malcolm a friendly smile.

Malcolm returned the smile. "Of course, I understand how fragile the dragon ego can be."

Malcolm left the room and heard the sword fight resume as he walked back to his bedroom with Chevalier slowly following along behind him.

CHAPTER XVII

As promised, Jean-Yves arrived at Malcolm's room several minutes later. He was carrying a large silver tray that was covered by a silver domed lid and a bathrobe draped over his arm. He set the tray down on the table and then helped Malcolm into the robe. Malcolm sat down in front of the tray as Jean-Yves removed the silver lid that covered the large platter. Malcolm chuckled to himself. He was growing accustomed to the eating habits of dragons and their desire for large amounts of meat and not much else. Breakfast consisted of a large plate of a variety of roasted meats, and what appeared to be an entire pound of fried bacon. The presence of the tray caught the attention of Chevalier, who got up from his morning nap to further investigate.

"Should I prepare something for Chevalier?" Jean-Yves inquired.

"No, there is more than enough here for both of us. We're used to sharing," Malcolm replied as he gave Chevalier a large piece of roasted beef from his plate.

"Very well, monsieur."

There was a knock at the door and Jean-Yves opened it, allowing the two footmen to enter carrying Malcolm's clothes, which had since been expertly repaired and laundered. Jean-Yves directed them efficiently as they put them away in the exquisitely carved armoire in the corner. Upon completing their task, the footmen exited the room.

"Monsieur, do you require help dressing?"

Malcolm gave Jean-Yves an odd look. "No, I think I can handle that myself."

"Will you require anything else, monsieur?"

"Chevalier should go out for a walk. Can you help with that?"

"We've been walking him in the garden. If you would like, I can take him to the garden now while you finish eating and dress."

"That would be a big help. I can meet you in the garden after I have finished. I could use some air, and a walk in the garden sounds great. That is, if I am allowed to go outside."

"As a guest, you may walk four miles in any direction without leaving Rodin's estate. I only ask that you not leave the grounds. I'll take charge of Chevalier, and you can join us when you're ready."

Jean-Yves put the leash on Chevalier, and led him out of the room, leaving Malcolm to eat and dress. After eating, Malcolm walked into the bathroom and removed the robe and allowed it to drop to the floor. He stood and admired his naked body in front of the full-length mirror. He ran his fingers over the red welts on his chest, and he now secretly admitted to himself that they fascinated him. He shifted his body and studied the outline of his ass. He had never realized how perfect the curve in his back was, and how it gave way to such a round ass. He had never looked at himself in a mirror this way before, but this morning was different. He was different. For the first time, the site of his own reflection, the same one that he had detested for so many years, was now starting to turn him on.

He showered quickly and went to the armoire. His familiar clothes seemed unfamiliar. They had been invaded by great care. Rips and tears had been expertly sewn and repaired. Stains had been removed, and everything appeared lightly starched and ironed. He dressed and then headed down the stairs to the back garden.

Malcolm joined Jean-Yves and Chevalier as they walked together through the garden in the cold morning air. They entered the side garden through a gate and Malcolm saw a handsome young man who was oddly dressed as an ancient archer prepared to enter battle. He was an attractive younger man with a strong but less muscular build than Trechus and Valerian. His outfit, while odd, further enhanced his male stature and made the sight of him more interesting and appealing. He was engaged in shooting arrows into a series of three brown burlap targets crudely stitched together and shaped like giant dragon stuffed animals. As they approached him, he was preparing to take a shot, when the wind stirred slightly and he caught their scent in the air behind him. With his eye fixated on the target and his arrow drawn back against the bowstring, he called out, "Who approaches, Jean-Yves? Is the other human friend or foe?"

"He is a friend, monsieur! This is Malcolm Quinn."

"Does he look like the sort of human who would allow me to shoot an apple off the top of his head?"

Jean-Yves stopped for a moment and looked at Malcolm, who shook his head with a definitive "no."

"No, monsieur, he does not," Jean-Yves called back.

"Pity," Leonardo said, as he took the shot, launching the arrow directly into the eye of one of the targets.

"A fine kill, monsieur!" Jean-Yves congratulated him.

"Merci, Jean-Yves." Leonardo turned and handed the bow to Jean-Yves. He approached Malcolm, who took a step forward to greet him.

"Stop!" he ordered Malcolm, who stopped dead in his tracks, "Never approach a dragon, always let the dragon approach you. It's bad manners."

Malcolm did not move as Leonardo stepped up to him.

"I'm Malcolm," he offered, his hand extended.

Without offering his hand in return, Leonardo looked down at Malcolm's extended hand and said politely, "Curious behavior, humans always wanting to touch each other when they meet. Does your world possess so many aberrations that you must constantly confirm the existence of an actual being?"

"I am a little out of my element here," Malcolm admitted, as he withdrew his hand.

"I assure you that I am real, not some ghost or phantom."

"I didn't think you were," Malcolm replied.

"Malcolm, remember, you're in our world now. Our traditions and customs come from a time long before your ancestors were even capable of walking upright," Leonardo advised.

"I realize I know very little about your world," Malcolm humbly confessed.

Leonardo's tone quickly changed from cautious and stern to animated and friendly as he offered, "Then you should learn. Come! I will show you!"

Leonardo started walking in the direction of the targets as Malcolm followed behind. As they reached the targets, Malcolm closely observed the three burlap makeshift dragons were skillfully riddled with Leonardo's arrows. The face of the first target was completely studded with arrows.

"Dragons have two layers of skin. We have an epidermis similar to yours, but then we have an under layer of skin that has the strength of steel. Think of it as our version of a bulletproof vest. It can stop most bullets. So, if it is your intent to either harm or kill a dragon, you need to target their body's weakest points. Eyes, nose, and mouth are excellent options if you're going for a face shot."

He moved on to the second target that had a series of arrows embedded in the side of the head.

"Of course there is the ear shot, but it is more difficult since you need a straight shot into the ear canal itself. It is only a theory of mine, but I believe I could put an arrow straight into the ear canal and penetrate the brain. Of course, if you can get close enough . . . ." At hyper-speed, Leonardo pulled a dagger out of a leather holder attached to his upper thigh, leapt up, and drove the dagger into the ear of the target.

"Now you have a dead dragon," he proclaimed.

He walked to the third target, which had over twenty arrows protruding from the buttocks. He brushed his hand across the exposed ends of the embedded arrows.

"When in doubt, go for the easy kill and shoot them in the ass. No protection and an easy shot right into critical vital organs. The shot is especially useful during a retreat. This shot is my personal favorite, though I'm not sure why."

"Is it the same for female dragons?" Malcolm inquired.

"You really don't know much about us do you? We have no females in our race. Well, for that matter, we have no males. We are intersexed creatures."

"I don't think I understand," Malcolm replied.

"We appear in the male form as you see, but for a short period of our lives we become fertile and produce eggs."

"So you can become pregnant?"

"NO! We come from the egg or better put we are born out of the egg."

"You mean you are hatched?"

"Did you know it is a slur to compare a dragon to a chicken in our world? Chickens are hatched. We are mighty dragons, not domestic fowl. We first develop inside the egg and then we burn our way out."

"Very cool!" Malcolm replied as he was truly fascinated by Leonardo's lesson on dragons.

"What about you and Trechus?" Leonardo asked with a cheeky grin.

"Does everyone here think there's something between us?" Malcolm asked, frustrated.

"You're with him, are you not?" Leonardo pressed Malcolm.

"Yes, I am with him, but I am not with him."

"You just contradicted yourself."

"I think I like this guy but then I find out he is not really a guy at all. So I am not sure where that leaves me or how I should feel."

"Are you afraid?" Leonardo asked.

"Afraid of what?"

"Afraid of what people might say if they found out you were making it with a dragon?"

"No." Malcolm smiled and chuckled. But I assure you nothing has happened between us."

"Too bad. Aren't you the least bit curious of what it would feel like to have him touch you? To have him take you in his arms and hold you?"

"Stop it!" Malcolm demanded as he blushed beet red.

"Are you blushing, Malcolm?"

"No, of course not."

"You know dragons do possess certain talents that are beyond the skill level of ordinary men. Why, their tongues alone . . . . " Leonardo teased.

"Stop! Just stop it!"

"I'm sorry, I'm having too much fun with you."

"OK, I think he's hot," Malcolm admitted. Are you happy now?"

"I think it's cute that you have a crush on a big bad dragon."

"Now you're making fun of me!"

"Seriously, you would benefit from Trechus' affections."

"What do you mean?"

"Rodin is the master of protecting the secrets of dragons. Your knowledge of us makes you a credible threat. You're fortunate that he maintains a high level of interest in you."

"Why me?"

"Trechus, of course."

"What does Trechus have to do with it?"

"Trechus is favored by Rodin."

"I see. So I'm some kind of prized possession?"

"No, it's not like that. Trechus shut himself off from the world a long time ago. It was a surprise when Valerian told us that you were staying at his home."

"I am not staying there. I just slept there a couple of nights on the couch."

"Valerian says you are the first man to be in the house since Peter died."

"Who's Peter?" Malcolm asked.

"Peter was the last man he allowed into his life."

"What happened to him?"

"He died a long time ago. It's not really my place to speak about Peter."

"I know almost nothing about Trechus," Malcolm admitted.

"You're having a good effect on him," Leonardo confirmed.

"I feel bad because he gives so much to me and I have nothing to give back. This is all new to me, and confusing at the same time," Malcolm explained.

"I can understand how difficult this is for you. Not because you're young, but because you've been thrown into a world that, before a couple of days ago, you could hardly imagine existed."

"Yeah, I'm not used to being taken outside and flogged in the dead of night. I'm still not sure what to make of it," Malcolm confessed.

"Don't give it another thought. I saw it. Taking a being to the edge of their limits to discover their true nature is a ritual that is deeply rooted in our culture."

"I can't tell you how embarrassed I was."

"You need to shed that ridiculous human notion of shame. You were beautiful, brave, and honest. Humans talk about these traits, but so few really possess them. You were glorious and magnificent. It even made me a little jealous—and I have never been jealous of a human before!"

"This is all so surreal," Malcolm admitted.

"You just need time to come to terms with the fact that something strange and wonderful is happening to you."

"I'm actually beginning to believe it," Malcolm said.

"I think there is a place for you in our world. The question is are you prepared to leave your old world behind?"

"Except for Chevalier, I have no world to leave."

"Valerian has explained your situation to me. We do think Rodin should allow you to stay among us."

"Well, as long as I am a 'guest' here, I can't really leave."

"You're a holder of the truth now. Your purpose in the world has been elevated to a level you have yet to fully comprehend."

"When you put it that way, I think I am beginning to understand."

"Now, come with me, there is something I want to show you."

The two headed toward the chateau while Chevalier stayed behind with Jean-Yves in the garden. They entered the chateau and Leonardo led Malcolm down a series of hallways.

As they walked through the main hall, Leonardo began to explain. "The current chateau was constructed by Rodin in 1722. It replaced a medieval castle, which was also constructed by Rodin in 1192. Every five hundred years he gets bored and starts tearing things apart. The chateau serves as his residence, but the main purpose for its location is to conceal what is below us."

"How old is Rodin?" Malcolm appeared surprised by the dates.

"He is more than five thousand years old."

"That can't be possible," Malcolm protested.

Leonardo turned and gave Malcolm a serious look that was reflected in his tone. "I said he is over five thousand years old."

"I'm not saying you're lying, I just can't comprehend being alive for even a thousand years. How old are you?" Malcolm asked curiously.

"I'm not an ancient like Rodin," Leonardo chuckled, "I am only four hundred and sixty-two."

"Only four hundred and-sixty two!" Malcolm reiterated.

"You sound surprised. Did you think I was older?"

"I'm really not sure what I thought."

"Are you ready to go down?" Leonardo opened the door to the cellars.

"This is where you take me to the dungeon and tie me up, right?" Malcolm teased Leonardo.

"Is that your fear or your fantasy? No, the wine cellar is more my style," Leonardo said to assure Malcolm of his intentions.

They descended a set of stairs. At the bottom, there was a second set of stairs followed by a third set of stairs. Beyond that, the passage was guarded by a massive iron door that had a large grotesque face contained in the center of the door. Leonardo unlocked the door by blowing a thin stream of purple fire from his lips into the mouth of the figure. The door opened and the two of them entered.

It was dark on the other side of the door and Leonardo turned a switch that lit the pathway ahead with modern electric lights. The final stairway was cut into the bedrock itself. Now far below the chateau, they entered a prehistoric cave system with hundreds of stalactites hanging from the ceiling. Malcolm was completely taken by the beauty of the cave and prehistoric rock formations.

They continued, walking above an underground river on a wooden walkway that was built into the sidewall of the massive cavern. The underground caves and caverns seemed more magnificent to Malcolm than the chateau that stood on top of it.

"I am sure you're wondering why Rodin wants to keep this cave a secret from the outside world," Leonardo said, as he led Malcolm further into the cave and down a corridor.

"This is so incredible down here. It's hard to believe that no one knows about this," Malcolm said, marveling as they walked under the thirty-foot long stalactites that hung from the ceiling and had taken nature millions of years to form.

"Wait, the best is yet to come," Leonardo said, leading Malcolm into a larger cavern. Leonardo stopped in the center of the cavern and pointed upward, shining a flashlight on the ceiling above. Malcolm looked up to see a series of what looked like hundreds of paintings on the cave ceiling, depicting dragons and humans interacting in prehistoric times.

"You're looking at 10,000-year-old documentation of the life shared by dragons and humans. We jokingly like to call these Rodin's baby pictures."

"Amazing!" Malcolm whispered.

"The principle reason for guarding the caves was first to protect the prehistoric paintings, and then later to conceal the paintings from educated humans and science."

Malcolm could hardly believe his eyes as he looked at the extensive collection of prehistoric paintings that covered the vast ceiling.

"Dragons are fully documented in ancient writings and throughout history. Rodin has made a tremendous effort over the last four thousand years to search out documents and artistic references of dragons and destroy them, or at least remove them from circulation. However, the oral tradition of story telling remained and the mythology of dragons took root."

"Why would Rodin want to extract dragons from history?" Malcolm asked.

"Ten thousand years ago, when the earth's population of humans began to rapidly increase and the human brain began to develop a higher level of intelligence, an aggression toward dragons developed. Look." Leonardo pointed with his flashlight to a ceiling painting that showed Black Dragons hunting humans.

"Black Dragons were enslaving humans and hunting them for food. This caused the humans to revolt and fight back. For eight hundred years, a bloody conflict known as the 'Black Dragon War' raged between the Black Dragons and early man.

"Eight thousand years ago the earth's human population exploded and expanded to foreign continents. The Black Dragons followed and sustained their practices of feeding and enslaving humanity. This continued until 4000 BC, when men began to keep a record of history, and the age of man became evident to the Black Dragons.

In 450 BC, Herodotus, the Greek historian, referenced the Black Dragons when he wrote, 'Winged serpents are nowhere seen except in Arabia, if they increased as fast as their nature would allow, impossible would it for man to maintain himself on the earth.' Marco Polo would later write about seeing White Dragons on his travels through China. Written history began to record the existence of dragons at an increasing rate. The dragons decided they did not want to be part of the emerging human world and began to live away from humans, in a world of their own. Things remained quiet for almost 5,000 years until, fearing a loss of their position of domination, the Black Dragons changed their course and began a massive genocide of humans in 1346. You would know it by its historical name, the Black Plague.

Witnessing the destruction and suffering of humankind, the Gold Dragons formed an alliance with the White Dragons to end the genocide. For five hundred years, Gold Dragons, with the help of the White Dragons, hunted and executed Black Dragons to the point that by 1850 it was believed that Black Dragons were on the verge of extinction. The Gold Dragons then called an end to the hostility, and peace has prevailed for the last one hundred sixty years." He paused as he illuminated a darker corner of the ceiling with his flashlight and said with a big grin, "Dragon Kama Sutra!"

Malcolm looked up to see a dozen different images of dragons engaged in sexual positions, and saw, to his surprise, that most of them portrayed dragons with humans. "Why did dragons start breeding with humans?"

"No one is exactly sure why or how it started, but it became possible for humans and dragons to produce offspring. These offspring more closely resembled humans. This became practical for dragons, as the hostility that began between men and dragons never ceased. Men continued to hunt dragons, even though they themselves were no longer threatened. The dragons of the time believed that the best way to coexist was to assimilate. By interbreeding, dragons did become more human looking, but were able to retain their unique dragon qualities."

"Are there humans who know of your existence?"

"Of course," Leonardo replied. "We have small devout groups of allies among humans that safeguard our secret. Eight hundred years ago we were closely aligned with the Vatican, but due to the instability of the church and corrupt behavior and practices, dragons broke from the church in 1086 under Pope Lucious III. Rodin has been a friend and benefactor to the church here in France. Look carefully on the sides of Notre Dame in Paris and you will see that the great cathedral is symbolically protected by dragons that are carved into the exterior. This was done to honor Rodin's contribution to the protection of the church here in France and also to thank him for his extreme generosity in funding its construction. The Italian-dominated Vatican has not always been, how should I put it, a friend to French Catholics."

"Does the Vatican still know you exist?"

"Without a doubt. We're written in the part of their history books that are not allowed beyond the walls of the Vatican's well-guarded private libraries."

"The church does protect you then?" Malcolm asked

"It is not protection. We are a monumental threat to modern-day Catholic beliefs, and therefore a key enemy of the modern church. The very foundation of the Vatican would crumble into dust if it was ever determined that the winged beings that dropped from the sky and caused bushes to burn in the middle of the dessert were not angels, but something entirely different. The church has conveniently rewritten us in their history. We have become, in some instances, what every human should fear, the fire-breathing devil. In other cases, we are elevated to the great heralds and winged angels of heaven."

CHAPTER XVIII

Later that morning, Valerian went to Trechus' room to ask Trechus to immediately meet with Rodin and him in the library. Trechus followed Valerian to the library in silence as there was little to say that had not all ready been said between them regarding the atrocities occurring in Paris and the resurgence of the Black Dragons. They both understood the exigent nature of what was about to be discussed. As they entered the room, Rodin was standing within the oak-lined recess of one of the great hand-carved Gothic windows of the library. His back was to the window, which allowed the sun to stream over his shoulder and illuminate the page of the ancient book he appeared to be studying. He looked up as they entered and promptly slammed the book closed with one hand as if the sound it made was meant to announce their presence.

"Please, sit down," he instructed.

Trechus followed Valerian to the library table in the center of room where they proceeded to sit down. In an attempt to surmise the direction of Rodin's thoughts, Trechus scanned the ancient books and maps that Rodin had laid out across the table. When it came to literary information, no one knew more than Trechus. From the books on the table, Trechus could determine the facts Rodin was using to guide his decisions, giving him an insight into Rodin's likely course of action.

After a brief pause Rodin began. "The Great Dragon War decimated the Black Dragons. We hunted and slaughtered over five hundred of them. Then, for five hundred years we tracked and systematically executed every Black Dragon we could uncover. Despite our victories, we suffered significant casualties on our side and our own ranks dwindled as a result.

"In the end, the Black and Gold Dragons entered into a war that drove both of our races to the brink of extinction. As we sit here today, there are only four of us left. Despite all our efforts to exterminate the threat of the Black Dragons, I knew deep in the recesses of my mind that it was inevitable that some dragons would escape, survive, and would rise up again one day.

"Almost ninety years ago, I was pondering the question of their return late one evening in this very room and, curiously, I made a simple calculation on the inside cover of the book I hold in my hand. I closed the book and put it back on the shelf. Ten years ago, I pulled it down to review my original calculation."

Rodin dropped the book on the table in front of Trechus who opened the ancient book to the inside cover where Rodin had made a written calculation:

$$1346 \text{ AD} + 666 = 2012 \text{ AD}$$
$$6 \text{ December } 1924$$

"I had hoped against all hope that I was mistaken. So, it comes to no surprise to me today that you bring me news that they have returned. In 1346 they unleashed the Black Death on human civilization for the first time, killing in excess of 100 million people. Over the next 500 years they made additional attempts on the human population but with lesser results. They have not returned from hiding to feast on humans or take over drug traffic—these are merely signs of their usual profiteering ways. Nor do I believe they would return unless they were absolutely certain that this time their attacks would succeed. I am most certain they now have the ability to unleash a force that could bring an end to human civilization as we know it."

"Hundreds of millions of people will die," Valerian said in a somber tone.

"No, Valerian, we should not make the mistake of underestimating our enemy. This time, billions of people will die."

Trechus studied Rodin's face carefully as Rodin sat down and joined them at the table before saying, "This just does not seem possible in our modern age."

"If the human race's innate fear of sickness, starvation, and death were properly manipulated, the Black Dragons could push the world to an irreversible state of anarchy and usher in the darkest age the world has ever known."

"How could they have possibly have amassed the resources to carry this out?" Trechus asked.

Rodin replied, "The Black Dragons have had over six hundred years to prepare for this. If they are here, then we must believe they are confident in their ability to carry this out."

"Are we to be the only defense against this attack?" Trechus asked.

"I have sent word to the White Dragons in China and they have dispatched a representative to Paris. However, things may happen before we have a chance to make a new alliance with the White Dragons. If this is so, we will face our enemy alone."

Valerian slammed his fist down on the table as he said with confidence, "We will crush them as we have before."

"I would like to believe our victory would be certain. However, let me remind you, we have no way to determine their numbers or their strength," Rodin cautioned Valerian. "They are hiding under the city in the catacombs and mines. That is more than 200 kilometers of tunnels. I trust you will do your best to try to track them before they begin their attack, but I fear your efforts will not benefit us soon enough."

"What is your plan for us?" Valerian asked.

"Valerian, it is important that you and Trechus return to Paris and put your efforts into hunting down the Black Dragons. Time is growing short and we need to find to them before they strike the city.

CHAPTER XIX

Malcolm and Leonardo made their way back upstairs from the caves and entered the chateau's kitchen. The room was full of activity as two chefs were busy working, shifting copper pots and pans across the giant black antique stove, and shoveling roasting pans in and out of the great ovens. Set in the middle of the kitchen was a sumptuous buffet table that was impeccably set, with a wild boar displayed in the middle surrounded by a variety of pheasant, quail and pigeon. There were also no less than five great platters of various kinds of large sausages.

"When you're hungry, Malcolm, just come down here and eat. These chefs have been specially trained and prepare the finest meats you will ever taste. Take a plate."

Malcolm followed as Leonardo piled large portions on his plate from the different meat dishes being offered.

"You sure can eat," Malcolm said, amazed.

"On average, I will eat about twenty kilos of meat per day, or about forty-four pounds."

"Are you bullshitting me? Forty-four pounds?" Malcolm asked.

"It takes a great deal of energy to blow fireballs. The fuel has to come from somewhere."

"Can you fly like the others?"

"Of course I can fly, we can all fly, but then you really have to eat because that takes a serious amount of energy, depending on the distance."

Valerian entered the kitchen and, seeing Malcolm, exclaimed with his Russian bravado, "Here you two are! I thought you might have come looking for me Malcolm, but now I see that you have traded me for Leonardo. I hope he is looking after you at least half as well as I would."

"He is. He took me down to the caves this morning," Malcolm replied.

"That would not have been my choice of outings. I would have taken you flying! You have not flown yet have you?" Valerian asked.

"No, I haven't," Malcolm replied.

"Regrettable! And here Leonardo has you crawling around in the cold damp air looking at Neanderthal drawings. However, I suppose there is some minor importance for you to see our caves."

Valerian went about filling up his plate from the assorted feast. Using his fork, he speared a giant sausage and held it in the air, studying it. "Rodin has the biggest sausage I have ever seen, anywhere. How is this even possible? What do you do with this?"

He plopped it on his plate and continued to load up with the other meats, and then proclaimed, "Now this is what I call a feeding!"

He joined Malcolm and Leonardo at the table, clearly attempting to outshine Leonardo.

He looked over the selection of wine bottles in front of him and then poured himself a large glass from one of the bottles. He began to eat and speak at the same time. "Be careful, Malcolm. Leonardo has some crazy ideas. If anyone is going to corrupt you, it should be me."

"You keep promising, but you might be all talk," Malcolm teased.

"Is that a challenge? I hope it is a challenge!" Valerian shot back.

"It could be," Malcolm responded.

"Then tonight we drink vodka! I will teach you how to drink like a Russian man! We will make a Russian out of you yet."

"I was hoping you would teach me how to drink like a Russian dragon!"

"Of course. First a man, then a dragon." Valerian laughed boisterously, but then stopped abruptly and said in a serious tone. "Have you spoken with Trechus yet this morning?"

"No, I've been with Leonardo," Malcolm replied.

"I think you should go and see him," Valerian proposed. "When he gets into one of his moods, he starts reading and that could go on for twenty years. I think your appearance would get him to put his books down and come join us for some fun?"

"I should talk to him. I feel bad about the way I reacted towards him in Paris. Every-thing just happened so fast. I was frightened, but I should apologize to him. I don't want him to feel bad."

"No! Never apologize, Malcolm, make him dance like a black bear in the circus ring for you. You're not at fault. Force him to work to regain your trust."

Malcolm grinned at Valerian as he rose from the table and said with confidence, "I think I can do that. I will go make him dance a little." He turned to Leonardo. "Thank you for this morning. The caves were incredible."

"Wait," Leonardo called after Malcolm. He got up from the table and followed Malcolm toward the door to the hall. "Don't listen to Valerian. Remember, Trechus is a mighty warrior who fears nothing with the exception of his own heart.

CHAPTER XX

Trechus retreated to his bedroom, quietly reading in his favorite chair. He had opened the large French windows and allowed the room to fill with cold autumn air. He heard footsteps approaching and placed his book on the side table. His keen sense of smell could not mistake Malcolm's scent. He immediately rose from his seat to open the bedroom door. Malcolm was only steps away and gave him a shy smile.

"I thought we might talk," Malcolm said in a conciliatory tone.

"Do you want to come in?" Trechus asked.

"I would like that."

"It's a little cold in here. I can close the windows, if you like," Trechus offered.

Malcolm entered the room, closing the door behind him. Trechus turned away to close the windows and said, "I wanted to speak with you sooner, but I understood that you would need some time to try to make sense of all of this."

"How could anyone make sense of this? Trechus, I was so terrified of you the other night. I really thought you were going to kill me."

Trechus turned to face Malcolm. "Please believe that I would never harm you."

"No, I don't think you ever meant to harm me," Malcolm admitted.

"Can we go forward?" Trechus asked.

"Part of me still wants to run and hide from you."

"I understand how you could still be frightened by me. What does the other part of you say?"

"The other part of me says you have been more kind and caring than I deserve."

"Malcolm, this was my mistake. Everything that happened is my fault. You had no idea who I was."

"Would you have told me who you were?" Malcolm asked.

"Eventually, I would have told you. When you were ready to understand."

"Do you really want me to be a part of your life?" Malcolm asked.

Trechus smiled a sad smile. "I didn't think I wanted anyone in my life until the other morning when I was crossing the street and looked up to see a young man giving coffee to a dog. My mind is usually filled with hundreds of thoughts, but when I saw you that morning everything stopped and my world stood completely still. I have walked the streets of Paris for a very long time now and all I ever see is a solid mass of people—a collage of people moving in one direction or another. No one person is ever distinguishable from the next. That morning, for the first time, I saw you—a single beautiful man sitting on the sidewalk with his dog."

"I didn't think you liked me when we first met," Malcolm admitted.

"It had been such a long time since I had spoken to anyone on a personal level that I barely knew what to say. I just knew I needed to say something. I admit, I was not the most personable or eloquent during that first morning. I was a bit out of practice."

"I'm glad you stopped and spoke to me. Even if you were a bit condescending," Malcolm replied.

"Even now, I admit I do not fully understand what draws me to you. Something inside me, beyond my own consciousness, has taken over. Can you even begin to understand how much you captivate me?"

Malcolm looked at Trechus, and, while he appreciated the kind words, he did need to help Trechus understand how odd they sounded to his ears. "You do know how weird this all sounds?"

"I know you think I am strange and freakish, but I really want us to be friends."

"It's probably not the best way to say this, but, no, I don't want to be friends. The opportunity for a friendship between us has passed. Too much has happened," Malcolm said. As he paused, he could see Trechus' eyes fill with disappointment.

Malcolm continued. "Friendship between us seems pointless. It will never be enough for me now. If you want me to be part of your life then you need to be prepared to give me more. Do you understand why I need more?"

"I think so," Trechus confirmed.

"Trechus, we both know that I'm pretty fucked up, emotionally. My only friend and connection to the world is a Great Pyrenees."

"I don't believe that about you. You're much more than that," Trechus asserted.

"I know I should have people in my life; but I am not comfortable around them, my heart is empty, I don't feel it, and physically I have never had the desires I think I should be having at my age."

"How can I be more to you?" Trechus asked sincerely.

"I just want someone who can make me feel good about myself every day. I need someone with a big heart who will care for me even when I don't deserve it."

"I really want to be that person."

"You know I hate my body," Malcolm added.

"You have a beautiful body."

Malcolm slowly started to pull his T-shirt over his head, exposing his chest to the cold air of the room. Goose bumps broke out across his arms and shoulders.

"Malcolm, it's freezing in here."

"I don't care," Malcolm said, as slipped off his shoes, unbuckled his belt, and unbuttoned his pants, letting them drop to the floor. He now stood in just his briefs before Trechus.

"When you saw me naked in your bathroom the other day, you looked at me in a way that no one ever has before. I didn't understand it and I felt ashamed—like I wasn't worthy of that kind of attention," Malcolm admitted. He removed his briefs and now stood naked before Trechus.

Trechus gave Malcolm a gentle smile. "You're beautiful."

"Do you really think I'm handsome?" Malcolm asked with a gentle shyness.

Trechus approached Malcolm, reached behind him, and slowly started to run his hand from the nape of Malcolm's neck down the center of his back. Malcolm shuddered, partially from the cold air, but mostly from Trechus' warm touch across the sensitive area of his back. Trechus wrapped his arms around Malcolm's shoulders and hugged him using his strength to pull Malcolm's body firmly against his. Malcolm's shaft started to swell and his balls twitched as the feel of Trechus' muscular body sent Malcolm's mind spinning.

Trechus released Malcolm and moved to stand behind him. Again he ran his hand down Malcolm's back. This time, instead of stopping at the bottom of his back, he allowed his hand to continue around to Malcolm's stomach and up toward his chest until he was able to squeeze Malcolm's entire right pectoral in his hand. He massaged his pec and then began to explore his nipple with his fingers. Malcolm's mind was racing in ecstasy as his cock continued to swell.

Trechus' other hand started to travel up Malcolm's stomach until both of his hands were massaging Malcolm's upper chest. Trechus looked down and saw that Malcolm was now fully erect, the head of his cock gently bobbing in the air. Trechus took Malcolm's two nipples in his hands and massaged them between his fingers. He slowly increased the pressure until he was pinching them. Malcolm silently endured the delicious pain as his cock became rock hard. Without easing up on the pressure, Trechus began to pull his nipples upwards. Malcolm arched his back and moaned out loud as his cock strained in front of him. Trechus raised his chest and lifted Malcolm off the floor by his nipples while supporting the weight of Malcolm's body on his own chest. Despite the pain, Malcolm could feel Trechus' large hard cock against his ass cheeks.

Trechus put Malcolm back down on the floor and started to kiss his neck as he reached around and grabbed his cock at the shaft and balls. He squeezed hard and Malcolm moaned again. He began to stroke Malcolm's shaft slowly at first but then faster until it felt like it couldn't get any harder. Trechus pulled down on Malcolm's shaft and let it snap up against his stomach. He did it again. He spun Malcolm around, wrapped him up in his arms, and began to kiss him deeply.

It was awkward for Malcolm at first as Trechus forced his large tongue into his mouth, but he quickly got the hang of it. As Trechus sensed Malcolm's comfort level increasing, he pushed Malcolm back against the wall. Malcolm put his arms around Trechus' neck as Trechus picked Malcolm up under his knees and began to grind his own cock against Malcolm's. As Malcolm looked into Trechus' eyes, he saw them beginning to turn bright metallic gold as the pupils elongated into narrow slits. Trechus' transformation turned Malcolm on even more and he began to grind harder against Trechus. Trechus was now getting to the point where his arousal had become so great that he started to shift. Malcolm could feel his back widen as his spine started to bifurcate. The transformation only increased Trechus' strength, and he moved harder against Malcolm.

Trechus' erect cock felt increasingly constricted by his pants. He continued to endure the pain as he was consumed by the sight of Malcolm losing control of himself and submitting to him. He now felt completely in control of Malcolm and craved every inch of him.

Malcolm started to pull at Trechus' shirt, tearing it open and sending the buttons flying everywhere. Trechus placed Malcolm back down on the floor. Malcolm tore Trechus' shirt from his body and immediately started working Trechus' nipples with his tongue until he was wildly sucking each of them.

Trechus needed relief from the pain of his erection so he started to undo his buckle and open the top of his pants. Malcolm took this opportunity to force his hand down the front of Trechus' pants and grab his cock. Trechus kissed Malcolm even deeper than before. Malcolm struggled to get his other hand into Trechus' pants. Trechus helped by pulling them down far enough so they dropped to the floor.

Trechus took control and threw Malcolm face down on the bed. Malcolm was almost out of breath as Trechus grabbed him by the ankles and spread his legs to expose his asshole. Trechus got on the bed and knelt between Malcolm's legs while spreading them apart with his knees. He started to gently massage Malcolm's ass cheeks and then began to pull them apart. He reached under Malcolm and grabbed his balls and shaft with one hand, forcing Malcolm's ass into the air. He bent over and licked Malcolm's hole. Malcolm let out a moan. Trechus licked it again around the outer edge and then started to flick his tongue directly on the hole.

"Oh my God! Oh my God! Don't stop!" Malcolm pleaded.

Trechus now started to lick Malcolm's hole in long strokes from the bottom to the top. Each time he pushed his large tongue in deeper, Malcolm's body shook with delight.

Trechus flipped Malcolm over. Malcolm grabbed him by the back of the neck and pulled him on top of him, kissing him deeply. Trechus grabbed Malcolm's shaft at the base and licked the head. Malcolm had never experienced anything like it before. As Trechus continued, Malcolm's legs began to convulse uncontrollably. Trechus then swallowed Malcolm whole as he licked hard between his balls.

Malcolm could barely stand it. He grabbed the back of Trechus' head and cried out, "Motherfucker!"

Taking this as a sign, Trechus stroked Malcolm's shaft as his tongue wildly licked his dickhead, bringing Malcolm to an explosive orgasm. Malcolm shot six loads, his pelvis lurching forward with a hard thrust each time.

Trechus pulled Malcolm's spent body on top of his own, and wrapped his arms around Malcolm, warming him with the heat of his body. Malcolm quickly fell asleep on his chest. Trechus remained completely still, watching for over three hours as Malcolm slept, gently inhaling and exhaling against his chest.

Malcolm awoke some time later, his body warm and rested. For a moment he didn't want to move. He couldn't recall ever having felt that incredible. He looked up to see Trechus awake and gazing down at him.

"How long have you been awake?" Malcolm asked.

"I was never asleep."

"How long have I been sleeping."

"About three hours."

"What have you been doing?"

"I've been watching you."

"You watched me the whole time?"

"You sleep like an angel."

"I don't sleep like an angel."

"How would you know?"

"I guess I don't know."

Looking into Malcolm's eyes, Trechus explained, "When you fell asleep, your eyes softly closed and your breathing became ever so gentle. Your breath slowly warmed as you exhaled onto my chest. A wave of peace came over your face and your body's tension diminished as you relaxed. You then moved closer to me until I felt as though we could be the same person."

"Is that really true?" Malcolm asked.

"You cannot appreciate how amazing you are. There is nothing in the world more stunning than a man like you. The world's greatest artists have only been able to capture brief moments or small pieces of men. They sculpt, paint, and sketch—but there is no statue, painting, or photograph that will ever capture the beauty of a living man. No artist, no matter how skilled, could ever capture you as you just lay sleeping here in my arms."

"There's no way I can ever offer you such eloquent words. I have no talent for words," Malcolm confessed to Trechus.

"Malcolm, words can be formulated, manipulated, made to be truthful, or turned into blatant lies. What I see when I look into your eyes is greater than any written or spoken words could ever express."

"What do you see?"

"When I look into your eyes, it causes a transformation in my being. There's this amazing glimmer that's like a continuous light warming everything around it."

Malcolm held Trechus tightly, as if he would never let him go. Suddenly there was a

loud pounding on the door.

"Trechus," Valerian yelled through the door. "You can no longer neglect us or keep Malcolm all for yourself. I absolutely insist that you join us for Dragon Balls downstairs. And bring your purse with you."

Trechus got out of bed and, without saying a word to Valerian, went to the door and turned the key to lock the door loud enough to make it clear to Valerian that he was not wanted. He crawled back into bed with Malcolm.

"Fine," Valerian shouted back. "I'll take that to mean you will be down within the hour."

"What are Dragon Balls?" Malcolm whispered.

"It's a game like billiards. It's a betting game. Valerian loves to play for gold and usually takes Leonardo for the contents of his purse."

"Do you want to go play with Valerian?"

"No, I would much rather stay here and play with you for a little while longer," Trechus said, pulling the covers over their heads.

CHAPTER XXI

An hour passed before Trechus made his way into the billiard room, where Valerian had just beaten Leonardo at a game of Dragon Balls. Valerian was looking quite pleased with himself as Leonardo placed the last stack of five gold coins in front of him.

"Finally, you have decided to come," Valerian exclaimed. "Leonardo has made an almost worthy competitor, but he has still managed to wager and lose all twenty of his gold ducats."

"Set the balls on the table, Leonardo. I will win back your twenty ducats for you, plus another hundred ducats from Valerian's own purse for myself. That is, if it's large enough to handle such a wager," Trechus teased.

"You know better than to question my deposits of gold," Valerian responded.

"And you know better than to knock on my door and interrupt," Trechus playfully shot back.

"You're gambling with unusual confidence this evening."

"Shall we say twenty ducats a game?" Trechus proposed.

"Twenty—now I am impressed. You must believe that Malcolm brings you luck. Where is this new amulet of yours?" Valerian asked.

"Here I am," Malcolm said, entering the room.

"Finally! The sunshine has arrived! Now we can have some fun together. Jean-Yves! A round of vodka for everyone!" Valerian said as he stopped to carefully study Malcolm. "Malcolm, I must say there is something new about you. Do you see it, Leonardo?"

"Valerian!" Trechus cautioned. "Allow Malcolm his privacy."

"No, I want to hear this too," Leonardo added.

"So it is true then. I love when men fall in love. Why do you hide it Trechus? It is ridiculous to hide such a treasure!"

"Who said anything about love?" Malcolm grinned.

"Valerian, it's not your place to involve yourself in Malcolm's affairs," Trechus warned.

"See—you admit it then! There was an affair!" Valerian teased Trechus.

"Valerian!" Trechus warned.

"Trechus," Malcolm interjected, "I am capable of defending my own honor. Even against a dragon as mighty as Valerian."

"Do you admit to an interlude?" Valerian asked Malcolm.

"Should I confide in him?" Malcolm asked Trechus with a sly look.

"If you want to," Trechus replied.

"Well, 'bottom boy' Trechus here was a real trooper. It was difficult for him at first," Malcolm explained grinning. "But then he got the hang of it."

"You see!" Valerian roared with laughter. "That is why I love this boy so much. Really, Trechus, I feel he is wasted on you. He really should come with me to Siberia."

"Where is Rodin this evening?" Trechus asked, just noticing his absence.

"He went to Paris to meet the White Dragon that was dispatched to France. He'll return before dawn," Leonardo confirmed.

Jean-Yves presented a silver tray of small cups, each filled with vodka.

Valerian spoke as they each took one. "Malcolm, in Russia we call these 'charkas.' So! I propose a toast to Malcolm and his elegant human beauty and captivating boyish charm."

"To Malcolm!" they said, as they each clinked each other's charkas and drank.

"Another round, Jean-Yves. I have many more toasts to make!" Valerian ordered. "Trechus, get the game started and break the balls. I am eager to win more gold."

Trechus surveyed the table.

"Is it like playing pool?" Malcolm asked.

"It's similar, but you start with the smaller metallic gold ball in the center. Each person has either blue balls or black balls. Then you have the red icosahedrons, which are twenty-sided balls that guard each of the pockets. Then it is like billiards. You win by getting all of your balls into the pockets before your opponent. The difference is if you hit an icosahedron, your opponent gets an extra shot. If you hit it and it rolls, your opponent gets two extra shots."

Valerian put his arm around Malcolm's shoulder and said, "Malcolm, with your next vodka you need to have some caviar. Here, take a plate and spoon. This is Russian Osetras Caviar. It was a particular favorite of the last Tsar. You will love it. They are little eggs that give off a delightful salty flavor. You put them in your mouth and smash them with your tongue."

Malcolm took one of the Mother-of-Pearl plates and spoons that had been laid out for the caviar.

"These look like these were made from seashells?" Malcolm commented.

"That is very astute of you," Valerian replied. "You must be very careful to maintain the delicate flavor of caviar. If you use metal utensils to serve it, you will destroy the flavor. Mother-of-Pearl makes the ideal material for serving plates and utensils."

Malcolm took a small spoonful of the caviar, placed it on his tongue, and gently smashed the tiny eggs in his mouth, releasing the flavor.

"Does it agree with your palate?"

"I love popping them, and the salty flavor!"

Jean-Yves presented the second tray of charkas. They each took one and held it up for Valerian's next toast.

"To victory and the end of the insidious Black Dragons!" Valerian roared.

"To victory!" they shouted.

Valerian put his arm back around Malcolm. "You can drink. We should go out together in Paris. Trechus never wants to go out. I have this favorite place and have probably not been there in close to a hundred years. It is where all the fashionable people go to drink and discuss ideas of the day. I remember the café, but what was the name? Le? Le Propay?"

"Café Procope," Trechus confirmed.

"Yes, that's it. Le Procope. That is where I met my first American. A good enough fellow. Loved to play chess and chase French woman."

"Valerian," Trechus interrupted. "It's your turn."

"Of course it is," he confirmed. "Malcolm, he was a famous Ambassador. He claimed to have ravished some countesses and madams. I was never sure if he was serious about it. He was quite old, did not move very fast, and had gout. He was a smart fellow, though. A very smart fellow. He got along wonderfully with the French and absolutely hated the English, but he did have the most repulsive body odor I can recall for a man or a woman."

"Everybody had body odor in those days. I can't say I have fond memories of yours," Trechus teased Valerian.

"Back then a good odor was your calling card. You could judge the size of a man's purse by how much eau de cologne he could afford to dump over himself to cover it up."

"I don't recall you using eau de cologne," Trechus said as he further attempted to tease Valerian.

"Now you're just trying to make Malcolm think less of me. I most certainly did bathe in the stuff, and I won't allow you to dispute me," Valerian retorted.

Jean-Yves arrived with another round of vodka, and they again raised their cups as Valerian continued. "In life, there are few things more important than friends. I have been more than fortunate to have enjoyed a very long friendship with my dearest friend and confidant, Trechus! My only regret is that he never loved me as much as he loved his books."

Valerian and Trechus looked at each other with an understanding that only could be shared between two beings who had experienced so much of the world over such an indefinite period of time.

"To Trechus' books," they all shouted, and laughed as they clinked their cups.

"Malcolm, drink a couple more of these and you'll quickly get hair on that smooth chest of yours. However, drink too many and you'll get hair on your back!" Leonardo joked.

"Which Ambassador are you talking about?" Malcolm asked.

Valerian thought for a second. "Franklin. The man's name was Franklin, Ambassador Franklin."

"He's talking about your Benjamin Franklin," Trechus clarified, as he took another shot and put two more balls in the pockets.

"You knew Benjamin Franklin?" Malcolm asked.

"Knew him! I beat him at chess so many times, he still owes me money! When you have lived as long as I have you meet a lot of people," Valerian asserted.

Leonardo cautioned, "Don't get Valerian started on the subject of historical figures who owe him money. It's pointless, since they're all dead now and unable to pay."

"I wonder if Le Procope is still there?" Valerian pondered.

"Yes, it's still there. I stop there for lunch from time to time."

"We are definitely going back there so I can show Malcolm where I beat Franklin at all those chess games!"

"That's another thing about Valerian and his stories of knowing all these great historical figures," Leonardo again cautioned. "Unfortunately, since they're all dead, there's no way for them to deny ever knowing him. Perhaps, it is he who owes Franklin money."

"Enough reminiscing about dead Americans who owe Valerian money," interjected Trechus. "I'd like to hear how you got along with Leonardo today."

"Yes, Malcolm, tell us about your morning with Leonardo," Valerian encouraged.

"Well, he did teach me how to kill a dragon," Malcolm admitted.

"Now there's an important skill to learn your first morning in the world of dragons! Be careful to be on your best behavior now, Trechus," Valerian laughed.

"I taught him more than that," objected Leonardo.

"He did," Malcolm confirmed. "We went down into the caves and he told me the history of the Black Dragons and the Dragon Wars."

Valerian spoke directly to Trechus in a low serious voice. "It is important that he understands this now. After all, he is here and he may be of some use to us."

"It is not my intention to involve Malcolm in any way. He's too young and this situation is becoming far too dangerous," Trechus said firmly to get his point across to Valerian.

"Involve me in what?" Malcolm asked.

Leonardo piped in, "The Black Dragons will attack Paris in the coming days."

Malcolm looked at Trechus and asked, "Why won't you let me help?"

Trechus replied sternly, "Because it is too dangerous and Valerian and Leonardo should not be filling your head with any thoughts of glorious battles. The reality will be far different."

Trechus took a shot and won the game and announced to Valerian in a perturbed tone. "You owe me 20 ducats."

"If you don't consider allowing me to win from time to time, I shall not play with you anymore," Valerian complained. "I will force you to play cards instead."

"You're even worse at cards than you are at Dragon Balls," Trechus replied.

"I believe a round of absinthe is in order," Leonardo offered.

"I'll pass on the green fairy juice. I need to eat something," Trechus replied. "Malcolm, are you hungry?"

"Sorry, but I can't look at another piece of meat tonight," Malcolm replied apologetically.

"Good, then you can remain here and continue to drink with us." Valerian smiled.

"Are you OK with that?" Malcolm asked Trechus.

"Sure, just as long as you have only one absinthe. These two can easily drink twenty and love to go flying afterward. Do not take him flying. He is not a toy."

"Trechus," Valerian interjected. "You speak as if we don't have Malcolm's best interests at heart."

"I'm just reminding you that he is young and human. I'm going to eat and trust you both will behave like the nice dragons you are," Trechus said as he left the room.

"Jean-Yves, bring out the absinthe glasses. And bring the good absinthe this time, I don't care how much Rodin complains that we drink from his special collection," Valerian asserted.

Leonardo turned to Malcolm. "Trechus has a big heart. He feels guilty that he is the reason you're here when we are entering a time of certain danger. He just doesn't want anything to happen to you."

"He's difficult to read sometimes. I don't always understand him," Malcolm confessed.

"He's making too much out of this." Valerian chimed in. "Malcolm, you're as much at risk in Paris as you are in London or Berlin. No one is safe now. Being with Trechus is probably the safest place for you. Tonight, I want to drink, laugh, tell stories and get merry. Tomorrow will be here soon enough and we can deal with it then."

"I agree!" Malcolm concurred.

"This is precisely why I love you," Valerian laughed.

Jean-Yves entered the room and presented a bottle of absinthe to Valerian for his inspection and approval.

"Yes, this is the good stuff with the right kind of wormwood."

"Shall I pour it, monsieur?" Jean-Yves asked.

"Yes, we will each start with one," Valerian confirmed.

Jean-Yves proceeded to set up the glasses under the fountain that was located on a corner table. Malcolm was intrigued by the fountain, which was made from a beautiful silver fairy holding a crystal water container above her head with four spigots emerging from each side of the water container. Jean-Yves filled the bottom of each glass with absinthe, then placed it under each tiny spigot of the fountain. He positioned a specially slotted silver spoon on the top of each glass and carefully placed a cube of sugar in the center of each spoon. He then opened the spigot and allowed the iced water to run over and melt the sugar cube as the glasses filled, and water and sugar mixed with the absinthe. When the glasses were adequately full and the sugar cube had melted, Jean-Yves removed the spoon from the top of the first glass, gave the concoction a quick stir, and presented the first glass to Malcolm.

"Now, you're permitted to have one, Malcolm," Leonardo said, "and then it is off to bed with you. Valerian will have you believing that wormwood spirits will expand your mind and soul—but that is a myth that was disproved long ago. Besides, you have something far more important waiting for you." He gave Malcolm a smile and looking overhead in the direction of Trechus' bedroom.

CHAPTER XXII

Bernard sat at the bar enjoying his second drink and checking his text messages. He knew he didn't have any but it was a way for him to look busy when he was alone at a bar. It was still early so the little gay bar in Le Marais had not begun to fill up yet. Businesses were suffering all over the city as the number of unexplained missing men put the people of Paris on high alert. Still, there were many people in Paris who, like Bernard, thought it was safe enough to go out as long as you kept your guard up. This had been Bernard's usual "lucky spot" for hooking up with men, but he had come out tonight with mixed feelings, considering all the unexplained disappearances in the city. He was always safe when it came to strangers, and there had been many. He prided himself on his character judgment. If something appeared to be the least bit out of place, he just wouldn't go. He planned to stay for an hour tonight and see if someone interesting might come along.

He looked up from his cell phone and noticed a dark-featured, masculine looking man walk in through the front door. While Bernard liked many types of men, this was the type that he found to be the most attractive. What was the chance that this guy was alone and would sit down at the bar? Most guys who are this good looking, he thought, are more often meeting a group of friends or, more specifically, a boyfriend.

Drakas' attention was caught by Bernard almost immediately as he entered the bar. Bernard was wearing a tight black T-shirt to highlight his thin but muscular French physique on a cold night when long sleeves would have been the more appropriate dress. Drakas knew that Bernard was obviously making an effort, and sustaining a little discomfort, to advertise himself. A vain guy like this, with open bar stools on either side of him and pretending to check his text messages, was easy prey. He sat down next to Bernard and nudged him as he asked, "What are you drinking? It looks good."

"It's a cucumber martini," Bernard said, somewhat surprised by the immediate presence of the stranger next to him and his apparent good luck.

"Is it strong? Drakas asked, looking deeply into Bernard's eyes. "I like strong things."

"Here, see what you think," Bernard said, pushing the martini glass closer to Drakas.

"I never drink out of another man's glass. That is, unless we've been introduced."

"I'm Bernard."

"Call me Drakas.'

"Interesting name. Is it Bulgarian?"

Drakas picked up the half-filled glass, finished it off, put it back down on the bar and said, "I owe you a drink."

"Are you waiting for your boyfriend?" Bernard inquired tactfully.

"No. No boyfriend." Drakas confirmed.

"Girlfriend?" Bernard asked.

"No. No boyfriend, no girlfriend either."

"So why is a guy as good-looking as you out and alone?"

"I guess many men are afraid of me. I don't get approached often," Drakas replied with a sly smile.

"You look like such a nice guy," Bernard said coyly.

"I like to think I am."

Drakas put his hand down to feel Bernard's upper thigh, "You have big legs for a French guy. I especially like meaty legs. You're a football player?"

"I was."

"I always go for guys with big leg muscles."

"What kind of guys do you like?" Bernard asked.

Drakas began to look Bernard over and formulated a description that exactly matched Bernard, "Tall, brown hair, blue eyes, nice shoulders, a nice tattoo, a little scruff on the face, nice lips."

"Sounds like I could be your guy," Bernard said, grinning.

"You do have the kind of body that I look for."

"And you really don't have a boyfriend, or is he just out of town?" Bernard asked.

"No boyfriend, but I'm looking for one, or at least one for tonight," Drakas said, smiling at Bernard. "Are you interested in going to a party with me? It's not far from here and I would rather not go alone. There are too many men disappearing these days."

"Yeah, the newspapers said today that over fifty men are missing in the city. Scary stuff."

"It is no longer safe for men to be alone on the streets, so I think it would be better for me to take you with me. You don't look dangerous."

"No, I'm a nice guy. You can trust me."

"Thanks for saying that. I'm trying to be careful with all that's going on."

"Where's the party?" Bernard inquired.

"It's in the basement wine cellar of my friend's apartment building just across the river. My friend has a great deal of money, so the wine he serves is always vintage."

The bartender came over. "What would you like to drink?"

"Do you want another drink or should we go to the party?" Drakas asked Bernard.

"Let's go to the party," Bernard replied.

"No thanks, we're good for tonight," Drakas told the bartender.

The two of them put on their jackets and scarves and left the bar together. They walked down past the Hotel de Ville and across the river to the left bank. It was a quick walk to the apartment building and they entered the door to the basement level where dance music could be heard below.

"Stop for a minute," Drakas said.

"Why? What's wrong?"

"Kiss me," Drakas said, putting his arm around Bernard's neck.

The two begin to kiss slowly and then more passionately.

"Ouch! You bit me!" Bernard said, pushing Drakas back.

"I like the way you taste."

"You're a bad boy!"

"Are you a good Catholic?"

"Yeah, on Easter and Christmas."

"After you," Drakas said, indicating the way with his hand.

Bernard smiled as he thought about his good fortune that evening. He continued down the stairs at an enthusiastic pace preparing to take in the party. As he reached the bottom of the stairs, he found a small empty room with an old stereo playing in the corner but no people. He turned back to look at Drakas in confusion. Drakas' eyes had shifted and Bernard was now looking into his silver metallic eyes. Bernard instantly panicked and tried to push Drakas aside to make his way back up the stairs, but he was easily overpowered. Drakas grabbed him by the arm, turned him around, and slammed him against the wall hard enough that it left Bernard slightly dazed. Drakas pushed the side of his face against the stone of the wall with incredible pressure.

"Are you a good Catholic?"

Bernard was breathing hard and tears filled his eyes as he tried to deal with the shock of the pain and fear.

Drakas now ordered him in the most sinister manner. "I said, tell me you're a good Catholic!"

Bernard could barely get it out as he started to cry. "I'm a good Catholic."

Drakas slammed his head against the stone wall and Bernard lost consciousness and fell in a heap on the floor. Drakas picked him up, threw him over his shoulder, and walked over to a door at the opposite end of the room. He unlocked it and headed into the tunnels beneath the city.

A short time later Bernard awoke when someone threw a bucket of cold water on him. He opened his eyes to see Kadar's face and sadistic smile only inches from his own face. As the water ran down the side of his face and into his mouth, Bernard realized by the salty taste that it was urine.

"Welcome to hell," Kadar said, as he stood up and walked around to inspect Bernard's tight, muscular body.

Bernard was stripped naked and fully restrained. He was bent over with his chest pressed against a young man who lay under him, who in turn was tied to some heavy wooden timber. Their arms were outstretched and tied at the wrists. The young man below him did not move and kept his eyes shut as he lay flat on the timber face up. Bernard was standing on his legs and bent over in a position which left his back arched and his ass pointing toward the ceiling. Bernard tried to get up but the position was awkward and the timber was too heavy. He quickly surmised that he and the man below him were tied to a giant crucifix.

Kadar ran his hand from Bernard's shoulder blade down his back and up over his ass, and slapped it hard. "This is one beautiful ass."

From behind, Bernard heard Drakas say, "If you want, when we're done its yours to eat."

Still exploring Bernard's ass with his hand as if he had never seen one before, Kadar replied, "I'm not hungry right now, but for this, I would definitely force myself."

"Do you love Jesus?" Drakas barked at Bernard.

"What?" Bernard asked in confusion.

"DO...YOU...LOVE Jesus?" Drakas repeated slowly.

The man below him now whispered, "Don't fight him, just say yes."

"Yes," Bernard said, submitting to Drakas. "I love Jesus."

Drakas stepped forward and grabbed Bernard by the hair on the back of his head, pulling Bernard's face up so he could clearly see the frightened face of the guy below him.

"Now can you see Jesus?"

"Yes . . . yes, I see him," Bernard said quietly, his voice trembling.

"Kiss Jesus and show us how much you love him," Drakas ordered.

Bernard hesitated and made a Herculean attempt to pull his arms free that proved to be futile.

"I said kiss Jesus now so he knows you love him." Drakas pushed Bernard's face into the man's face below him, grinding their lips together.

Bernard tried to resist and started to choke.

"Kiss him!" Drakas ordered.

Bernard relented and kissed the man.

"Again, like you mean it!" Drakas insisted.

Bernard followed the order and kissed the man again.

Angrily, Drakas gripped Bernard's hair tighter and started moving Bernard's lips over the guy's face. "Use your tongue, slut. I want to see some serious tongue action."

Terrified, the two men began to simulate passionate kissing as the two dragons watched.

"There. Now why is it so hard to show Jesus how much you love him. Rub your body against his. Go on! Rub your body against his six pack."

"I'm loving this shit!" Kadar exclaimed with sadistic glee.

Drakas bent down and looked into the other man's terrified eyes. "How is it that all the pretty boys are the stupid ones?" he asked.

Kadar moved between Bernard's legs and pulled his ass cheeks apart as he barked, "Were you planning on being a little slut tonight? Out on the town, hoping to get your hole plugged?" Kadar pushed his two thumbs into Bernard's exposed hole past his sphincter muscle.

Bernard cried out in pain as he tried to pull his ass away from Kadar.

"I don't think this little snack appreciates your generosity. These boys are never very thankful when you give them what they came for," Drakas said to Kadar.

Kadar pushed his thumbs as deep into Bernard as they would go.

Bernard cried out, "AGHHHH!" He was breathing hard and begged, "Please stop. Please stop! Oh, dear God, please stop."

Kadar pulled out of Bernard, grabbed a leather horsewhip from the wall, and hit Bernard squarely across his back.

Bernard screamed as the whip tore into his skin.

"You just can't seem to keep your ass or your mouth closed," Kadar said, circling Bernard. "Let's have some fun and play a game. Every time you make a sound, I use my whip. I'll stop when you stop your screaming." He grabbed Bernard's hair and pulled his head up and back to an extreme position. "GOT IT!?"

Bernard's eyes were filled with terror and his neck was strained, but he managed to whimper, "Yes."

Kadar let go of his hair and brought the whip down on his back with full force. Bernard screamed out in pain.

"I told you not to make a sound! Now you're forcing me to hit you again." He looked at Drakas. "You have to train these stupid boys like dogs."

Again he hit Bernard, who struggled but managed to stay silent.

"One more time just to make sure you learned the lesson," Kadar said, bringing the whip down hard on Bernard's back tearing even deeper into his skin this time. Bernard held back his cry with all his might.

"See Drakas, it's not the student, but the skill of the teacher. He walked around to look Bernard in the face. "Are those tears I see?"

Kadar took his thumb and wiped a single tear off of Bernard's face, holding it up to examine in the light. He marveled, "Is there anything more precious than a man's tear?" He licked the tear off his thumb. "So much tragic human emotion concentrated into a single tiny droplet. Delicious!"

Drakas broke in. "I'm getting bored with these two, maybe they would be more exciting squirming around on my fists. These whore boys look like they would enjoy some heavy fisting action!" Drakas positioned himself and began to push his hand into the lower man's ass.

I'Lagore, a massive, muscular Black Dragon appeared in the doorway. After observing Drakas' behavior for a couple of seconds, his nostrils flared and he blew a stream of steamy smoke from them. "Stop! You idiotic sloth!" He threw a beer bottle that he had been drinking from and it smashed against the side of Drakas' head.

I'Lagore hissed, "You morons waste too much time playing these trivial games."

I'Lagore breathed out a giant plume of red fire onto the two men. The fiery gel entirely engulfed the men. It stuck to their bodies and their skin quickly formed giant red blisters that burned and then charred from the intense heat.

Fearing further retaliation from I'Lagore, Drakas backed against the far wall. Kadar, untroubled by I'Lagore's anger, continued to circle the bodies as he watched them burn. He seemed oddly fascinated and delighted by the blistering and bubbling of the skin, despite having seen it countless times before as the two bodies strained slightly and then became motionless as they continued to burn.

The flames from the dead bodies subsided as the wood from the cross continued to burn below. A combination of gray smoke, steam, and a terrible stench rose from the corpses. I'Lagore grabbed what was left of Bernard's charred right arm and with a single action, ripped it off the body. He took a machete that was attached to his belt and tossed it at Kadar as he said in disgust, "Chop up the rest of them. I'm fucking hungry."

CHAPTER XXIII

Trechus returned to his bedroom and sat in front of the fire, reading only by the light of the candles burning in the room. He had stripped down to his briefs as it was warm for him, and he enjoyed the heat of the fire against his bare skin. As he turned the page he raised his nose into the air. He could tell by the growing presence of the scent that Malcolm was coming down the hall toward him. He put the book down and remained seated as Malcolm tried to quietly open the door and enter the room.

"Hey," Malcolm said softly, "I didn't want to disturb you."

"You are not disturbing me. I am happy to have you back."

"How many did you have?"

"Why do you think I had any?" Malcolm grinned.

"You forget I have a superior sense of smell. I can smell the absinthe on your breath."

As Malcolm sat down in the chair opposite Trechus, Chevalier got up from his place in the corner of the room and went over and pawed at Malcolm to pet him.

"Chevalier, are you having the time of your life?" Malcolm asked as he scratched him behind his ears.

"What about you? Are you happy here?" Trechus asked.

"I don't think I know what real happiness is. This is still all very new to me. Chevalier has certainly adapted well. All this attention and walks in the garden six times a day. House arrest has its benefits."

"I will be going back to Paris tomorrow with Valerian."

"I guess I'm staying here," Malcolm said regrettably.

"I don't think Rodin is ready to let you leave."

"How many years do you think he'll keep me locked up for?"

"He will come to trust you. It won't be long."

"Is he like your boss?"

"He is over me, yes."

"Could you do me a favor when you get back to Paris?"

"Certainly."

"Go to the square and find Charlotte. Tell her that Chevalier and I are OK. Otherwise, she may assume the worst, that I have disappeared like the others."

"I will make sure to tell her."

"Thank you."

"Are you angry with me about having to stay here? I wouldn't blame you if you were," Trechus asked.

"I'm OK with it, really. I wasn't going to be able to sleep outside much longer. With any luck, Rodin will keep me locked up until spring. It's better for Chevalier. Living on the streets of Paris in the winter is not an ideal life. I think maybe I am being too selfish. I should find Chevalier a real home with some land. Now that I see this, I realize I'm not giving him the right kind of home."

"You're being ridiculously hard on yourself. He's just as content now as he was the first day I saw him. I think he misses his morning coffee and croissants."

"Thanks, but I don't believe that."

"Malcolm, you need to realize how incredible you are."

"Someday," Malcolm said with a sad smile.

"There is something I want to ask you."

"What is it?"

"Would you spend the night with me?"

"You mean sleep here with you?"

"Yes, spend the night with me in my bed."

"You don't breathe fire in your sleep do you?" Malcolm teased.

"No, not unless I have a head cold." Trechus said teasing him back.

"I guess I could agree to that. Actually, I'm quite tired and you do look very sexy right now."

Without saying another word, Malcolm stood up and began to undress, leaving a trail of clothes until he reached the bed. He crawled naked into the large bed and got comfortable under the sheets. Trechus went back to reading his book.

"How old are you?" Malcolm asked.

"I was wondering when you were going to ask me that question," Trechus said without bothering to look up.

"It's not that I mind older men. I'm just curious."

"I'm almost three thousand years old."

"That's old," Malcolm said in a concerned tone, attempting to tease Trechus.

Trechus looked up at Malcolm. "Does that make you uncomfortable?"

"No, it's not like you're some kind of old guy hitting on me."

"No, I'm an ancient relic hitting on you."

"Maybe I should hit on you. I did have a couple of drinks, and you're looking mighty fine from where I'm sitting."

"You're drunk."

"So what if I am? Now, I think you should put that smelly old book down and stand up so I can see that hot body of yours."

Trechus put down the book and stood up.

"Turn around and face the window so I can see your ass," Malcolm instructed. "Ummm . . . why don't you lose the shorts so I can get a better look?"

"Lose the shorts?" Trechus asked.

"Yeah, I want to see your butt-naked ass. You're not bashful are you?"

Trechus removed his briefs and stood facing the window. The light from the fire and candles lit his body beautifully.

"You know you're going to cause me to shift. Are you sure you want that?" Trechus cautioned Malcolm.

"I think I can handle Puffy the Magic Dragon."

Trechus turned around and looked at Malcolm. "You know, you can be a real smart ass."

"HEY! I did not say you could turn around. Turn around and show me your ass and this time arch your back more and spread your legs a little."

"Ok boss," Trechus said as he smiled and complied.

"Now pull your ass cheeks apart."

Trechus looked over his shoulder at Malcolm in defiance.

"You heard me boy. Spread them," Malcolm ordered.

Trechus obeyed.

"That's it," Malcolm said. "A little more. Pull them far enough apart that they start to hurt a little bit . . . perfect!"

Malcolm tried hard not to laugh. He was enjoying his role as manipulator. And with each new set of orders, he became more and more aroused. His own throbbing cock was becoming so engorged with blood that it felt like it might explode.

"Now, turn around and let me see you."

Trechus turned around and Malcolm could see that Trechus was becoming erect himself.

"Stroke it for me. I want to see you make yourself hard as you shift."

"Are you sure about that? Don't start something you can't finish. Once I start there's no going back."

"Puffy, I can handle you."

Trechus closed his eyes and began to stroke himself in front of Malcolm. His cock got harder and he began to breath hard. Trechus opened his eyes and Malcolm could see them beginning to change. Trechus' breathing became heavier.

"Why don't you come over and get into bed?" Malcolm suggested.

Trechus slowly walked over, still stroking himself, and stopped at the edge of the bed, looking down at Malcolm with his eyes now shifted and his shaft fully erect. He reached down with his free hand and pulled the covers off Malcolm, who was now stroking himself. Trechus climbed into bed and put his arm around Malcolm's shoulder as the two continued to stroke themselves.

Malcolm could no longer resist and reached over and grabbed Trechus' thick shaft and started stroking it as Trechus' own hand fell away. The more Malcolm stroked Trechus the more he knew he had to taste it. Malcolm shifted himself in the bed and got between Trechus legs and, still stroking the lower part of the shaft, Malcolm licked the head of Trechus' cock. He had never tried oral sex before and the very action sent a shiver of excitement down his spine. Malcolm began licking the upper shaft and head slowly at first and then more rapidly.

Sensing that this might be Malcolm's first time, Trechus was surprised at his dedication to the task. Malcolm was working Trechus hard and watching him at the same time. He knew that he was only really doing it right if he could get Trechus to shift. Malcolm stopped the stroking action and now moved his hand down under Trechus' large ball sack and cupped the underside of them as he ran his tongue over his balls.

"I thought you'd never done this before," Trechus teased.

"I'm a natural." Malcolm grinned up at Trechus and then pressed his nose hard into his pubic hair, enjoying the musky smell as the tip of his tongue traveled up to the tip of Trechus' shaft.

Malcolm pulled Trechus' large shaft back so his cock head was sticking straight up in the air, and he put the head in his mouth. A wave of euphoria overcame Malcolm. He sucked hard as he worked Trechus' cock, bobbing his head up and down on it as his mouth filled with the taste.

Trechus was becoming more turned on just by watching Malcolm enjoying himself. Trechus took his hand and brushed the hair out of Malcolm's eyes so he could see them. Malcolm grabbed Trechus' ball sack and pulled forcefully as he sucked harder.

That little bit of pain in his ball sack really turned Trechus on and he arched his back off the bed and closed his eyes. He could feel his back start to shift and bifurcate. Malcolm repeated the action, but this time pulled harder and went down deeper down on Trechus. The pain was greater, which was an awesome feeling for Trechus, and as he lay back he couldn't believe this young man's virgin mouth was giving him so much pleasure.

Trechus' breathing started to intensify and this only encouraged Malcolm to work harder. Trechus decided that he couldn't hold himself back and he grabbed the back of Malcolm's head and begin to encourage him to go even deeper on his shaft. Even though Malcolm started to choke, he continued to go deeper until the tip of Malcolm's nose was again in Trechus' pubic hair. Malcolm inhaled, taking in the smell of Trechus' body as he pulled away from Trechus shaft.

Malcolm climbed on top of Trechus and went to work on his pectoral muscles. He licked his nipples but quickly graduated to biting them as he realized that a good dose of pain was Trechus' weakness. As his bit down on his nipple, Trechus encouraged him by pushing the back of his head into his pec as he repeated,

"Harder . . . harder . . . harder!"

Malcolm worked his way up Trechus' chest and bit him hard on the shoulder and kissed his way up to his ear lobe as he whispered into Trechus ear, "I want you to fuck me."

"Are you sure?" Trechus whispered back.

Malcolm looked Trechus in the eye and nodded.

"Yes. I'm sure."

Trechus flipped Malcolm off of him and onto his back and then rolled him over onto his stomach and ran his hand between his ass cheeks. Trechus got off the bed and then pulled Malcolm by the ankles to the edge of the bed. Malcolm was now bent over the mattress as Trechus reached into a drawer of the bedside table and took out a container of lube. He poured a healthy amount down on the top of Malcolm's ass crack and let it run down. He caught the excess and gently worked it into Malcolm's tight hole. At first he could only get his index finger in, but then he slowly worked in a second and then a third finger as Malcolm let out a moan each time a new digit was added.

Trechus worked two fingers on either side of his prostate gland and Malcolm moaned loudly. Trechus pulled his fingers out and pulled Malcolm off the bed. Trechus wrapped his arms around Malcolm and they began to kiss. Trechus slid his tongue into Malcolm's mouth and gently played with Malcolm's tongue as they continued kissing. Malcolm put his arms around Trechus' neck and Trechus pushed him back up against the wall as they both started to lose control.

Trechus pinned Malcolm's wrists over his head against the wall as he kissed Malcolm and pushed his body hard against his. Malcolm pushed back against him. Trechus picked him up and Malcolm wrapped his arms and legs around Trechus. This positioned Malcolm's eager hole just above the head of Trechus' engorged cock. Trechus teased Malcolm by lowering him down so that the head pushed firmly against his hole before lifting him up again. He did this several times until he began to allow Malcolm's body to slide down onto his shaft and his cock head popped inside Malcolm. It was a mixture of pain and excitement for Malcolm who held onto Trechus' neck as tight as he could.

Trechus allowed Malcolm's body to go lower as he slid a few more inches up inside him before he lifted Malcolm up again. Now he pushed him up against the wall and started to enter and exit him more rapidly. Each time he pushed in, he pushed him hard against the wall. Trechus' thick shaft stretched Malcolm's hole as it repeatedly rammed against his prostate. Waves of delight ran through Malcolm's muscles. His legs loosened up as the waves became so intense they seemed to take over his body.

Trechus now used his hands to cup Malcolm's ass cheeks as he raised and lowered Malcolm's ass onto his shaft. Malcolm was breathing heavily as he passionately kissed Trechus. Trechus' cock twitched and swelled as Malcolm's tight ass stroked the shaft and head.

Trechus began to increase the speed as he lowered Malcolm all the way down to the base of his shaft. Malcolm stopped kissing him as he threw his head back, moaning loudly.

"Are you alright?" Trechus asked, making sure Malcolm wasn't in pain.

"Don't stop, don't stop!" Malcolm pleaded.

Trechus began ramming Malcolm, while still holding firm to his ass cheeks, and pinning him up against the wall with his chest. Malcolm's legs dangled as he held on tightly to Trechus' neck, pulling himself up after each inward thrust.

Both Malcolm and Trechus were lost in the moment, focused only on each other. Malcolm had given himself entirely to Trechus in a way that was completely foreign to him, but at the same time he felt electrified.

Trechus began to sweat hard. His sweat was different from Malcolm's as it had a thicker consistency than human sweat. This added to the lubrication between their two bodies. Malcolm eagerly licked Trechus' neck and shoulders, finding the taste of his sweat to be seductively sweet.

Trechus put Malcolm's ass down on the edge of the bed as he reached under Malcolm's knees and pulled his legs up into the air by his ankles. Holding firmly onto his ankles, he spread Malcolm's legs as far they would go, and lifted his ass up off the bed. He pushed his cock firmly against Malcolm's hole and increased the pressure until he was inside him. He repeatedly began to slowly enter Malcolm, going in as far as he could, and then pulled completely out. Malcolm grasped the duvet hard as each penetration of his body filled him with painful pleasure.

Trechus pushed himself into Malcolm until his shaft was buried deep inside Malcolm. He let go of Malcolm's ankles and leaned toward Malcolm as Malcolm lifted himself up to support himself on his elbows. Malcolm was eager for Trechus' kiss. Trechus gently cupped Malcolm's face with his hands and kissed him, their two tongues meeting in delicious union. Trechus pulled back slightly so he could gaze into Malcolm's face. Looking into Malcolm's sparkling blue eyes he said,

"You're so incredibly beautiful." He leaned in and kissed Malcolm again. Malcolm responded more aggressively this time, grabbing the back of Trechus' head and pulling hard as he furiously kissed him. Malcolm couldn't get enough of Trechus' lips, tongue, hands, or body. With all his strength he pulled himself hard against Trechus, wanting to feel every bit of him.

Malcolm finally dropped back against the bed from physical exhaustion. He was dizzy as his endorphin levels were elevated far beyond anything he had ever experienced. His body had become so sensitive that he could feel Trechus' warm breath against his body as Trechus stood above him, looking down at him. Malcolm had an uncontrollable craving to be touched, handled, and ravaged in any way that would please Trechus.

Trechus was breathing heavier now and hesitated for a moment as he looked down at Malcolm. Without warning, he forcibly wrapped his arms around Malcolm's thighs just under his knees and entered Malcolm, ramming him repeatedly. His pace quickened to a speed beyond what was humanly possible. Malcolm jacked himself off as Trechus continued to fuck him as hard as he felt Malcolm could stand without injury. Malcolm began to accelerate his strokes until he shot a massive load up across his chest and it went as far as his own forehead.

Trechus let go of Malcolm's legs and let them rest over the side of the bed. Malcolm was breathing hard as he looked up at Trechus. Trechus started at the tip of Malcolm's shaft and began to gently massage Malcolm's cum over his abs, working his way up his chest and finally across Malcolm's face to his forehead. He bent over and gently kissed Malcolm and said, "You're not done yet."

Trechus flipped Malcolm over so he was bent over the bed face down and thrust himself hard back into Malcolm, who again moaned loudly. He pumped Malcolm a couple of times and then pulled his body off of the bed. Malcolm's upper body fell forward as Trechus bent him over and kept him steady on his feet by holding onto his hips. He expertly pulled Malcolm's hips against him, rapidly working himself into a frenzy.

Trechus' wings began to grow from his bifurcated spine. With each thrust the wings became larger and larger until they were full size. Then, with one final mighty thrust that lifted Malcolm clear off the floor, Trechus orgasmed and exploded inside Malcolm. He let go of Malcolm's hips and Malcolm collapsed on the floor.

"Are you OK?" Trechus asked, breathing hard. "I'm sorry, I didn't mean to drop you."

Malcolm was gasping for air, but managed to say, "That was so awesome! . . . I want to do it again?"

"Can you even stand up?" Trechus asked.

"I don't think I can move," Malcolm replied.

Trechus knelt down and picked Malcolm up in his arms and kissed him sweetly. He carried him into the bathroom and into the shower where he put him down, helping him to stand on his own feet. He turned on the shower and he got under the stream of cold water, which turned to steam as it hit his body. He began to soap up as he cautioned Malcolm, "Wait a minute for the water to warm up."

Malcolm watched Trechus soap himself. Never had a simple bar of soap been so interesting to Malcolm. As the water warmed, Trechus pulled Malcolm into the shower against his soapy body and kissed him as he wrapped him in his wings.

Malcolm looked up at Trechus. "I feel like I'm trapped in a sexy fairy tale."

"Let's hope you never escape," Trechus replied as he kissed him again. "Can you stand on your own now?" he asked with concern.

"Yeah, I'm fine now," Malcolm replied confidently.

Trechus pulled his wings back and handed Malcolm the soap. "You should clean yourself good, your skin is not used to my sweat and I don't want you to get a rash."

"Rash? There goes my fairy tale," Malcolm joked.

Trechus rinsed off and stepped out of the shower. Malcolm watched as Trechus stood looking at himself in the mirror. He was surprised to see that Trechus was almost instantly dry without having used a towel.

As Trechus walked out of the bathroom, his wings began to shrink in size.

Malcolm finished his shower and dried off and walked back into the bedroom where Trechus had turned back into his human form. He watched as Trechus removed two heavy leather sacks from the armoire.

"How did you do that?" Malcolm asked.

"Do what?"

"Dry off without a towel?"

"I just increased my body temperature."

Malcolm ran his fingers through Trechus' hair. "Even your hair is dry."

"Cuts down on laundry," Trechus said as he carried each of the sacks over to the bed and opened them up and emptied their contents of gold coins onto the center area of the mattress.

"Are you trying to impress me with your wealth?" Malcolm teased.

"No, this is how I sleep. I'm ectothermic."

"You're ecto-what?"

"Despite my big heart, I am still a cold-blooded creature. My metabolic rate depends on my body temperature. All dragons sleep better by lowering their body temperature. Gold is the most efficient thermal conductor. These coins draw the heat away from my body, cooling me down and allowing me to sleep more soundly."

Trechus got into bed and looked at Malcolm who seemed unsure of what to say. "Look, I know I'm weird. But, maybe you'll fall in love with me anyway."

Malcolm smiled at Trechus' admission and crawled into the bed next to him. Trechus, put his arm around Malcolm's shoulder and pulled him in close to him. Lying on the cold coins felt strange to Malcolm, but being next to Trechus' warm body made him feel wonderful. Within minutes Malcolm was fast asleep.

CHAPTER XXIV

I'Lagore had grown disgusted with Drakas and Kadar and their lack of focus on their ongoing efforts to make sure he and the other dragons were well fed. He wouldn't deny that it was the right of a dragon to profiteer and indulge themselves on humans, but their commitment continued to dwindle. He had chosen Drakas and Kadar from his team of eleven dragons in anticipation that they could walk among the humans with the least amount of detection.

I'Lagore preferred to feed on the adult flesh of human males and therefore insisted his dragons do the same. Male human protein and testosterone made dragons stronger, hyper aggressive, and ultimately more deadly than did other types of animal proteins. This mission was too critical to the future of his race to have it ruined by the antics of two dragons.

I'Lagore headed down to the main sewer tunnel, entered it, and walked along the elevated walkway. He stopped to smell for humans, and when he didn't detect any, he began to breath heavily as his wings emerged from his back as he shifted. With his wings now at full size, he took off from the ledge and flew through the main tunnel, following it to the outskirts of Paris. He emerged from the tunnel at the edge of an abandoned industrial complex that the dragons were occupying for the purposes of their mission. He walked to the back of one of the dilapidated buildings and banged on the rusted steel door. Waiting for one of the other dragons to unlock the door, he reflected on how, with their mission underway, Drakas' and Kadar's antics could no longer be tolerated or it could negatively affect the outcome. He would deal with each of them personally once they returned to Rome.

The door opened for him from the inside. He was greeted by Belazare, who appeared hyper-excited.

"They're here! They're here!! They arrived this afternoon from Rome, just as you said they would. Do you want to see them? Can I show them to you?"

"Don't be an imbecile, of course I want to see them. Right away!!"

I'Lagore followed Belazare, whose exuberance only irritated him more. When he entered the lower room he was instantly furious to see that the crate in the middle of the room had been opened. The precious cargo had been disturbed in his absence.

"Who did this?" I'Lagore demanded.

"I did. I had to see them," Belazare replied like a child who had unwrapped a Christmas present early.

"They are not yours to see. I should rip your arm off and beat you to death for exercising such moronic behavior."

"No, look," Belazare said, as he pulled one of the heavy rectangular units from the top of the crate. It had a half-inch thick metal plate on both the top and the bottom, and the plates were separated by six hollow glass tubes that contained a green liquid. Each unit had a series of wires running into each tube with a complex electrical component at one end with an attached handle. Belazare held the unit up to the light by the handle for I'Lagore to see. "Look how beautiful it is."

I'Lagore took it from Belazare and studied the glass tubes within the unit. Each tube contained a thick clear green liquid that appeared to glow in the presence of light. The liquid contained tiny dark blue bubbles that moved in a swirling motion through the liquid, traveling from the bottom of the tube up to the top and then down the center of the tube to the bottom again. As they swirled through the liquid, each bubble randomly flickered on and off like a firefly going from dark blue to light blue and then back to dark blue again.

"Put this away and close it up. Securely!! Just like you found it!" he said angrily, exercising great care as he handed the unit back to Belazare.

I'Lagore stormed out of the room and started up the stairs to the second floor. Belazare put the unit back into the crate and then ran to catch up with him, asking, "When is more food coming? Kadar and Drakas have been gone for hours."

I'Lagore wasn't ready to hear this, but before he could say anything there was pounding on the back door.

"That will be them now," he told Belazare. "Go let them in."

As Belazare turned and headed down the stairs to open the door, I'Lagore reached the second-floor landing and pushed opened the large metal door to a vast industrial space. He walked past more than a dozen oversized canvas bags that hung on large hooks along the wall. Some of the bags moved slightly as their contents were shifting. In the center of the room stood a large industrial wooden table littered with crushed beer cans, glass from broken beer bottles, and a series of different daggers plunged tip first into the table. Each dagger defined a different dragon's position at the table. At the far end stood a rusted fifty-five gallon drum. Eight dragons were seated at the table. Seven of them sat smoking crystolyan out of a large hookah in the center of the table. The eighth dragon had obviously smoked too much and was passed out, leaning back in his chair.

At the sight of I'Lagore, the seven dragons jumped to their feet. Disgusted, I'Lagore flipped the sleeping dragon's chair into the air. The chair flew eight feet into the air before crashing to the floor. The other dragons laughed as the dazed dragon struggled to his feet.

Kadar, Drakas, and Belazare entered the room, each carrying an oversized canvas bag on their shoulder.

"Who has the goods?" I'Lagore demanded.

Belazare threw his bag up on the table and announced, "I do."

He proceeded to dump the contents of the bag onto the table. Clothing, shoes, wallets, and jewelry—all begotten from their victims of the day. The dragons rummaged through the goods, each selecting from the different items. I'Lagore picked up a wallet from the pile, removed the euros and put them in his pocket, and then discarded the wallet, tossing it into the drum at the end of the table.

He opened up a large bottle of beer and drank from it as he sat at the head of the table watching the other dragons. He quickly became frustrated with the process and yelled, "Enough! Food! Now!!"

Drakas and Kadar dumped out the contents of their two bags—the charred and hacked up remains of their latest two victims. The pile of blackened charred parts was almost unrecogniz-able as being human as it was strewn across the table.

The dragons showed little regard for each other as they pulled at pieces from the charred remains creating their own food piles. Eagerly they began to feed in silence, using the daggers that marked their spots to strip the remaining flesh from the bones. After consuming the flesh, they threw the bones into the drum at the end of the table. A series of hollow thuds continually sounded throughout the meal as discarded bones hit the side of the drum. They guzzled beer, and when finished, smashed the can flat with their fist against the table, or, if it was a bottle, threw it against the adjacent brick wall.

"Drakas, Kadar, you lazy sloths, you barely brought enough food tonight to feed three dragons. Go get more. Now!" I'Lagore ordered as he stared at them with his dark eyes, exhaling a stream of steam from his flaring nostrils demonstrating his extreme dissatisfaction with them.

The two dragons immediately got up from the table, headed downstairs, and went back out into the night. I'Lagore took one of the hoses from the hookah and breathed in deeply and exhaled. He leaned back in his chair and asked, "Belazare, what do you have for me tonight?"

Belazare went to the corner by the entry door and took one of the heavy canvas bags down off its hook and dropped it to the floor. He dragged the bag across the floor and heaved it in front of I'Lagore, saying, "I think you'll like this one."

I'Lagore opened the top of the bag and dropped the sides down to reveal a young blonde man in his early twenties. He was alive and his mouth was covered by a piece of gray duct tape and his wrists were bound together with rope. He wore only a T-shirt, briefs, and a pair of athletic shoes. I'Lagore roughly grabbed the man by the T-shirt and pulled him down to the floor so that he could see the man's face at eye level. He briefly studied the man's face that was wrought with fear before he finally said, "Yes. . . I like him."

The other dragons at the table pounded the butts of their daggers on the table's top in approval. I'Lagore tore open the front of the man's T-shirt, leaving the rest of it to hang on his shoulders. He began to indiscriminately manhandle the young man by running his hands up from his abdominal muscles to his pectorals, grabbing his nipple hard and twisting it as he said, "Nice. This one is very nice!"

The young man watched helplessly as I'Lagore ran his hands down over his body and groped him through his briefs.

"Look at those eyes. Such pretty eyes. Let's see if you have a pretty mouth." I'Lagore violently tore the duct tape away from the man's mouth.

The man reeled from the pain as he gasped for air.

"Yeah, you will do just fine. Not much into pain though. Don't worry, we can work on that. Now, let's see your pretty mouth."

I'Lagore forcibly grabbed the man under his chin and squeezed his cheeks with his fingers, causing the man's lips to distort. He carefully eyed his face. "You know how to suck dick with that mouth, boy? I bet you've had all kinds of dick in that mouth."

"He's good at it," Belazare confirmed. "I had him at the train station this afternoon."

"Collar and cuff him," I'Lagore ordered.

Brud, a smaller dark-haired dragon, brought over a collar, put it on the man, and attached a thick heavy chain to it. Brud wrapped the chain around his hand and pulled it hard and the man's head jerked. "Hold your hands out," Brud barked.

The man held out his hands and I'Lagore took his dagger and cut off the ropes with a strong flick of the blade. The man rubbed his sore, bruised wrists. Belazare attached a pair of wrist restraints to the man's wrists as Brud grabbed the back of the man's T-shirt and cut it with his dagger, pulling off the two pieces and leaving the man in his briefs.

"This one can dance. He dances at clubs," Belazare announced as he turned on some dance music on an old boom box.

"Really," I'Lagore said with interest, grabbing the chain leash near the collar and throwing the man forward onto the top of the table.

"Get up on the table and let's see you crawl around!"

The man lifted himself up and began to crawl around the table, trying to avoid the broken glass and beer cans. As he reached I'Lagore, who was smoking more crystolyan from the hookah, I'Lagore grabbed the man by the hair.

"Breathe in!" He blew a stream of the exhaled smoke into the man's face.

Not pleased with the man's progress, I'Lagore stopped half way through his large exhale and said, "Suck this all in or I will drive my knife into your eye." As he continued to exhale, the man did everything he could to inhale the smoke.

The crystolyan didn't take long to take effect. The man was soon on top of the table gyrating his hips as Brud turned the music up louder. Lucky or not, the man was high enough at that point to be oblivious to the dangers below him. Brud jumped up on the table and started dancing with the man, but soon got bored, so he grabbed the chain and pulled the man's head down, forcing him to his knees. Brud attached the man's wrist restraints to either side of the collar. With his hands attached to his collar, the man trembled as he struggled to remain on his knees without falling over.

Brud grabbed him by the back of his head and pulled him into his crotch. Brud pulled his pouch down and rubbed his cock and balls against the man's face as his shaft began to get erect.

"Suck my cock, boy!" Brud ordered. The man complied and took Brud's cock head and then his shaft into his mouth. Brud grabbed the man by a big tuft of blond hair and held his head steady as he continued to pump his shaft into the man's throat. The man started to gag, but Brud was relentless. The other dragons laughed and jeered. Belazare pulled the man's briefs down just far enough to expose the man's young ass.

Brud's eyes began to shift while the man continued to suck his cock. I'Lagore had removed his own shirt and stood behind Brud and started to pull hard on the chain, causing the man to slam hard into Brud's pelvis.

"That's it, fuck that mouth hard. That little cock whore needs it real bad."

Belazare took his knife and cut away the man's briefs and tossed them into the drum as his eyes began to shift. I'Lagore's eyes began to shift as well as he watched Brud continue to work the man over.

"Hoist him up. Let's have some fun," I'Lagore ordered.

Brud pulled the man off of his cock and the man collapsed onto the table, gasping for air. I'Lagore grabbed the man by his collar and dragged him off the table and across the floor to a large metal hook that was attached to a rusted chain hanging from a hoist. He detached the wrist restraints from the man's collar and attached the hook to the wrist restraints while Belazare began to pull another chain, causing the hoist to pull the man's hands over his head.

I'Lagore sat in a large chair that was positioned in front of the hoist to give him a good view of the action. Brud sat on the arm of the chair and put his arm around I'Lagore shoulder as another dragon brought the hookah over so I'Lagore could continue to smoke.

"Nice, very nice," I'Lagore commented as he watched. "Put a spreader on his ankles."

Belazare grabbed the metal spreader and clamped each of the man's ankles to the alternate ends. He pulled the rusted chain further and it pulled the man up toward the ceiling. Belazare only stopped when the man's toes barely touched the cement floor.

"Oil that pig up!" I'Lagore directed.

Belazare grabbed a mop that was soaking in an industrial-sized five-gallon bucket of corn oil and slopped the head against the man's face. The other dragons laughed. He dunked the mop head back into oil and slopped more oil on the man's chest, working the mop over the front of the man's body. He dunked the mop again and this time moved behind the man and slopped it against his shoulders. He worked the mop down the man's backside almost to his feet. He dunked the mop a final time and slopped the oil against the man's ass as he began to move the mop head up and down over the man's crack. He finished by pressing the mop head hard against the man's hole. The force of the mop pushed the man forward and caused him to strain as the restraints dug into his wrists and ankles. The other dragons laughed and jeered as they called for Belazare to push harder.

I'Lagore watched with interest as oil dripped from every part of the young man's body. He stood up and stripped down to just his work boots and walked toward the man, fully erect. He walked around to the back of the man and grabbed the man by the hips and forced his cock completely into the man's anus. The man moaned loudly. The dragons laughed as I'Lagore pumped him. Periodically, I'Lagore stopped and grabbed the man by the hair, pulling his head back and ordering him.

"Tell me to fuck you harder!!"

To which the man replied dazed from the crystolyan, "Please, Sir. Fuck me harder!"

This continued for a while until I'Lagore orgasmed and shot his load deep inside the man. I'Lagore, exhausted and stoned, grabbed a liter bottle of beer, went into the far corner of the room where the floor was covered with a couple of old dirty mattresses, and fell asleep.

Belazare took the man off the hoist and led him over to the hookah where he gave him three more powerful hits of crystolyan. He then led him over to the mattress area. The other dragons followed them and they descended on the man and continued to use him as they pleased. The man floated in and out of consciousness as this continued throughout the night.

Kadar returned in the middle of the night after meeting up with Jean Paul in Montmartre. He had gotten Jean Paul so high on crystolyan that the young man could barely even comprehend where he was now or what sort of danger he was in. Kadar gave him another hit of crystolyan from the hookah that sat on the main table before forcing him to remove his clothes. He stripped him down to his socks and underwear before stuffing him into a white canvas bag and hanging it on the wall with the others. He took the pile of clothes and rummaged through the pockets opting to keep his cash and watch before throwing the rest of the clothes into the pile with the other discards.

CHAPTER XXV

It was approaching midnight when Rodin returned to the chateau and found Valerian and Leonardo playing cards and drinking absinthe in the billiard room. Upon seeing Rodin, the two footmen moved quickly and assisted him out of his long cashmere overcoat, taking his gloves and scarf as he asked, "Where are Trechus and Malcolm?"

"Together, upstairs," Valerian replied.

"Perhaps something good may come from all of this," Rodin commented.

"It would appear Trechus has finally parted ways with his hundred year mourning ritual," Valerian added.

"Want a drink?" Leonardo offered.

"No, I have nothing to celebrate," Rodin said, his voice tired. "I just came in to say goodnight."

Both Valerian and Leonardo said goodnight. Rodin walked out of the room, following Jean-Yves, who led the way through the dark halls with a candelabrum. The two footmen followed dutifully behind Rodin. They climbed the stairs together and went down the hall to Rodin's bedroom where Jean-Yves opened the door, allowing Rodin to enter first. There was a large fire burning in the fireplace and the room was entirely lit by candles as they entered. Jean-Yves went to the corner and started Rodin's victrola, which began to play "Nessun Dorma" from Puccini's Turnadot in the background.

Rodin walked over and stood in front of the roaring fire as Milos expertly removed Rodin's pocket watch and cufflinks. Janos, gently unbuttoned and removed Rodin's waistcoat. As the items were removed, Jean-Yves stood by and collected them. The two footman removed Rodin's shirt and undershirt. His belt was removed and then Milos lowered Rodin's pants and briefs while Janos placed a chair behind him. Rodin sat down in the chair and Milos removed his shoes, socks, and finally his pants and briefs. Janos went into the bathroom and returned with a big porcelain bowl and lowered Rodin's feet in the water. Rodin stood up in the water as Milos removed the dragonhead jewelry from Rodin's cock head, while Janos stood behind Rodin and massaged his shoulders with frankincense oil. Rodin stepped forward onto the hearth of the fireplace, his feet drying themselves in the process. The bowl was set aside and he stood on the hearth while the footmen continued to massage the rest of his body with oil.

Meanwhile, Jean-Yves took two sacks of gold coins from the armoire, pulled back the duvet cover, and spread the gold out on the bed.

"Monsieur, will you require the footmen tonight?" Jean-Yves asked Rodin.

"Yes, I may require something later in the evening," he replied.

"Very well, monsieur."

Rodin got into the bed and watched as the two footmen smiled at each other and began to undress, handing their clothes to Jean-Yves, who collected them and folded them, leaving them on a side chair. When they were both completely naked, they got into the bed on opposite sides. Rodin wrapped a muscular arm around each one. Jean-Yves snuffed out the burning candles and left the room after saying goodnight.

Jean-Yves returned to the billiard room for a final check before going to bed. Leonardo playfully gloated after winning another game as he dealt a new hand of cards to Valerian.

"Pardon messieurs. I took the liberty of preparing your beds the way you prefer them," Jean-Yves announced as he entered the room.

"Merci, Jean-Yves," Leonardo said, looking up.

Valerian was frantically looking through the large hand of cards he was just dealt.

"Will you require anything else tonight?" Jean-Yves inquired.

"No, Jean-Yves. I think we're finished for the evening," Leonardo replied.

"Very well, monsieur. If either of you should need something, just ring for me. Bonne nuit," Jean-Yves said, and then left the room.

Valerian threw his cards down on the table in disgust and said, "I can't bare to lose any more gold tonight. I'm finished here."

"Good, I want to go flying." Leonardo got up from the table.

"You always want to go flying when you drink," Valerian replied.

"Maybe I just like to fly after I drink."

"Flying is boring," Valerian said flatly showing no interest.

"Then you obviously are not doing it correctly," Leonardo retorted.

"What are you implying?" Valerian asked as he was beginning to get offended.

"Let's make it interesting," Leonardo proposed with a grin.

"What did you have in mind?" Valerian's curiosity was now piqued.

"A little free-fall action."

"Too dangerous," Valerian warned.

"What are you flying with these days?"

"What do you mean?"

"I wasn't sure if you were still using your dragon wings or if you had decided to start flying with little chicken wings."

"I said dangerous, I never implied I was afraid," Valerian said gruffly.

Leonardo stood up and started to unbutton his shirt as he goaded Valerian. "There's only one way you can prove to me that you haven't started flying about Siberia with flocks of clucking feathered fowl."

"How dare you imply that I'm a coward. I should take your head for that," Valerian said proudly, and he jumped up and started to remove his own shirt.

Leonardo looked up at Valerian. His eyes had started to change. "I can take you in a five-minute race."

"Five minutes is for children. We will do a ten-minute race, and the winner goes down on top," Valerian fired back.

"You don't want to try to win your gold back?"

"No, my interest is in you now."

"I'm beginning to like this even better," Leonardo said with a sly grin. The first to undress, he raced across the room, opened the French doors onto the patio, and sprinted out into the cold night air. Valerian was undressed and now in hot pursuit. As the two ran across the back lawn they both continued to shift, their spines bifurcating—and each one sprouted their full-sized wings.

Leonardo was the first to take to the air, and he started to fly straight up, with Valerian trailing behind him. It was a ten-minute flying race heading straight up into the sky, which would take them to almost 100,000 feet above the chateau. Leonardo had the lead until the eight-minute mark, and then Valerian surged ahead and maintained his lead for the last two minutes. At the ten-minute mark, Valerian stabilized himself by flapping his wings in the air. The full moon lit the sky. He never got tired of seeing the curve of the earth from this height. The air was too thin to breath and he comfortably held his breath at the high altitude. Leonardo reached him five-seconds later and flew into Valerian's arms. The two dragons embraced and kissed as they collapsed their wings and went into a free fall, head first, back toward Earth.

They kissed passionately as they fell. Valerian flipped Leonardo over in the air and grabbed him hard by the belly as they continued to fall back toward the earth. Leonardo spread his arms and legs out, helping to slow the decent. Valerian was able to work his cock deep inside Leonardo. Valerian now had about four minutes to work himself up to an orgasm. He wildly thrust himself into Leonardo, who skillfully balanced the two as they fell.

Leonardo collapsed his body several times causing wild free-fall summersaults. At the three-minute mark, Valerian pulled out of

Leonardo and shot his load into the air, and then spread his wings and began to fly again, blowing a stream of purple fire to mark his victory. Leonardo allowed himself to fall for an additional twenty-seconds so that he would at least beat Valerian to the ground.

CHAPTER XXVI

The next morning, the sun streamed into Trechus' bedroom, awaking Malcolm first. He had crawled on top of Trechus during the night for warmth and now lay on top of Trechus' chest wrapped in his arms. Malcolm buried his nose in Trechus' chest, taking in his incredible body aroma and causing Trechus to stir. Trechus awoke and looking down at Malcolm said, "Hey, handsome. How did you sleep?"

"I slept incredibly. You were so warm and your skin has this intoxicating aroma." Malcolm ran his hand up Trechus' arm and then examined his fingers as he said, "It's almost like an oil."

"It is called 'pharnum.' It is a substance our body secrets through our skin. It's what makes our outer layer of skin highly resistant to heat and fire."

"Then my tongue is definitely fireproof after last night," Malcolm said with a smile, as he proceeded to seductively lick Trechus' nipple. "It has an awesome flavor."

"Only humans can taste and smell it."

"Dragons can't taste it?" Malcolm asked.

"It does not taste or smell like anything to us."

"You don't know what you're missing," Malcolm said as he went back to tonguing Trechus nipple.

"Don't get me started," Trechus cautioned.

"What? You're not ready for a second round?"

Trechus smiled, "I would love a second round and a third and a fourth."

There was a knock on the door and Trechus said, "Come in."

Jean-Yves opened the door and entered the room, "Bonjour, messieurs, Rodin would like Malcolm to collect his things and meet him in the library."

"Thank you, Jean-Yves," Trechus replied. "Please tell Rodin he will be down in ten minutes after he dresses."

"Yes, monsieur." Jean-Yves left the room and closed the door.

Malcolm turned to Trechus, "This is good news right?"

"It would appear you're getting your freedom."

Malcolm slid off of Trechus and rolled off the bed, landing on his feet. He started putting his clothes on as he jokingly proposed, "I guess all I really had to do was bang a dragon."

"No, you got banged by a dragon. You did not bang a dragon," Trechus corrected him.

"Rodin doesn't know that," Malcolm informed Trechus.

"Maybe, you should stay here a little while longer," Trechus teased, getting out of bed.

"It beats sleeping in the cemetery, for sure, but all the same, I miss Paris."

"What are your plans for Chevalier?"

"He's coming with me."

Trechus walked over to Malcolm so he could look him in the eye, "Are you sure that is the best thing for him right now, considering all that is going on?"

Malcolm stopped putting clothes into his backpack and looked at Trechus.

"Why don't you let him stay here? Just for a couple weeks. If it doesn't work out for either of you, we can always come back and get him. At least until you find a proper place to live," Trechus proposed.

"It would be hard to go back to Paris alone."

"You're not going alone. You'll be going back with me," Trechus assured him.

Malcolm thought about it, "We're talking about two weeks, right?"

"Two weeks," Trechus confirmed.

"It is better for him to sleep here instead of sleeping with me on the street."

"I am not letting you go back to Paris so you can sleep on the street."

"Trechus, I can take care of myself. I don't need you to 'let me' do anything."

"That came out the wrong way. I only mean that I want what is best for you. I want you to be safe."

"Look, it would be a dream come true for you to take me back to Paris and for us both to live happily ever after, but I don't have that kind of luck in my life."

"Let's just take it one day at a time, OK?" Trechus asked.

"Trechus, you're incredible, but that's the problem. Nothing ever incredible happens to me."

"One day at time, OK?" Trechus reiterated.

"OK," Malcolm said in humble agreement.

Trechus walked over to the bed and took a gold coin from the pile and walked over and placed it into the palm of Malcolm's hand.

"What is this for?" Malcolm asked.

"I want you to have it. Keep it with you."

Malcolm looked down at the ancient coin in his hand and said, "It's beautiful Trechus, thanks."

"Now, grab your stuff and get yourself downstairs. It's best not to leave Rodin waiting." Trechus smiled. "He can be a real dragon in the morning."

Malcolm put the coin in his pocket and grabbed his bag and headed toward the door. As he got to the door he stopped, walked back to Trechus, and gave him a kiss. "Thanks," Malcolm said. "Look, I know I'm weird. But, maybe you'll fall in love with me anyway."

CHAPTER XXVII

Rodin was slowly and methodically pacing back and forth at the far corner of his library when Malcolm appeared at the door. Rodin reached into his pocket and pulled out his watch and opened it to check the time.

Malcolm spoke up, "I hope I am not late."

Rodin looked up at Malcolm, "No, you're right on time. Forgive me, I can be obsessed by time." Rodin closed his pocket watch and smiled warmly at Malcolm.

"I would think for someone who has lived as long as you have, that time wouldn't be that important," Malcolm replied.

"In the end, time is all we have," Rodin said as he looked out the window appearing to be disinterested in Malcolm.

"You wanted to see me?" Malcolm asked.

Rodin turned back toward Malcolm, "You will have to forgive my manners this morning, I have a lot on my mind. Please, come in and sit down."

Malcolm entered the room and took a seat at the reading table in the center of the room. Rodin returned to the window and looked out as if he was searching for something in the distance. While he studied the horizon, he started to speak. "We are the last of our kind." He paused and turned to face Malcolm. "We are all that is left now. A once great race of thousands now reduced to four dragons."

Rodin crossed the room and pulled out a chair across from Malcolm and sat down. He looked at Malcolm. "I have decided to release you from the chateau provided you give me your most solemn word that you will never reveal what you have witnessed here."

"I give you my word. I will take it to my grave," Malcolm said with sincerity.

"I believe you. Now I must decide where to send you."

"I'm going back to Paris," Malcolm blurted out.

"I am not inclined to return you to Paris. There is a wave of death and destruction that will overtake Paris in the coming days." Rodin pushed an envelope across the table and let it rest in front of Malcolm.

"What's this?" Malcolm asked.

"You will return to the United States. Inside that envelope there is an airline ticket and ten thousand U.S. dollars. I will send you more money when you arrive back home and set up a bank account."

"The United States is no longer my home. Please let me go back to Paris with Trechus," Malcolm said.

Rodin held up his hand to silence Malcolm. "Paris is no longer safe for you. The Black Dragons have returned to Paris with the sole purpose of inciting anarchy by decimating the population. As a human, you will be defenseless. Trechus will return to Paris to aid Valerian in hunting down the Black Dragons. This will only provoke the Black Dragons and they will retaliate against us in a most brutal fashion. You would be caught in the middle."

"If you release me as you claim you will, then it should be my choice as to where I go."

"I may release you from the chateau, but as long as you're alive, I am and will remain your Lord and Master!"

"I accept you as my Lord and Master but, I must protest! It is wrong for me to abandon all of you at your greatest time of need."

"I admire your commitment but I do not see how you can be of any use."

"You haven't been able to locate the dragons. They know your scent and are hiding from you. I could get closer to them. They don't know my scent from any other human. I have seen a Black Dragon with Trechus and I know what he looks like. I even have a sketch of his face." Malcolm said this as he pulled the sketch Charlotte made for him from the pocket of his backpack and handed it to Rodin. "Here, look."

Rodin took the sketch from Malcolm and studied the picture before saying, "I know of this dragon from long ago, his name is Belazare."

"Give me some time. Give me a week to help Trechus and Valerian. If I don't prove myself useful to them, then I promise I will go back to the States, or wherever you send me."

"You understand you would be risking your life?"

"I do."

"Malcolm, I can see in your eyes that your concern is not for yourself but for Trechus."

"Why is that wrong?"

"Listen to me. There is nothing more precious in this world than life. Once it is taken from you, it can never be returned and all that you have is lost. It is noble that you would risk all that you have for Trechus or it is foolish."

"Why would you say foolish?"

"How much value do you place on your life."

"I guess very little."

"Why is that?"

"I am nothing but a homeless boy who sells stuff on the street. I have no future beyond what I am today."

"You may return to Paris with Trechus under the direction of Valerian on the condition that you disregard what you think about yourself and begin to strive toward the potential I see in you. You don't know it yet, but you have the capacity to do extraordinary things in this world. You will soon come to realize that your life has an incredible value. Malcolm, the world is in dire need of more people like you."

Tears came to Malcolm's eyes. Rodin stood up and walked around the table to Malcolm. "Stand up," Rodin said.

Malcolm stood and Rodin wrapped his arms around him and hugged him as he told him, "You're very special. You should not fear me because I see parts of you that you have yet to discover. Above all else, you need to stay alive. Terrible things now lay in your path and you must remain strong."

Trechus appeared at the door and asked, "May I interrupt?"

Rodin released Malcolm and looked up. "Trechus, come in. I have decided that Malcolm will return with you and Valerian to Paris."

"Respectfully, Rodin, after thinking it over, I would ask that you send him back to the States."

Malcolm blurted out, "Why would you say that?!"

Valerian appeared in the doorway behind Trechus and stood there in silence, listening.

Trechus approached Malcolm and took his hand as he said, "Malcolm, I thought it over, and it is selfish of me to bring you back to Paris where you won't be safe. I would rather lose you for a period of time than to have something terrible happen to you and lose you forever."

"Nothing is going to happen to me," Malcolm confirmed.

"You can't say that with certainty. If anything were to happen to you, I would blame myself."

"What if something happens to you? How should I feel?" Malcolm asked in desperation. "Chevalier can stay here, but I am coming with you to Paris."

"Please, Malcolm, there is no need to take the risk, I am only saying this because I care about you. I really do care about you," Trechus said in a sincere and loving tone.

Malcolm looked up at Rodin. "Rodin decided I am to return to Paris, I am bound by what he says."

Valerian stepped into the room as he broke into the conversation. "It's time for us to leave. Malcolm may be of use to us. His argument is strong. He could get closer to the dragons and he at least knows what one looks like."

"I heard his argument," Trechus said.

"The decision is made, Trechus. We should go," Valerian urged in a serious tone.

Trechus stood up and they all filed out of the room and began to walk down the hall. Valerian put his arm around Malcolm's shoulder as they walked. Malcolm turned to Valerian and asked, "How did you know what I said when I was in with Rodin?"

Valerian tapped on his right ear with his index finger, "We hear most things. This is a small house."

"I see," Malcolm said thoughtfully, as they walked out the front door of the chateau to the waiting car. "Valerian, last night, could you hear me and Trechus?"

"Don't worry. Leonardo and I barely listened at all," Valerian said nonchalantly.

Milos and Janos loaded the car with the luggage as Jean-Yves stood by with Chevalier. Malcolm stopped and bent down to scratch Chevalier on his head and rub his ears. "I'll be back soon," he assured the dog.

"He'll have the best of care in your absence," Jean-Yves assured him.

"Thank you, Jean-Yves. You're kind to look after him."

Jean-Yves leaned in close to Malcolm. "Most days, it's quite boring around here. Chevalier will give us something to do."

Milos and Janos stood on either side of the car and opened the doors for Valerian, Trechus, and Malcolm to get in.

"Wait," Leonardo called out as he ran down the front stairs dressed in his archer's uniform, his cloak flowing behind him like a cape, and carrying an ancient looking travel bag. "I'm going with you."

Milos took the bag and put it in the trunk as Leonardo prepared to get into the car.

"You know that there are people where we are going? Human people?" Valerian cautioned.

"Yes, I know." Leonardo sounded a bit irritated.

"Good," Valerian confirmed. "At least you made the effort to blend in," he said sarcastically as he eyed Leonardo's outfit.

"Yeah, Valerian, like you blend," Leonardo shot back as he got into the car.

Rodin stood with Jean-Yves and the footmen as they watched the car pull away and exit the front gate.

Jean-Yves turned to Rodin. "It's not good, is it, monsieur?"

"No, Jean-Yves. I never believed this day would come and we would be standing here on the brink of our own extinction."

CHAPTER XXVIII

Later that afternoon, Valerian and Trechus sat in Trechus' dining room, closely studying several maps of the city, including the one that showed the sprawl of underground tunnels and catacombs. Valerian made notations on the map with a red pen as he spoke to Trechus.

"I suspect that their base is in this general area. There is a great deal of movement in and out of this area here on the Left Bank. So, if we assume that, then Le Marais would be their prime hunting ground."

Malcolm entered the room wearing his jacket and scarf. Trechus looked up at him and asked with concern, "Where are you going?"

"To work. I have books to sell. Hungry dog to feed. Remember?"

"Malcolm, I really think it's best for you to remain here."

"Trechus, I need to work. I also need to go and see Charlotte and let her know that I am still alive."

"Wait, and I will go with you," Trechus insisted.

"Trechus, I don't need you to babysit me. I can handle myself," Malcolm said as he eyed Trechus.

"Let the boy be a man," Valerian urged Trechus.

"OK, you're right," Trechus relented.

"Thanks. I'll take care," Malcolm replied.

"Wait," Trechus beckoned.

"What's wrong?" Malcolm asked.

"Take my mobile phone. Call me on Valerian's number every half hour while you are out." Trechus held out his phone for Malcolm.

"For real?" Malcolm asked, not wanting to be forced to take the phone and report in.

"Just do it for me. Please?" Trechus asked.

Malcolm took the mobile phone from Trechus and shook his head as he walked out of the room. As he headed toward the door he could hear Monique's bare feet running toward him on the marble floor.

"Wait! I have something for you," she called out after him.

As she reached him she pulled a small pewter disk strung onto a black leather cord out of the pocket of her skirt. She carefully put the necklace on him.

"What is this?" he asked.

"This is a talisman and will protect you from any harm or evil that might come to you."

"Thank you, I will never take it off."

Monique hugged Malcolm and he left the house. Immediately outside the door, sitting on the cold bare sidewalk, was a Chinese man in his early thirties. The man was poorly dressed for winter and, despite the frigid temperatures, had no shoes but wore only traditional Chinese corn husk sandals. Seeing this, Malcolm stopped and asked the man, "Parlez-vous français?"

The man stared at Malcolm and shook his head. Malcolm removed his backpack and put it down on the sidewalk and began to go through it, pulling out a pair of socks, a sweatshirt, and a pair of old sneakers. He gave the objects to the man along with sixty euros. The man graciously accepted them and began to put on the socks and shoes. Malcolm continued on his way, walking the four blocks to the square.

When he crossed the street, Charlotte spotted him and jumped up, knocking her easel over. She ran toward Malcolm. "Mon garçon, don't ever do that to me again!" She grabbed Malcolm and hugged him in the middle of the street. "You never miss a day and then you disappear without a word? It scared me to death! I imagined the worst! Wait, where is Chevalier?"

"Trechus took me to the country for a few days, Chevalier is staying behind with Trechus' friends for a couple of weeks. A little vacation."

She stood back as she carefully inspected him, "You're different."

Malcolm grinned. "Yes, I am very different."

"Very good. Your heart has finally blossomed. I wish you had found a Frenchman and not a Greek. Onassis was such a pig, but I suppose Trechus is French enough!"

"I am finally finding my way toward happiness!" Malcolm confirmed.

"This is wonderful news!" Charlotte exclaimed.

"Come on," Malcolm urged. "I have some books to sell tonight."

Malcolm helped Charlotte reset her easel and went about displaying his books. As he finished, he looked up to see the Chinese man from earlier standing over him. The man put his hand on his chest and said, "Long Ji." He smiled at Malcolm.

Malcolm put his hand on his chest and smiled and said, "Malcolm." He stood up and took a bottle of water from his pack and handed it to Long Ji, who drank from it. Malcolm searched another pocket in his pack and pulled out a candy bar and handed it to Long Ji, who accepted it with a gracious smile and began to eat it.

"Who is this?" Charlotte inquired.

"His name is Long Ji. He was outside my door. He doesn't speak any French."

"So, he is to be your new Chevalier?"

"No, there's only one Chevalier."

Long Ji left the two of them and crossed the street to sit on the curb. He continued to watch Malcolm as he ate the candy bar and drank the water.

"I think you have an admirer," Charlotte observed.

"He's breaking my heart," Malcolm confessed.

"Falling in love already?" Charlotte teased.

"He's handsome, but no. It just pains me to see someone alone on the street," Malcolm replied.

"You truly have a heart of gold, Malcolm."

Malcolm looked at Charlotte sadly.

"What's wrong?" she asked.

"I don't know how to put this. If I asked you to do me a favor, I mean a really big favor, would you just try your best to do it?"

"Yes, I suppose if it was that important to you. What is it? What's wrong?"

"You told me you have a cousin with a farm in the south."

"Yes, my cousin, Patricia."

"I want you to go and visit her right away. I mean tonight."

"Why, what's happening?" she asked cautiously.

"I can't really say, but please go and see your cousin. Promise me you'll take a train tonight and go and stay with her for at least a week."

"Tell me what is going on," Charlotte insisted.

"I can't. I mean, I don't know. I just know something really bad is going to happen here in Paris."

"I knew Trechus was a cop all along," Charlotte said.

"Yes," Malcolm said. Lying did seem to be the best option. "He's a cop and there are some serious, deadly threats to the city. Promise me you'll go tonight."

"You are really serious about this." She paused as she studied his face. "I will go if you think it is important."

"Call Patricia right now so I can see you talk to her."

"OK, I'll call her," Charlotte said as she removed her mobile phone from her coat pocket and started to dial the number. Within seconds she was speaking with her cousin.

Malcolm looked across the street to see if his admirer was still there. He was, but he had fallen asleep. Malcolm looked around the square as the cold wind blew into his face. At the far corner of the square he spotted someone who looked like Belazare, walking. Could he be this lucky? Could it be him? Malcolm started to walk across the square. It was difficult to tell as he could only now see the back of Belazare's head. Malcolm continued to follow him around a corner and then another. As he reached the third corner there was no sign of him. Half way down the block there was a bar. There was no place for him to go except the bar, so Malcolm went in to look for him.

He entered the bar and spotted Belazare again from behind. He worked his way around the room so he could clearly see his face. Malcolm could not believe his luck, it was him! He excitedly scrambled to pull Trechus' phone out of his pocket as he rushed outside. He searched the phone for Valerian's number and dialed it. He waited for the call to connect. Malcolm watched through the window as Belazare began to talk to a young man sitting on the bar stool next to him.

Trechus answered Valerian's phone and asked, "Malcolm are you all right?"

Malcolm excitedly explained, "I found the Black Dragon we saw the other day! He's sitting in a bar here in Montmartre!"

"Where are you?" Trechus asked.

"I'm outside, watching him through the window." Malcolm looked up at the sign. "The name is Barre de Jazz Manouche."

"I know it! Don't move and don't go inside," Trechus warned. "We will be right there. And don't hang up!"

Malcolm continued to stay on the phone as he watched from outside. He was surprised to see that Long Ji had followed him and was now sitting across the street on the curb. He looked back in the window and saw that Belazare had gotten up and was starting to put on his coat.

"Trechus, he's getting ready to leave. Where are you?" Malcolm said, starting to panic.

"We are three blocks away," Trechus said reassuringly.

"I think the guy he's talking to is going to leave with him," Malcolm told Trechus.

"Malcolm, if they start walking, try to stay with them, but stay far behind and don't let him see you or suspect you're following him."

Belazare exited the bar with the young man, who lit a cigarette. The two conversed for a moment before a taxi came down the street. Belazare hailed the taxi and it stopped. He reached for the door handle.

Malcolm put the phone in his pocket and called out to the young man Belazare was with. "Where are you going?"

The man and Belazare stopped and looked up at Malcolm.

"I said, where are you going?" Malcolm asked again, but louder this time.

Belazare cautioned the man, "Let's leave, this guy is drunk!"

Malcolm stepped forward and asked the young man, "Why are you leaving with him? You know nothing about him."

"Shut up," Belazare said angrily to Malcolm. "Mind your own business you stupid American!"

"Tell him," Malcolm urged Belazare. "Tell him what you are."

Belazare examined Malcolm as he breathed in his scent and asked curiously, "Who are you?"

"Why don't you buy me a drink, sexy boy, and I'll tell you all about myself?"

Belazare took a step toward Malcolm. Malcolm looked over at the young man and said, "Get lost!"

The young man replied, "Fuck you!" He got into the taxi and it pulled away, leaving Malcolm alone with Belazare. Malcolm quickly went into the bar as Belazare followed behind him. He took a seat at the bar and waited for Belazare to sit down next to him.

"So, you think you know all about me?" Belazare said as he eyed Malcolm.

"Sure, you're a handsome foreigner making plays for young French guys. We get a new crop of tourists just like you every week."

"Really, and that's what you think I am?" Belazare asked in a perturbed tone.

"Yes, I do," Malcolm replied.

"Do you think I'm a fucking moron?"

Malcolm simply replied, "No."

"Tell me, why do your clothes carry the scent of dragons?"

"I really don't know what you're talking about," Malcolm replied as he realized he had put himself into a dangerous position.

Belazare's face turned dark as he grasped Malcolm's leg hard just above the knee.

"Do you believe that I can crush your leg right now?" Belazare asked.

Malcolm stared back at him, realizing he was in serious danger.

Belazare could now sense Malcolm's fear and his suspicions were confirmed. "Of course you do because you do know what I am."

He continued to grip Malcolm's knee as he began to heat up his hand. The heat of his hand started to transfer to Malcolm's leg.

"It's getting hot, isn't it? Is it starting to burn yet?" Belazare smiled with a sadistic confidence.

Malcolm remained silent and looked at him with growing fear in his eyes as his leg started to burn under Belazare's grasp.

"Here is what we are going to do," Belazare proposed. "We're going to get up and we're going to head out of here quietly. If you make trouble, this place is going up in flames and everyone will die. Understand?"

Malcolm nodded. Belazare released his leg and grabbed Malcolm by the base of the neck with his other hand as he instructed him, "Now, get up slowly and don't call any attention to yourself. The lives of these people now depend on you."

Malcolm obliged and stood up as Belazare started to lead him toward the entrance. Trechus and Leonardo entered the front door and immediately saw Malcolm with Belazare. An inebriated woman, getting up from her bar stool, accidentally bumped into Belazare causing him to momentarily release his grip on Malcolm's neck. Malcolm used the opportunity to pull away and slip through the small crowd toward the back of the bar. He made his way to the back staircase with Belazare in pursuit. He climbed the first staircase, but as he reached the second landing, Belazare caught up to him and grabbed him by the arm.

"Stupid boy! Head toward the roof and no more bullshit," Belazare sternly ordered him.

Belazare pulled Malcolm up the second and third flights of stairs and then kicked in the door to the roof. He pulled Malcolm through the door and threw him down hard onto the rooftop.

"You think you're better than me? Do you really think you can outsmart me?" Belazare taunted him as Malcolm scrambled across the roof trying to put some distance between them.

Malcolm made it to his feet but was dangerously close to the edge of the roof.

"Tell me about your friends," Belazare ordered as he stepped closer to Malcolm.

Malcolm looked behind him, realizing there was no escape—it was too far to the ground to jump and survive.

"I don't have any friends," Malcolm said defiantly.

"Then you're no use to me. Will you jump or should I burn you to death?" Belazare took another step closer toward Malcolm, forcing him to the very edge of the roof. As Malcolm struggled to keep his balance on the ledge of the building, Belazare asked, "Any final requests?"

Leonardo and Trechus quietly appeared in the rooftop door behind Belazare.

"I'll tell you whatever you want to know," Malcolm said, his voice trembling.

"You're a liar. I really think you need to die." Belazare blew a fireball at Malcolm as a whizzing noise cut through the air, causing Belazare to stumble forward.

As the fireball traveled toward Malcolm, he fell backwards off the edge of the roof, locking eyes with Trechus as he tipped back over the side.

"NOOOO!!" Trechus cried out.

Malcolm fell backward toward the sidewalk below. As he fell, his thoughts were of Trechus. Suddenly, something hit him from below, causing his neck to snap hard, and he was swooped up, unconscious from the severity of the impact.

On the roof, Belazare spun around to face Leonardo and Trechus. Leonardo had his bow drawn and a second arrow pointed squarely at Belazare's right eye.

Belazare was breathing heavily. He looked Leonardo in the eye and said, "Go ahead and kill me, you murderous dragon. It won't stop us. It won't stop what's coming next." He fell to his knees as green blood began to pour from his mouth. He fell forward onto the deck of the roof. Leonardo's first arrow buried deep in his ass.

Valerian ran through the roof door in time to see Belazare go down. Trechus ran to the edge of the roof and looked down. Malcolm's body was missing; it had not hit the sidewalk. All was quiet below as a couple of women stood outside the bar smoking cigarettes as if nothing happened.

Trechus turned in shock and looked up at Leonardo. "He's not there! I saw him go over the edge, but he's not there!" Leonardo walked to the ledge and looked over the side and looked up at Trechus. "There must have been a second Black Dragon."

"We have to find him!" Trechus cried.

"Focus, Trechus," Leonardo warned. "It's too late. We will never find him now."

Valerian made a call on his mobile phone. After speaking to Rodin, he hung up the phone. "Rodin wants us to bring the body back to the chateau."

Leonardo knelt down next to the body and studied the green blood. "Did you see this?" he asked Valerian.

"I realized it right away. They've gone back to breeding solely with dragons."

"There's no way the blood would be this green unless they were only breeding with other dragons," Leonardo noted as he stood up and looked around. "Where's Trechus?"

"He went after Malcolm."

"You let him fly off and leave. We needed him here."

"How could we stop him? There is little hope Trechus can reach him in time," Valerian said sadly, "but he needs to try. We at least owe that much to Malcolm. You and I can handle this on our own."

CHAPTER XXIX

In the dead of night the Panamera went roaring down the gravel driveway and made an abrupt stop in front of the chateau causing the tires to spatter gravel everywhere. Valerian and Leonardo jumped out of the car as Jean-Yves ran down the front steps of the chateau, followed by Milos and Janos. Valerian opened the back trunk to reveal Belazare's dead corpse covered in drying green blood and partially wrapped in plastic sheeting. Rodin descended the front steps of the chateau looking at his watch. He approached the car to inspect the corpse.

"The color of the blood suggests they are no longer interbreeding with humans but have gone back to breeding only with dragons," Valerian noted over Rodin's shoulder.

"What concerns me most is that they are breeding. Now, we have no idea what their numbers could be," Rodin said cautiously. He turned to address Jean-Yves. "Considering the direction of the wind into Paris, we will take the body and go to the fields by Kermorvan."

"Yes, monsieur." Jean-Yves replied.

Rodin continued, "Fill the truck with firewood and wrap the body in burlap. We will leave here on the hour."

"Right away, monsieur," Jean-Yves said and turned and ushered the footmen into the house.

"What's the plan?" Leonardo asked Rodin.

"We will take the corpse of the dragon and burn it. The westerly winds will carry the smoke and its scent into Paris. When the Black

Dragons pick up on the scent, they will certainly know we are behind it. Demanding retaliation, they will follow the trail back to us. There we will face our enemy."

An hour later, just before dawn, the truck was loaded with wood. Jean-Yves sat behind the wheel as Valerian and Leonardo came out of the chateau and approached Rodin, who said, "You two go with Jean-Yves, I will meet up with you later. I should be here when Trechus returns."

Valerian and Leonardo pulled away in the truck. Rodin went back inside and went to his library and watched the sun come up, frequently checking the time on his watch. After dawn he grew concerned that Trechus still had not returned. He opened the large windows in his library and was relieved when he caught Trechus' scent in the air. Several minutes later, he could hear Trechus' footsteps far off as he walked across the frozen lawn toward the chateau. Moments later, the front door opened and Trechus made his way to Rodin's library.

Trechus walked into the room; his clothes were disheveled and his eyes were puffy and red while the rest of his face had lost its color. Rodin looked up at him as Trechus blurted out, "Malcolm was taken by the Black Dragons. I tried to find him but it was impossible. He's gone and I now fear that he is dead."

"Trechus, I am deeply concerned that your emotions are running uncontrolled and guiding you during this time of great crisis. This is completely out of character and not what I expect from you."

"I apologize, Rodin. You know I am loyal to you."

"I do not doubt your loyalty. You forget that Malcolm is under my care and I made my own arrangements to safeguard him. He was not taken by the Black Dragons. He is alive and asleep upstairs in his bedroom."

"How is this possible?" Trechus asked.

"Two nights ago the White Dragon, Long Ji, arrived in Paris. I went to meet him and decided it would be best for him to remain in Paris. When I decided that Malcolm would return to Paris, I had Long Ji watch over him. Long Ji caught Malcolm as he fell off the roof and flew him safely back here to the chateau."

"I must see him," Trechus insisted.

"I will bring you upstairs."

The two dragons left the library and headed up the main stairs.

"I should warn you, Trechus—White Dragons are very different from us. You should not expect a warm reception from Long Ji."

"I know of their feelings toward outsiders," Trechus replied.

"Then you understand you will not be welcome," Rodin confirmed.

"There is no reason for hostility."

Rodin stopped walking and looked at Trechus. "Get a hold of your emotions. Understand and respect the traditions of the White Dragons. I have asked Long Ji to protect Malcolm, and he has done that."

"What are you saying? Malcolm needs protection from me as well?"

"What I am saying is that Long Ji is now protecting Malcolm. He does not know you and therefore, he has no reason to trust you. You will need to be patient when dealing with Long Ji."

Rodin knocked lightly on Malcolm's bedroom door. The door was unlocked and opened barely an inch. Rodin spoke to Long Ji through the partial opening. "We have come to check on Malcolm."

Long Ji opened the door far enough to look at Trechus and replied with deep suspicion, "I do not know this dragon. You may come in, but he is not permitted."

"He is a companion to Malcolm. Please allow him to stand in the doorway so that he may see that Malcolm is alive."

"I will allow that but he is not to enter the room," Long Ji cautioned.

Rodin turned to Trechus. "You must respect his wishes and stay in the doorway."

"I understand," Trechus said.

Long Ji warned Trechus, "If you enter the room, I will kill you."

Long Ji opened the door all the way to reveal Malcolm lying face up and unconscious on the floor, his body expertly supported by blankets. Hundreds of acupuncture needles had been applied to Malcolm's body and a series of colored pastes had been painted in complex patterns and symbols to the sides of Malcolm's face and down across his naked body.

Long Ji wore only a brief made from a long strip of white silk that was wrapped and then tied across his midsection. He returned to Malcolm and, kneeling down next to him, resumed painting Malcolm's body with the colored paste.

Rodin looked down at Malcolm. His eyes were closed but there was something very peaceful about his face. Rodin said to Trechus, "He will be fine."

Trechus could not restrain himself and took a step into the room toward Malcolm. Without looking up Long Ji said to Rodin, "Tell him that he is to leave now or I will kill him."

Rodin moved to stop Trechus, and ushered him out of the room and closed the door behind them. "Calm yourself. He is in good hands. White Dragon medicine is highly effective. Give Malcolm some time to heal. Remember, Malcolm is alive because Long Ji saved his life

CHAPTER XXX

The truck laden with firewood and supplies followed by the Porsche Panamera traveled the winding country road until they stopped in a field near the coast overlooking the Kermorvan lighthouse in Le Conquet. Jean-Yves, Milos, and Janos got out of the truck and began to unload the split French oak. Valerian and Leonardo got out of the Panamera and joined the other men. Within the hour they had stacked the wood on end to form a base where they placed the burlap wrapped corpse of Belazare. A second layer of oak was piled around the corpse, and finally a third layer was added to cover it. As Valerian and Leonardo inspected the pyre, Jean-Yves directed Milos and Janos as they erected a large purple Medieval style tent on the edge of the field.

Upon completing their task, Valerian suggested, "Jean-Yves, it is best for you to leave. You don't want to be here when we light this. Burning Black Dragon is the most putrid smell you can imagine."

"I appreciate that, monsieur. I have set aside supplies of meat and wine in the tent for you."

"Thank you for your help here," Valerian replied.

Jean-Yves called, "Janos and Milos take the truck back to the chateau."

Jean-Yves got into the Panamera and started the engine. He rolled down the window and called out to Valerian, "Monsieur?"

"Yes, Jean-Yves," Valerian replied.

"Good luck, monsieur," Jean-Yves said with a tone of concern.

"Thanks, Jean-Yves, but it should never be about luck and always be about skill," Valerian said proudly.

"Of course, monsieur," Jean-Yves said with a smile.

Jean-Yves drove off, leaving Valerian and Leonardo with the funeral pyre.

"Leonardo, it was your expert kill—it is your right to light the pyre," Valerian proposed.

"We should offer some words of respect," Leonardo replied.

"I trust you're right. We should show respect for our fallen enemy."

There was a silent pause before Leonardo looked at Valerian and asked, "Do you have some words you can offer?"

"Words of respect, yes I do," Valerian said, and then cleared his throat. "We stand here today to mark the passing of this Black Dragon who . . . tried to fight us off . . . but sadly was poorly trained and not smart. He died a fool's death. May his putrid stench bring those other sons-of-bitches out of their holes so I may personally slay them one by one. May their scourge be wiped from the face of this fair earth. . . . How was that?"

"Well, one might say that you were a touch weak on the respect part . . . but I think it will suffice," Leonardo replied, and then took in a deep breath and exhaled a plume of purple fire that consumed the pyre. The fire shifted in color from purple to the usual color as the oak began to burn. The smoke emerged randomly at first, but was quickly taken by the wind and blown inland. Black flecks of ash began to float out and spiral off in patterns toward the inland.

Valerian watched the ash spiral off towards Paris. The smell of the burning corpse was horrible, prompting Valerian to say, "It will take a couple of hours for this stench to reach the city. By now the Black Dragons will have surmised that their comrade is dead. Once they pick up his scent, they will know for certain. It won't be long before they trace it back here. By midnight, we shall have the results that we desire."

The truck did not appear again until close to sundown. Jean-Yves stopped the truck only long enough for Trechus and Rodin to exit, and then, without fanfare, he drove off. Rodin ignored everyone and went directly to inspect the burning pyre. He stood upwind of the fire and looked to the sky and in the direction of Paris.

"Trechus!" Valerian called out. "This is good news about our boy, Malcolm."

"I am relieved that he is alive and safe at the chateau," Trechus replied somberly.

"I would expect you to be elated by the news." Valerian looked at Trechus with concern.

Trechus smiled slightly as he said, "I am pleased and relieved that he is safe. However, the news from Paris is not good. The dragons have begun their attacks on the city this morning. It is far worse than we thought."

Rodin turned his attention away from the pyre and approached Valerian, Trechus, and Leonardo. "The Black Dragons have released a deadly toxin into the air that causes massive hemorrhaging in human lungs. Hundreds of thousands of people are dead or dying as we speak." He looked away and out into the night. "The unthinkable has begun."

"How is this even possible? There cannot be enough Black Dragons to carry out an attack of this size," Leonardo asked.

"I believe I have gravely underestimated their numbers," Rodin said shaking his head. "It is clear to me now that they have been actively breeding and planning for this very moment. For them to carry out an attack of this magnitude, their numbers are likely to be closer to fifty, perhaps higher. I concede that we do not know the size of the force that will meet us on this field tonight, but we will face them."

CHAPTER XXXI

Earlier that morning at 4 o'clock, all the Black Dragons assembled dressed as Métro maintenance workers in the lower level of their building around the cargo crate that held the shipment from Rome. I'Lagore entered the room with purpose and, looking around, immediately asked, "Where is Belazare?"

"I did not see him return after he went out last night," Drakas offered.

I'Lagore let out a deep grunt in anger as steam spewed from his flaring nostrils. "Call him on his phone, see where he is!"

Drakas took out his mobile phone and dialed the number. I'Lagore began to pull boxes one by one out of the crate. The dragons lined up and each one approached I'Lagore with an open black backpack. I'Lagore put two boxes in each backpack. Carefully handling the cargo, each dragon zipped the backpack closed and moved on.

Drakas interrupted the process. "He isn't answering."

I'Lagore stopped what he was doing and said with certainty, "Yes, something is wrong."

The others dragons looked to him for guidance. I'Lagore stared them down and barked angrily, "This means nothing! We will continue without him. He is no longer necessary."

I'Lagore handed a full backpack to Drakas. He picked up his own and the one meant for Belazare and said, "I will take care of the work Belazare was to do. The taxis are waiting outside. Take a taxi to your first drop location and then, travel on foot to your second drop location. Your first installation should occur in one hour at five o'clock. The second should occur at five-thirty. The units will begin to deploy every half hour until nine. Sit in a cafe and wait until ten. Then return and collect the units, leaving the shell behind. You're to meet back here no later than noon. I will be delayed since now I have to do the work of the incompetent Belazare as well. Do not stop! Do not let anyone stop you!! Kill anyone or anything that gets in your way. Now go!"

The dragons exited the building in silence to meet the line of waiting taxis. I'Lagore stood there in the early morning darkness and watched as each dragon left in a taxi. There were two remaining taxis. He went to the window of the taxi meant for Belazare and knocked on the window. The driver rolled down the window as I'Lagore handed him a hundred euro note and said, "We do not need you. You can go."

I'Lagore got into the remaining taxi and said, "To Gare du Nord." The driver nodded and pulled away from the curb. It was close to a thirty-minute ride to the train station. I'Lagore got out of the taxi and paid the driver. He entered the station and went directly to the lower level. He knew exactly where he was going as they had all rehearsed their movements several times in the last four weeks. He passed a security camera and then entered a second smaller hall without one. As a few early morning commuters passed, he opened the first backpack and slid a unit out of its cardboard box. Each unit had a large piece of adhesive tape applied to its flush back side. He stripped away the protective liner, exposing the wet adhesive, and stuck the unit to the wall at waist level. He pressed against it to ensure that it was securely affixed to the tiled wall and then took a key from a retractable chain clipped to his belt and inserted it into the top of the unit. He turned the key to the right as the electronics inside lit up and the unit's digital timer came to life. He stood next to the unit leaning against the wall for a moment to make sure there was no one who was suspicious of his actions. He watched as the earliest morning commuters walked by. No one paid him any attention so he moved on to his next location.

The process was duplicated by the dragons in twenty of France's busiest commuter points, including the cities five train stations and the Métro's fifteen busiest stations. At five minutes to six, I'Lagore installed the last unit at the Les Halles Métro Station. A female street musician entered the tunnel with her cello and began to set up. I'Lagore watched her as she sat down and began to play. As he left, he dropped five euros in her collection box. As he exited the tunnel, there was a small pop inside the unit and a puff of green neon smoke emerged as a swarm of tiny blue bubbles swarmed out into the tunnel.

At quarter passed ten, he returned to the Les Halles station to collect the unit. The musician was still in the same place but she was now visibly ill. She was sweating profusely as she coughed and hacked. I'Lagore stopped and stuck his key into the unit and turned it the opposite direction. This released the electronic component from the shell and he pulled it out of the unit. He opened his backpack and slid it into the original cardboard box and closed the backpack. He stopped as he passed the woman and bent over and studied her face for a moment before commenting, "Mademoiselle, you do not look so well."

She looked up at him with heavy bloodshot eyes and said as she coughed, "No, I feel terribly ill all of a sudden." She began to have another coughing fit, but this time it was more violent. As she tried to cover her mouth, blood began to spatter into and drip from her fingers. Petrified by the sight of so much of her own blood, she managed to scream. She continued coughing and hacking even harder as blood flowed from her mouth down the front of her face and onto her chest. She tried in vain to breath but she was rapidly suffocating as blood filled her failing lungs. As the crowd of commuters gathered in horror around her, she fell over onto the floor of the tunnel, blood running from her mouth and nostrils in a continuous stream.

I'Lagore called out in French, "Please someone call an ambulance." It was his own dark joke. For at that moment, thousands of commuters exposed to the first blast were suffering the same fate and it would be impossible to even get through on the jammed emergency lines. He walked out of the Métro station with a proud smile on his face. As he walked down the block, he passed a café where a waiter lie choking on the floor as a small concerned crowd of people gathered in an attempt to aid the dying man. Further down the block, a woman came out of her apartment building with blood on her hands. Hysterically crying, she begged him for assistance as she tried to explain her husband was dying in their apartment. I'Lagore simply smiled at her and said coldly, "Madame, surely you should call an ambulance."

He collected his other three units as death continued to spread in the wake of his path. People panicked in the streets as sirens wailed and people lay dead or dying all around him. Chaos and fear quickly took over the city. This was turning out to be the best day of I'Lagore's ancient life. Then, without warning, he thought he smelled something that would mean something quite different for him. He could be wrong, but then he picked up the scent again as the wind shifted. This time it was stronger. He ran down the street saying aloud to himself, "No! No! This is not happening!"

He reached the corner and stood directly into the oncoming westerly wind and sniffed the air. There was no mistaking the distant smell. He was certain. Far to the west, a Black Dragon's corpse was being burned. He now understood the fate of Belazare. He knew immediately that this could only be the work of the Gold Dragons. No one but the Gold Dragons possessed the knowledge to taunt him in such a matter.

Enraged, he stepped out into the street and up to a car stopped for the traffic light in front of him. He forcibly put his fist through the window, shattering it, and grabbed the female driver by the collar of her coat. He opened the driver's door and tossed her onto the sidewalk. He got into the car and sped away, heading back toward the factory complex while cursing the Gold Dragons in an ancient tongue known only to the Black Dragons.

When he arrived back at the complex he was met by Kadar, who was also just returning. Kadar had also smelled the burning body of Belazare and was seething as he approached I'Lagore.

I'Lagore immediately sensed Kadar's overwhelming anger and said, "I expect you to remain in control. There will be time for you to unleash your anger and make the Gold Dragons pay dearly for what they have done."

Kadar's lips quickly formed a sinister smile as he stood contemplating I'Lagore's response.

I'Lagore entered the building and sprinted up the stairs to the second floor; a celebration had been started by the dragons who had returned before him. Enraged, he stormed into the room picking up objects and throwing them with superhuman strength across the room as his loud voice deepened, "You dare to rejoice? You think this is all good? Do you realize what has happened, you stupid, stupid fools?"

He grabbed Drakas by the collar and pulled him over to the window on the west side of the building. He opened the window and forced Drakas' head out of the window, demanding, "Tell me what you smell!"

Drakas smelled the air, his face turned dark, and, outraged, he cried out, "They will pay for what they have done to Belazare!"

I'Lagore turned to the other dragons in disgust. "As you waste your time celebrating, our enemy is murdering us off one by one!"

CHAPTER XXXII

As the sun descended below the horizon bringing darkness to the evening skies of Paris, the Black Dragons departed from the rooftop of their compound and flew west toward Le Conquet. Within thirty miles of Le Conquet, Kadar and Drakas broke away from the other nine dragons and flew north and then west toward Saint Renan and Rodin's chateau. Drakas and Kadar landed downwind on the eastern lawn of the chateau, careful that their scents not be picked up by any dragons inside the chateau.

Inside the chateau, Janos was heading up to Malcolm's room with a dinner tray. Malcolm was still recovering under the watchful eye of Long Ji. Milos had just returned to the kitchen with Chevalier after a brief walk in the garden as one of the two chefs had prepared a bowl of food for the dog. As Janos carried the tray down the main hall toward the great staircase there was a heavy rapping on the front door. He carefully set the tray down and went to the door. As he looked through the glass door, he seemed perplexed, as there was no one there.

As Milos tried to enter the back door of the kitchen with Chevalier, the dog stopped as his keen sense of smell detected something in the air that bothered him. Milos, unaware as to the meaning of the dog's strange behavior, pulled gently on the leash to coax the dog into the chateau. Chevalier started to growl and then bark wildly as he pulled on the leash with all his strength. Trying to restrain him, Milos pulled Chevalier into the chateau and put the end of leash around the back-door handle. The dog continued to bark and whine, warning them of the impending danger.

Long Ji was upstairs sitting on the floor of Malcolm's room meditating by the fire when he, in a single move, instinctively leapt to his feet. He awoke Malcolm and as Malcolm became conscious he said sternly, "Get up now and hide yourself!"

Back in the main hall, Janos opened the door to investigate and was immediately blasted with a flume of red fire from Drakas. The energy from the blast sent Janos and several pieces of furniture burning and flying across the hall. His body was engulfed by flames and landed near the middle of the hall and withered slightly as the intensity of the burning fire extinguished his life.

Drakas boldly walked into the main hall taking in the opulent surroundings before looking down at Janos' burning body. Extremely proud of his first kill of the night, he called out loudly, mocking anyone who might be in earshot, "Trick or treat!" Milos came running from the kitchen below into the hall to investigate the strange commotion. Drakas smiled broadly at the site of Milos as he was pleased to see another helpless human and eagerly approached his next victim. Looking at the twin brother, he cocked his head slightly to one side as he pointed at him and asked, "Didn't I just kill you?"

Milos looked down to realize the burning fire in front of him was his brother. Instantly overcome with grief, he fell to his hands and knees in front of the body as he watched in shock as his brother burned. Behind him the two chefs emerged from the doorway from the kitchen stairs into the hall. Stunned by what they saw, they paused long enough to give Drakas the opportunity to blow a red fireball that easily engulfed both men before they had the opportunity to retreat.

Long Ji appeared at the railing on the second floor and briefly observed Drakas before jumping over the railing and landing squarely on the hall floor behind him. Through scent and sound, Drakas quickly determined there was a dragon behind him. As he turned to face the dragon, Long Ji blew a blue fireball that Drakas barely deflected from his body by shielding himself with his wing. The presence of a White Dragon took Drakas by surprise. While Drakas had never seen a White Dragon before, he was aware of their legendary speed and lethal strength. Facing a White Dragon alone was not something he was prepared for. Drakas panicked in the moment and he took off running down the hall in the opposite direction. With no place to go, he crashed through a set of French doors and flew as fast as he could into the night sky. Long Ji pursued him, seeking to eliminate any danger to Malcolm.

In the kitchen below, Chevalier managed to rip the door handle off the door that was restraining his leash and freed himself. He charged up the stairs, jumped over the burning bodies of the chefs that blocked the doorway, and ran down the hall, jumping through the opening where the French doors once stood, following after Long Ji.

Meanwhile, as Drakas was entering the front door, Kadar flew around the castle several times focusing in on Malcolm's room which seemed to be the only room on the second floor that appeared occupied. He dove down from above at full speed and, counting on the element of surprise, he smashed through the window and completed a controlled roll across the rug, landing on his feet. He stopped for a moment to stretch his neck as he smelled the warm air of the room. He easily picked up Malcolm's scent and knew he was still present and hiding somewhere in the room. He began to walk around the room, nonchalantly picking up items and examining them as he called out, "Little piggy, little piggy, come out, come out, wherever you are!"

Malcolm was behind the closed door of the armoire. The door on the antique piece of furniture was slightly warped, so he had a partial view of Kadar as he walked about the room.

Kadar was enjoying the game and moved about slowly, relishing each second of the suspense and fear he could feel growing in his victim. He picked up the book Malcolm had been reading earlier, held it to his nose, and inhaled deeply appreciating the scent as a fine connoisseur of human flesh would. He called out to Malcolm, "Yes indeed, you are a fine little piggy and I am a very bad wolf." Getting no response, Kadar continued with a slight tone of frustration, "Little piggy, come out, come out . . . I won't hurt you." He returned the book to the table and said with a big smile, "I am only going to kill you."

Kadar could hear Malcolm breathing and stopped and turned to face the armoire. He could see one of Malcolm's eyes looking out from the partial opening. Their eyes locked.

"Little piggy . . . I can see you now. Why don't you come out so I can see if you are as beautiful as you smell?"

Kadar walked across the room to the armoire and opened the door to fully reveal Malcolm squatting behind the door. He looked down at Malcolm and offered his hand to him, "Little piggy, look at how beautiful you are."

Terrified and shaking, Malcolm was unable to move. Tears filled his eyes as his death now appeared certain. Kadar coaxed him kindly, "Come on, little piggy, come out and play with the big bad wolf. Come on, you can do it."

Malcolm took Kadar's hand as he was gently pulled from the armoire.

"There now," Kadar said in a comforting tone. He reached for the bottom of Malcolm's T-shirt and pulled it over Malcolm's head and handed it back to him. "Here, wipe your eyes now. It won't hurt for very long."

Malcolm did as he was told and wiped his eyes with his T-shirt.

Kadar examined Malcolm's eyes. "You have such pretty eyes for a human."

Kadar sat down in the chair next to the fire and studied Malcolm as he stood there trembling. Suddenly he ordered, "Take off your clothes! All of them!"

Hoping Long Ji would return in time to save him, Malcolm moved very slowly, trying to buy as much time as he could. He removed his shoes, socks, pants, and then briefs. He stood before Kadar who ordered him, "Get down on your knees."

Malcolm hesitated.

"Don't make me hurt you any more than I have to," Kadar told him.

He got down on his hands and knees in front of Kadar.

"You're a very well trained little piggy. Now crawl over here to me."

Malcolm slowly crawled over next to Kadar's feet.

Kadar reached down and gently put his hand under Malcolm's chin, lifting it upward so he could look him in the eyes. Kadar smiled politely as he brushed Malcolm's hair away from his eyes with his free hand as he said, "You really have such pretty eyes. I think I am going to make you mine. You know how I am going to do that little piggy?"

Malcolm looked at him and gently shook his head "no," his chin still being held up by Kadar.

Kadar's face turned very dark as he tightened his grip on Malcolm's chin until Malcolm was obviously in extreme discomfort. A tone of self-assured cruelty grew in his voice as he said, "I am going to burn my name on your chest, arms, legs, and face. This way, when they do find your body scattered about the room in pieces, they will know that they all belong to me." Malcolm attempted to pull away. Kadar released his grip and allowed him to. Kadar stood up and took a step forward, grabbing Malcolm by the hair and yanking him mercilessly across the floor toward the bed. Then he easily picked Malcolm up and threw him on top of the bed.

Kadar walked toward the bed as Malcolm attempted to scramble away. He grabbled Malcolm's leg and easily pulled him across the bed where he was able to grab and hold him by the throat. As Malcolm lay there helpless, Kadar stood over him generating a pencil thin blood red flame from his lips. Malcolm could feel the intense heat of the flame as it came down on his chest and he cried out in agony as the tip of the flame seared the skin of his chest.

"I have something for you!" Long Ji's stern voice called out as entered the room through the door behind Kadar.

Kadar spun around to see Long Ji standing in the doorway holding a single black dragon wing, bloodied with green blood. Malcolm quickly rolled across to the other side of the bed and fell uncontrollably to the floor below.

Long Ji held up the wing for Kadar to see as he said proudly, "I was only able to pull one off his body before he died. As I desire a pair, I will be taking the second one from your body."

Kadar's face grew red with rage. "Why have you dared to kill one of our own?"

"One life for one life," Long Ji assured him.

"You murderous traitor!" Kadar stepped toward Long Ji, spewing a flume of red fire at him.

Long Ji threw back a larger blue flume that engulfed most of the red flume and forced Kadar back.

Kadar turned and ran as the blue flame was about to engulf him, escaping out the broken window and flying off into the night sky.

Long Ji helped Malcolm up off the floor asking, "Are you hurt badly?"

"I'm OK, but this burn really fucking hurts."

"Collect your things. We are to leave now. This place is no longer safe for any of us."

Malcolm quickly put his pants on as Long Ji grabbed a small wooden box from his belongings. He opened the box and dipped two fingers into the greasy contents, removing a large glob that he proceeded to apply to Malcolm's chest wound. Immediately relieved from the pain, Malcolm put his T-shirt on.

They took their bags from the room and ran out into the hall and down the main stairs to the hall below. Jean-Yves was in the hall below covering the charred and smoking remains of Janos with a tablecloth. Milos sat nearby in a chair with his face buried in his hands as he wept uncontrollably.

"We all must leave now," Long Ji yelled down the hall.

"Yes, we will be leaving momentarily. I have an envelope for you, monsieur," Jean-Yves informed him as he quickly walked towards Long Ji reaching into his breast pocket and handing him a sealed envelope. "The envelope contains the location of a secure place where you can take Malcolm. He will be safe there until we can collect him. Do you need a vehicle?"

Long Ji opened the envelope and studied the map for a moment. Looking back at Jean-Yves for a moment he said, "No. Not for this location. I do need a large tarp, a sheet of plastic, and warmer coat for Malcolm."

"Right away," Jean-Yves said as he disappeared.

"What about Chevalier?" Malcolm asked Long Ji.

"Where is he?" Long Ji asked.

"I don't know," Malcolm replied.

Jean-Yves returned with a painting tarp, some plastic sheeting, and Rodin's large overcoat and handed them to Long Ji.

"Jean-Yves, do you know where Chevalier is?" Malcolm asked.

"No, I am sorry I don't. If we are able to locate him before we leave, I promise we will take him with us."

"I can't leave him behind," Malcolm replied.

"There is real danger here. We must leave now," Long Ji insisted.

"Please, give me just a few minutes to look for him," Malcolm pleaded.

Long Ji disregarded the request and said, as he handed Malcolm the large coat, "There is no time. Put the coat on."

Long Ji pulled Malcolm outside to the front of the chateau as he struggled to put on the coat.

Malcolm began calling out, "Chevalier! Chevalier! Chevalier!"

Long Ji spread out the tarp, lined it with the plastic sheeting, and ordered Malcolm, "Sit in the middle."

"What are you doing?" Malcolm asked, still frantically looking around the front of the chateau for his dog.

"Sit in the middle, now!" Long Ji grabbed Malcolm by his arm to stop him from moving about.

The seriousness of his tone persuaded Malcolm to do as he was told. Long Ji pulled the ends of the tarp up over Malcolm's head and tied the ends of the tarp into a knot. Long Ji walked across the lawn until there was more than a hundred feet that separated him from Malcolm. He bowed his head and stood for a moment clutching his hands together and pointing them downward. His magnificent white wings sprung from his back as he shifted. He ran toward Malcolm as his wings lifted him into the air. He grabbed the top of the tarp and he pulled Malcolm up with him into the air. They flew off into the night as the makeshift tarp cocoon swung wildly back and forth before it steadied itself into a gentle swinging motion as Long Ji flew.

CHAPTER XXXIII

As Drakas and Kadar began their siege of the chateau, the four Gold Dragons waited in the fields in Le Conquet beyond the Kermorvan Lighthouse. The funeral pyre had become reduced to a pile of smoldering ash. Valerian built a fire next to the tent to provide a proper beacon so the enemy would have no problem locating him. The only other light in the field came from the near-full moon overhead and the distant light from the lighthouse.

Valerian turned his head to the sky as he heard the almost silent swish of I'Lagore's wings slicing through the air above as he glided toward the field. He calmly warned the other dragons, "Prepare yourself, a black bitch approaches."

I'Lagore landed alone thirty feet away in full view of the waiting dragons. He ignored the presence of the Gold Dragons and approached the smoldering pyre and knelt down on one knee as he paid his respects to his fallen comrade. Standing up, he turned to face Rodin, who had started to approach him from behind. I'Lagore's voice reverberated as his rage overtook him. "Which one of you is the murderous traitor? Who among you dared to take the life of another dragon?"

Rodin stepped forward. "I am responsible for bringing justice to this criminal," he fired back with equal intensity.

"Which life among your kind did he take?" I'Lagore demanded.

"He attempted to take the life of a friend."

"Friend? Friend??" I'Lagore stammered in anger. "Who is this friend?"

"He is a human," Rodin confirmed.

There was a blast of steam from I'Lagore's nostrils as the word "human" enraged him further. "You mean to tell me Belazare was slaughtered because of a common piece of meat?"

Rodin retorted, "Do not pretend your murderous actions are noble."

I'Lagore took a step closer to look Rodin squarely in the eye. "Your rotting brain has left you sick and misguided. You will give me the lives of the human and the dragon responsible for this murder."

Rodin's voiced lowered as he assured I'Lagore, "This is my land. You will not enter it and attempt to impose your will and destruction."

In disgust, I'Lagore replied, "I piss on your antiquated ways. The world belongs to those who take it. Today, we have proven that we are the superior race capable of mastering all."

"Inflicting mass genocide does not make you a superior race."

"Did you know we have been watching you for more than a hundred years now? Living out your life in that grand chateau as the world around you closed in, trapping you within your own walls. Humans have reduced your existence to nothing more than house arrest."

"In my land I take responsibility for the well being of all creatures."

"What are humans?" I'Lagore asked Rodin. "As long as humans have governments and possess weapons of destructive force they are a threat to all of us. Take those things away and they are nothing, nothing more than a food source. One magnificent dragon is worth more than a million humans, and yet you so easily slaughter one of your own kind."

Rodin struggled to restrain himself as he replied, "Do not attempt to elevate yourself by claiming you're our kind. You have violated our lands, killed our people and disregarded the order in our world. There is a penalty for that."

"What have humans done for the mighty Gold Dragons? They force you to live a life in hiding, fearful that one day you will be discovered. Are you free to fly the skies at will? Are you free to hunt? Are you free to live in the open? You have subjugated yourself and become the willing prisoners of a junior race of pitiful, disgusting animals. Animals who are destroying the world for all creatures."

"We coexist with the humans on terms that we set."

"Your words and beliefs are ludicrous. You protect a toxin that continues to poison your world, our world—where is the great wisdom in that?"

Rodin fired back, "You are driven solely by your instinct to slaughter and destroy. If the world was left to you it would be nothing more than Black Dragons feeding off a heap of rot!"

"I would gladly hand you over to the humans. How long before you would end up dissected into many parts floating in jars of chemicals in a military lab."

"You seek to deny the part of you that is human, but you will never escape it," Rodin replied.

"If I could cut it out and cast it away, it would be gone from me. It is the part of me that makes me weak. We no longer breed with humans, our blood line has grown polluted. We have returned to the ancient ways to flush out the poison that is destroying us."

"As long as I am alive, you will not have France."

"France? In less than a week there will be no Europe, only chaos as the masses of people start killing each other for food. The veil of human civility is so easily removed and discarded. No governments, just beautiful anarchy and humans behaving like the animals they are. Trust and compassion among humans is so easily morphed into fear and hatred. Brother killing brother for survival. This is the race you believe to be so noble. In the end, they will be nothing more than a pack of wild dogs."

"You know you are wrong," Rodin assured I'Lagore.

I'Lagore began walking toward Valerian, Trechus, and Leonardo who stood twenty paces away. "Your leader even lacks the ability to be a convincing liar, so tell me, which one of you killed Belazare?"

From behind I'Lagore, Rodin reiterated, "I told you, I killed him."

I'Lagore turned back to look at Rodin as he said coldly, "You lack the talent. Let your dragons speak for themselves, or do you control their free will as well?" He turned back to face the three Gold Dragons. "Is that it? Are you so collared and leashed to your master that you have no voices of your own?"

The three Gold Dragons remained silent.

I'Lagore eyed the three dragons with suspicion and focused in on Leonardo who stood holding his arrow ready in his lowered bow. He approached Leonardo and looked into his eyes as he said, "It is clear you're the killer. It is in your eyes. Tell me how wonderful it was for you to kill. How long has it been since you were allowed the glory of murder, or does your mighty leader have you wasting your life away arranging flowers in pots? Well, speak!!! Has your master removed your tongues as well?"

Leonardo remained silent.

"Puppets, you're all nothing more than his puppets," I'Lagore said. "Unlike your pathetic leader, I take no pleasure in killing dragons."

Rodin retorted, "I do not relish killing dragons, but if you force my hand I will strike you down with all my might. You're no match for me."

"You underestimate me!" I'Lagore turned to Rodin and blasted him with a plume of red fire.

Rodin instantly blasted him back with a larger plume of purple fire. The purple plume consumed the red plume.

I'Lagore eased his tone as he said to Rodin, "You possess such strength and beauty but so easily waste it away for nothing. You disappoint me. I have heard tales of the great warrior, Rodin, but as it turns out the legend of the Rodin appears to be nothing more than a myth."

"Must I destroy you to demonstrate my strength?" Rodin demanded.

"Destroy me?" I'Lagore laughed. "You're the ones who have been destroyed. As you stand here, your little chateau is being destroyed, and I assure you by now every living thing in it lies dead on the floor."

Trechus could no longer hold back his temper and he shot back, "You do not speak the truth!"

I'Lagore looked at Trechus and smiled as he said, "So you can speak after all."

Valerian quietly warned, "Trechus, silence yourself. He only seeks to provoke you."

I'Lagore approached Leonardo again and looked him in the eye. "All you have been thinking about since I landed in this field is how you would kill me. This master of yours wants me to believe otherwise, but you're a killer. You want nothing more than to slaughter and destroy me."

"I do not deny it," Leonardo said, breaking his silence.

"Then we should have war. One epic battle here and now to determine which race of dragons will inherit the earth." I'Lagore turned and began walking across the field away from the group.

"How many are there?" Rodin asked Valerian as he looked upward toward the night sky.

"I count eight about 10,000 feet above us just to the east," Valerian confirmed.

"Nine against four," Rodin concluded. "Are you concerned?"

"Me, no," Valerian replied. " 'Killer' over here is going to take five out on his own with that bow of his. Sadly, it won't leave much work for the rest of us."

"Trechus," Rodin said. "You're the one I am worried about."

"Don't be. If something happened at the chateau, Malcolm is alive. Long Ji would have seen to it. My head is clear."

"I'm ready," Valerian confirmed. He called over to I'Lagore, who now stood at the opposite end of the field. " I don't mean to rush you, but we have a reservation for dinner at nine o'clock and they only hold the table for fifteen minutes."

I'Lagore shot a fireball high into the sky.

"I guess that means go," Valerian confirmed.

"Watch the sky," Rodin warned, looking up.

Leonardo lifted his bow and pulled back the arrow and released. From across the field I'Lagore watched as the arrow traveled directly toward his head. Just before hitting him in the eye he snatched the arrow out of midair with his hand. He held the arrow up in victory, but Leonardo had already launched a second arrow, planning the first as a diversion. I'Lagore caught sight of the second arrow, but only in time to slightly turn his head. The tip of the arrow missed the eye socket, but the arrow shattered and the tail of the arrow did manage to hit I'Lagore squarely in the eye. I'Lagore cried out as he pulled the end of the arrow out of his eye socket as blood streamed down his cheek.

"I guess I can't make fun of you anymore for shooting arrows into your collection of oversized stuffed animals," Valerian admitted to Leonardo.

"I would say you just lost that right," Leonardo confirmed.

"Congratulations," Valerian said to Leonardo. "You just started a war."

Rodin warned, "They are dropping down on us."

"Are we ready to fly the not so friendly skies?" Leonardo asked.

"After you," Valerian gestured with his hand.

Leonardo made a running start and took off from the ground. Valerian and Trechus followed him as Rodin headed across the field toward I'Lagore, determined to finish him off before joining the others in the air.

The Black Dragons dropped from the sky in pairs. The first pair shot past Valerian but did not attack him, despite shooting a fireball at them. Valerian immediately sensed there was an orchestrated plan of attack that none of the Gold Dragons were counting on. He gave chase to the pair who opened their wings as they neared the ground below him. As they began to separate from each other they stretched a net between them and flew toward Rodin. As they reached Rodin from behind the dragons released the net. It contained a type of spring-loaded mechanism that contracted the net as it hit Rodin, causing him to roll violently across the field ensnared in the netting. He attempted to burn himself free but the netting was constructed of some type of metal and proved to have a high resistance to heat.

As Valerian turned to look for Trechus, he saw Leonardo ensnared in a net as he fell from the sky and hit the ground. With only seconds to spare, Valerian made the difficult decision to retreat. He knew that if he flew hard and never looked back, he could outfly his attackers. He deeply regretted not returning to the field and, had it been his choice, he would rather return to take a stand even if it might be his last. The decision he followed was the one he knew Rodin would want him to make. He flew away, his heart feeling like a hundred-pound stone in his chest as he thought about the friends he had to leave behind.

CHAPTER XXXIV

Malcolm was flown by Long Ji for five hours across France in the makeshift canvas cocoon. Malcolm continued to shift his body as he struggled to keep from freezing or suffocating in the plastic. Without the plastic lining which blocked most of the wind, he would certainly have been killed by the wind chill factor, which was well below zero. Even though he was starving, his mind was running wildly between thoughts of fear, the loss of Chevalier, and possibly Trechus. Anxiety set in as he thought about where he was going and what was waiting for him next. Too much had happened in the last five days, and now he was having a hard time processing it all. He began to long for his old life on the streets of Paris when it all seemed simple and under his control.

He felt the flight pattern change as Long Ji began to circle and descend. The circling continued for a period until he felt the bag go into free-fall for a couple seconds before landing hard on something soft. Malcolm was stiff from the long journey, but still managed to move and get the top of the canvas tarp untied and open. As he struggled to stand, he realized that he had been dropped in deep snow and the sack had sunk into the snow during impact. As he looked around in the darkness, he could barely make anything out in the moonlight except the snow that surrounded him.

Long Ji was about six yards away and called out to Malcolm, "Make your way to me."

Malcolm started to struggle through the deep powdery snow, half crawling and half swimming, until he made it to where he thought he had heard Long Ji's voice coming from. Long Ji pulled him by his right arm out of the snow and across the threshold of a door onto a wooden floor. Malcolm lay there exhausted and out of breath. Covered in snow, he began to shiver as the sweat he had generated from his crawling started to freeze against his body.

Long Ji lit a couple of old German oil lanterns by igniting their wicks with a blue flame from his lips. The lanterns easily illuminated the small one room cabin. He walked over and pulled Malcolm up from the floor and helped him over to a bed in the corner of the room. He pulled back the old quilt on the bed and helped Malcolm get under the covers.

Malcolm was starting to lose consciousness as his body shivered and his breathing became shallow. Long Ji quickly shed his own clothes and got under the covers with Malcolm. He pulled Malcolm close to him. Long Ji began to pull Malcolm out of his clothes, and when his warm hands finally touched Malcolm's freezing skin, it was as if hundreds of pins were piercing Malcolm's flesh all at once. Long Ji continued to pull off Malcolm's clothes under the covers until Malcolm wore only his socks. As Long Ji lay on top of Malcolm, the heat of his body began to warm him.

Long Ji rolled Malcolm over and lay on top of the cold skin of Malcolm's back; he wrapped his warm arms around his chest. Malcolm was warming up and gaining more consciousness. Long Ji rolled him back onto his back and again lay on top of him, skin to skin. Malcolm wrapped his arms around Long Ji and pulled him as close to him as possible to extract all the heat that he could into his own body. Malcolm pushed his cold face into the warmth of Long Ji's shoulder.

"Are you getting warm?" Long Ji asked.

"Yes," Malcolm whispered. "I am feeling better."

"Keep yourself warm, I am going to start a fire," Long Ji said as he left the bed. He placed a couple of logs in the small cast iron stove in the corner and blew a stream of blue fire that was so hot that the logs burst into flames, and he closed the door of the stove.

He crawled back into bed with Malcolm who eagerly clung to him for the warmth of his body. Like Trechus and Rodin, there was something about Long Ji's body scent that was intoxicating—but Long Ji's scent was different. It was less like musk and more like the smell of small wild flowers. Long Ji's skin was also unlike anything he had ever felt. It was like warm silk.

Malcolm began to think about Trechus and wonder if he was even still alive. "Do you think the others are all right?" he asked.

"I cannot say. We must wait for the outcome of this night to reveal itself."

Malcolm rolled away from Long Ji. Long Ji put his arm around Malcolm and gently pulled him back towards him as he said, "You are not alone."

Malcolm's mind remained focused on Trechus and Chevalier, but he was comforted by Long Ji who held him tight and continued to warm him. Exhaustion quickly overtook him and he was soon asleep.

CHAPTER XXXV

The next morning Malcolm awoke to bright sunlight streaming into the tiny cabin through the two small windows that flanked the crude wooden door. Long Ji was not there, but he had left a fire burning in the wood stove that provided ample heat for the small cabin. Malcolm's clothes from the night before had been hung to dry in front of the small stove. Malcolm got out of bed wearing only his socks and went over and opened the door, trying to determine where he was. As he looked over the landscape, the only thing he could determine was that he was high up on a mountainside well above the tree line. Was he somewhere in the Alps? France? Switzerland? Italy? He had no way of knowing.

He closed the door and noticed Long Ji's bag in the corner next to his backpack. He remembered that he had left the bags outside last night in the tarp. Long Ji must have gone and gotten them this morning. At least with Long Ji's bag still there, Malcolm could be certain that he had not gone off and left him.

His stomach growled loudly, reminding him that he had not eaten in a day, so he began to look around the room for some food. It was sparsely furnished with a bed, a table, two benches, a wood stove, and a small hutch. He searched the buffet but there was only a small collection of dishes, bowls and utensils. There was no food. He decided to dress and try to see if there was a road nearby, or at least some form of civilization.

He went outside but quickly realized that the cabin was built into the side of a remote section of a steep mountain. At this altitude there were only rocky cliffs and snow. Damn the dragons for being so safe with their houses, he thought. Long Ji better come back or someone better come; if not, he could die alone from starvation. He returned inside the cabin and noticed that there was barely any firewood.

He sat on the bench and began to realize that this was not going to work for him. Hearing a noise outside, he jumped up to open the door. Long Ji stood there undoing the knots on the top of the canvas tarp and opened the extremely large bundle that contained a pile of firewood.

"This wood will keep you warm," Long Ji told him. "This should last until someone returns for you."

"Where are you going?" Malcolm asked.

"I must return to my home."

Malcolm looked at him in disbelief. "You can't leave me up here. You can take me down to the nearest town and I can take a train back to Paris."

"The town is closed. The trains are not running. Everything is shut down."

"What are you saying?"

"There are many problems down there. You will be safe here."

"I want to go back. I can't stay here."

"You must remain here."

Malcolm sat down in frustration and disbelief as tears came to his eyes and he began to think about being left alone. He asked, "When are you leaving?"

"I will leave just after dark," Long Ji confirmed.

"I'm scared," Malcolm admitted.

"Luck has decided to keep you alive."

"You have kept me alive," Malcolm corrected him.

"Then luck has delivered me to you. Luck will always be with you."

"Will my luck bring me some food?"

"You're lucky, Gold Dragons live well. There is plenty of food here."

Malcolm was confused as he looked around at the meager surroundings.

Long Ji removed the envelope from his pocket that Jean-Yves had given him the night before. He opened it and read further down the page. He folded it up and put it back into his pocket. He went over to the left corner of the room and counted out nine wooden floor tiles from the wall and six into the room. He got a butter knife from the drawer of the hutch. He began to work the blade of the knife into the edge of the square wood end-cut cedar tiles that made up the cabin's floor. He removed the tile and below it was a large iron handle. He pulled hard on the handle and a well concealed trap door opened upward. Standing up and looking down into the dark hole, Long Ji said, "Below us you should find everything you need to keep you comfortable."

Long Ji blew a stream of blue flame from his lips lighting the oil lantern. He handed it to Malcolm. Malcolm carefully held onto the lantern with one hand as climbed down the steep wooden ladder to the room below.

As he reached the bottom of the ladder and held up the light, he saw that the room was packed with objects that he would best describe as more suitable for Gold Dragons. There were books, cured meats, cigars, furs, blankets, candles, crystal glasses, a selection of silver serving pieces, two large leather sacks of gold coins, and then another door. He opened the door and discovered a well stocked wine cellar with what appeared to be more than 1000 bottles of vintage wine, cognac, and armagnac.

"Now," he said aloud, taking in the splendor of the storeroom. "Now I can believe that a Gold Dragon could endure spending a night in this place."

He went about collecting a bottle of wine, wine glasses, silver utensils, and a collection of cured meats that hung from hooks on the ceiling and headed back up the ladder.

When he reached the top he smiled at Long Ji as he pulled the treasures he found below up and stacked them on the floor around the opening. "You won't believe what's down there!"

"The dragons will take care of you," Long Ji assured him. "I must rest now. It will take all my strength to return home tonight."

Long Ji went to the bed and slept while Malcolm sat and ate. He stuffed himself not just because he was starving, but because the meat and wine tasted so incredibly good. He pulled the chair closer to the window and spent the afternoon with a book he had found below, finishing the bottle of wine as he read. As the sun started to go down, Malcolm returned to the cellar and collected provisions for a large meal for Long Ji. He quietly laid out the meat and wine on the table careful not to disturb Long Ji.

As the sun set, he sat watching Long Ji as the final rays of light illuminated the sleeping dragon's face. He could see how Trechus could see beauty in a sleeping man. Long Ji had a beautiful face but it was the sense of peace that struck Malcolm as profound. Just as the final ray of light disappeared behind the mountain top, Long Ji awoke.

"Thank you for watching over me while I slept," Long Ji said.

"I am not sure you need me to watch out for you."

"Even the mightiest of creatures need to feel they are cared for."

Malcolm smiled at his wisdom. "I know you have a long way to travel so I have put out some food for you before you go."

"It is kind of you to take care of me," Long Ji said as he got out of bed and walked over to the table and sat down.

"It seems small after all you have done for me," Malcolm said as he sat down across the table and poured some wine into Long Ji's glass.

"The size of the deed is not as important as where the deed comes from. Your deeds originate in a pure heart. That is what makes your deeds significant."

Long Ji pulled out a pair of chop sticks from his pocket and started to eat heartily. All Malcolm could do was watch as he was still quite full from eating earlier.

"Will you help the Gold Dragons?" Malcolm asked.

"It is not for me to say. The decision of war requires deep reflection and thought by my kind."

"I doubt Rodin would retreat or surrender."

"I believe you are right. They have found themselves on an unfortunate path that has led them to war with their enemies."

"Can they win?"

"A war is not about winning. It is only about losing less than one's enemy. He who suffers the least amount of devastation is the winner. Or it is the side who is capable of enduring the most amount of pain who is often the victor."

"I guess I am lucky to be far from any danger."

"Luck does follow you like an obedient servant."

"I only fear I will be left here alone. That Trechus will forget about me."

"May I ask you if Trechus ever gave you a gift?" Long Ji inquired.

"He gave me so much," Malcolm replied.

"Yes, but did he ever give you an object that was his? A precious object that was personal to him."

"He gave me a framed picture. He also gave me this," Malcolm reached into his front pocket and produced the piece of gold Trechus had given to him.

Long Ji took the coin and studied it. "In ancient times, the Gold Dragons were named this because they were known hoarders of gold. They were so obsessive that they could never even part with a single gold piece. If you believe this legend, then you had to be someone of extreme value to Trechus for him to make such a gift to you."

"Do you believe this to be true?" Malcolm asked

"I know it to be true," Long Ji said as he handed the gold piece back to Malcolm. "When you were unconscious after the fall in Paris, Trechus came to see you with Rodin. I threatened Trechus with death if he entered the room. It was my way of testing him. It caused him great pain not to be close to you and he did potentially risk his life in making an attempt to enter the room."

"I'm glad you shared that with me."

"I must go now. Thank you for the food." Long Ji replied as he got up and went over and picked up his bag.

"Will I ever see you again?" Malcolm asked.

"I will return in two weeks. Perhaps the Gold Dragons will come for you sooner."

"You're kind to make sure I am not left here."

"It is the kindness that you have earned."

Malcolm and Long Ji hugged each other and Long Ji went out the door. Malcolm watched as he shifted into his dragon form. He took to the air and blew a brilliant stream of blue fire across the night sky as Malcolm watched him fly away. Malcolm hoped in his heart that he would see Long Ji again.

CHAPTER XXXVI

Malcolm returned inside to begin an undetermined period of waiting alone in the cabin. He had not been alone since the night he had met Chevalier on the streets of Montmartre. He resisted thinking about anything that had happened before he had arrived in France and met Chevalier, as he did not want to consider the prospect that he would not be reunited with his friends. Of course, it was most frightening to consider that no one would return for him at all; he had no idea if he could even get down off the mountain alone.

He went to his bag and pulled out the picture of Chevalier that Trechus had given him the second day they had met. He felt guilty not knowing where Chevalier was or even if he was still alive. Trechus could be dead. Any one of the dragons or all of the Gold Dragons could be dead.

He went outside to get some air. A storm was rolling in across the sky. He watched as the dark gray snow clouds came across the horizon and the snow began to fall. How wonderful it would be to see a purple flame shoot across the sky right now, he thought. He returned inside and put another log into the wood stove before lying down on the bed. The bedding carried the strong intoxicating scent of Long Ji. Malcolm buried his face in the pillow to take it all in. He began to think back to the previous night that Long Ji had warmed him with his body and how Malcolm had pulled so hard against Long Ji's limbs to gain any bit of warmth. He had been so cold and Long Ji's body had been all that he desired.

The wood stove gave off plenty of heat for such a small space so the cabin had been quite warm all day. Malcolm pulled off his shirt. His skin was healing from Rodin's flogging, but he could still trace the faint outlines of the welts with his fingers. His body was still sore in spots, but at least he could feel his body, and for the first time his body was wanting. Wanting more than it was given. He rolled over and again took a deep breath of Long Ji's scent from the pillow. The aroma sent his mind soaring and his body tingled as his cock became rock hard. He breathed in again and this time the tingling was more intense and he got even harder. He began to grind the front of his body against the sheets and the mattress as he continued to stimulate himself with Long Ji's scent until after the tenth time he inhaled, his back arched as he exploded in an orgasm that lasted nearly thirty seconds. His mind spun wildly as he collapsed exhausted on the bed, his body still twitching.

"God, I love dragons!" he whispered in a total state of euphoric bliss as he fell off to sleep.

During the night, a blizzard rolled in as the snow fell heavily, and the wind tore violently against the face of the mountainside causing the small windows of the cabin to rattle in their frames. Malcolm slept soundly through the night and awoke in the morning to a full-blown blizzard. Nearly three feet of snow had fallen overnight, and now he became concerned that if this continued it would not be long before the snow buried the door and the two windows.

For the rest of the morning he tried to lose himself in books, but he found himself becoming overwhelmed by his own anxieties as he started to panic. He would open the door every hour to witness the snowfall increase by another six inches. He began digging out the snow from the doorway with his hands to at least allow for a continued flow of oxygen into the cabin. Each time he would call out Trechus' name several times at the top of his lungs wishing and hoping for a miraculous reply.

Returning inside, he pulled a bottle of cognac from the cellar, which he drank a little at a time to help calm his anxieties. He seriously began to ponder what would become of him if no one returned for him. He believed he had enough food and wine to make it through to spring, but he would certainly run out of firewood. He could begin to burn the wooden floor tiles, but that would still not take him to spring.

By late afternoon, the snow depth was increasing to a height whereby the view through the windows was in danger of disappearing. Malcolm searched below for a shovel but the best he could come up with was a silver champagne bucket. He began digging the snow from the doorway again and tried to clear some of the snow in the area of the windows. He could not venture out far enough to get on the roof, but he hoped that the heat from the stove's pipe would at least melt the snow around it keeping it clear.

As he dug in the snow with the bucket, out of the blue he heard his mother call his name. The voice was as clear as if she were standing behind him. He spun around, fully expecting to see her standing there. He had only imagined it. There was no one there. He dropped the bucket and went into the cabin. What he would give to talk to a person, to any person. He lay on the bed and started to cry, consumed by his fears of being abandoned and his own loneliness.

Evening came and he did not feel like eating, but continued to drink cognac. He fell asleep early fully expecting to wake up with the blizzard still raging. When morning came he was thrilled to see the snow had stopped and that there was a small amount of sunshine coming in through the very tops of the snow covered windows.

He was reminded of Long Ji telling him that he was lucky. Maybe there was such a thing as being blessed by luck. He ate a hearty breakfast but was beginning to tire of meat at every meal. An apple, an orange, or even another birthday cake would have made his day.

He spent the morning digging out around the door and the windows. It was especially hard work without a shovel, but he was able to do a decent job. He was proud of himself. He had made it through another day. All he needed to do was take it day by day. Trechus would come, now he was sure of it. His luck was changing.

In the late afternoon he sat on the bed reading, when he heard a faint but growing roar. The sound was getting progressively louder and he got to his feet as the cabin began to shake. As he looked out the windows in the late afternoon sun, he saw that an avalanche of snow had started on the next ridge above the cabin and a flood of snow and ice was crashing down the mountain, burying everything in its wake. Suddenly everything went dark and the cabin began to fill with smoke as the stovepipe was ripped off by the tons of snow overhead. Malcolm quickly doused the fire by smashing two bottles of wine against the inside walls of the cast iron stove.

In the darkness he felt his way to the hutch where he had stashed his flashlight. He turned it on and could see there was still smoke coming into the room from the stove so he smashed two more bottles inside walls of the stove to end the smoke.

"FUCK!!" Malcolm cried out as he realized he was trapped under tons of snow with no means to escape. His luck had finally run out.

He pulled the blanket from the bed and went below to the wine cellar to escape the smoke that had filled the cabin. He sat on the floor with his flashlight and tried to calm himself, but began to tell himself that he was not going to survive this.

"I'm OK with this," he said aloud. "God damn it, I am not going to cry either. I am really OK with this." The tears ran down his face as he wondered how much air he had before he would suffocate.

He stood up and located a bottle of cognac on the shelf, opened it and said, "Here's to my sad, fucked up life." He held the bottle up and took a long swig. He sat back down on the floor and proceeded to drink from the bottle for a while before passing out.

He found himself walking back down the same snow-covered road, just as it was in his past dreams. As he got to the bend in the road where the car wreck usually was, it was no longer there. Instead, in its place was pristine snow. He stood there alone when a woman in a white gown approached him from behind. Her skin was snow white and her blond hair was closer to silver. The only vibrant color in her beautiful face was her brilliant red lips and beautiful blue eyes. She walked in the snow in ballet slippers but left no footprints.

"Malcolm, is that you?" she asked in gentle voice.

From behind, Malcolm heard his mother's voice and froze, frightened to turn around.

"Where's the car?" he asked.

"It's gone. It was cleaned up a long time ago," she reminded him.

"It was here the last time," Malcolm asserted.

She put her hand softly on his shoulder. His eyes filled with tears as he confirmed her presence by reaching up and touching her hand.

"It is time for you to move on. You don't need to visit this place anymore. We have all gone on. You need to go on as well."

Malcolm turned to see his mother, who was more beautiful than he had ever remembered.

She smiled proudly as she gently brushed the hair out of his eyes. "Look at you, Malcolm, you're all grown up now. And you made it to Paris all on your own."

"I never wanted to leave you and Dad. I wish . . ."

"No," she said compassionately, gently touching his lips to silence him. "You should never wish for the end of your life. Treasure each hour with all your heart and might . . . even in the most difficult of times."

"I'm in so much pain," Malcolm confessed, the tears continuing down his cheeks.

"I know. It hurts the most when you lose the things in your life that you love dearly. Your capacity to love is the cause of your pain. That is never a bad thing."

"I'm nineteen years old and I all ready feel like I'm seventy. For the last five years I've been consumed by this constant pain. I'm tired of this life. I'm sorry Mom, I can't do it anymore. Let me just lie down, go to sleep, and finally have it all be over."

"Would you want to be alive if Trechus were there to wake you in the morning?" she asked.

"Yes . . . yes, I would."

"Then you're not ready to end your life. All is not lost for you," she assured him lovingly. "There is someone here who wants to see you and he would be awfully upset with me if I didn't share my time with you."

Malcolm's hand was gently nudged by Chevalier's muzzle. He looked down to see him and dropped to his knees and hugged him.

"I never knew what happened to him or how he died," Malcolm said, looking up at his mother.

"Now you can remember him this way, as he was in life. He loves you so very much and is so thankful you loved him, and cared for him, when no one else would."

There was a flash of light, and Malcolm was left standing alone in the snow.

Malcolm awoke and struggled to his feet. The air was cold and thinning out as he was battling to breathe in enough oxygen. He slowly climbed the ladder out of the cellar to the cabin above. Using the flashlight, he found his backpack and took out a small pad and a pen. He sat at the table and wrote Trechus.

Dear Trechus,

I hope you're alive and find this note someday. I waited for you until my last hour. I would have given the world to have seen you one last time. I love you now and forever.

Malcolm

Malcolm took the pad, put it in the breast pocket of his shirt, and went over to the bed to lie down. He thought back to his first days with Trechus in Paris and tried to fill his mind with the details of his birthday with Trechus and Chevalier. These happy thoughts comforted him. He let himself drift off again and hoped his life would end while he slept.

As the next hour passed, his breathing became shallow and the flashlight dimmed as the batteries continued to drain. In the near darkness of the room, there emerged a faint purple glow in the windows as water began to drip through the edges of the door. The glow became more pronounced and provided minimal light to the room as the flow of water increased and flooded the main section of floor. The light went dark.

The door was pulled open and it burned from the outside as water from the melted snow rushed in, flooding the entire floor and pouring through the trap door into the cellar below. A figure appeared out of the darkness and entered the cabin.

CHAPTER XXXVII

The next afternoon Malcolm stirred from a deep sleep when he felt a sharp pain in his right arm. The pain repeated itself, causing him to waken. He opened his eyes to see the familiar sight of Chevalier's large head and big brown eyes. Chevalier pawed at his arm a third time, again scratching at his arm for his attention.

Malcolm quickly moved to sit up. Sun was streaming brightly though the windows as Malcolm sat up in the bed in the unfamiliar dark-colored bedroom. A fire roared in the fireplace next to the bed, warming the room. He looked at Chevalier in disbelief. He reached out and scratched him under his left ear just to make sure he was real. Finally convinced that this was not an apparition, he said to Chevalier squarely, "I keep telling you, if you keep waking me up like this we're not going to be friends."

Malcolm was hungry and his legs were weak but he still managed to get himself out of bed. He was naked and his feet were cold on the decorative parquet floor. He was eager to go to the window to determine where in the world he was now. The view of the frozen lake below was splendid in the morning sun. In the distance he could see a large brown bear crossing the frozen terrain below. He watched as another larger bear came around the corner of the house and turned to look at him through the window. Chevalier let out a fierce series of barks at the sight of the bear. The bear roared back at Chevalier and resumed his lazy walk down the hill towards the frozen lake.

"Welcome to Siberia," a deep familiar voice said behind him. Malcolm turned to see Valerian standing in the doorway. "You will note that Chevalier has not yet learned to get on with the bears."

"Valerian!" Malcolm exclaimed.

"I expect a large hug in exchange for your fortunate rescue last night."

Malcolm flung himself at Valerian, hugging him as hard as he could.

"Now back into bed with you. You're not well enough yet to be walking around naked."

"Where are we?" Malcolm asked.

"We are at one of my safe houses deep in Siberia. Far from where anyone will find us. We must now take precautions as the Black Dragons are certainly looking for us."

"Where are the others? Where is Trechus?" Malcolm asked.

"Trechus is sleeping. Come on, get back into bed and I will explain," Valerian said in a more somber tone.

"I don't like the sound of that," Malcolm said, as Valerian helped him back into the bed and adjusted the blankets around him.

"Are you comfortable? I will have Jean-Yves bring you some tea, or would you prefer some vodka?"

"I think it would be best if I started with some tea." Malcolm smiled.

Valerian pulled the red bell cord next to the bed.

"When I saw the results of the avalanche, frankly, I thought we had lost you," Valerian confessed.

"I can hardly believe I am still alive," Malcolm replied.

Valerian sat down on the edge of the bed with a serious look in his face. "I should start by telling you that you have returned to a very different world. The Black Dragons have launched a series of attacks across the major cities of western Europe. Almost a million people are dead and more continue to die each day. Anarchy is rapidly spreading across Europe. The financial markets have all collapsed and the governments are powerless in stopping the further outbreaks and ensuing riots. People are turning on each other as food and medicine have all but run out. Human society is in a state of near collapse. Entire countries are now quarantined and the world is in a state of panic."

Jean-Yves appeared at the door. He smiled for the first time that Malcolm had witnessed and bowed slightly, saying, "I am glad to see you're well, Malcolm."

"Thank you, Jean-Yves," Malcolm replied.

"Jean-Yves, let's start our friend here on some tea. Something dark and strong that will put hair on his chest."

"Oui, monsieur. I will take Chevalier so that I can feed him."

Jean-Yves exited the room with Chevalier who happily trotted behind him sensing a meal was at hand, leaving Malcolm alone again with Valerian.

Valerian continued, "The night you were attacked at the chateau, we were ambushed by the Black Dragons in Le Conquet. Luckily for me, I managed to escape. Rodin, Trechus, and Leonardo were not so lucky and were captured by the Black Dragons. I immediately returned to the chateau and found the bodies of Janos and the chefs in the hall. I searched the chateau and was relieved when it appeared everyone else had managed to escape. I left the chateau and flew along the main road until I spotted Jean-Yves' truck parked in a field several miles away.

Jean-Yves and Milos had found Chevalier and were suiting up in a nearby barn where Jean-Yves had hidden an impressive arsenal of weapons. Knowing you were safe with Long Ji, I used the remaining hours of darkness to try to track the Black Dragons and determine the whereabouts of Rodin, Trechus, and Leonardo. I flew back toward Le Conquet and then toward Paris in an attempt to pick up some scent of the dragons. With daylight approaching, I returned to the chateau but as I got close I picked up the scent of the Black Dragons and realized several of them had returned to the chateau with Trechus and Leonardo. Meeting back in the barn, Jean-Yves and I decided to wait until we had the cover of darkness to storm the chateau. Milos kept close surveillance over the chateau during the day. I had to keep my distance from the chateau and mind the wind direction as I did not want to risk having the

Black Dragons pick up my scent and lose the element of surprise. As the sun set, we received a frantic call on the radio from Milos. He told us there were dreadful screams coming from the chateau and he believed it was Leonardo.

Jean-Yves and I rushed to the chateau. When we arrived we knew we had to act immediately. Jean-Yves took down the first dragon with a near impossible shot as the dragon passed by a window inside the chateau. He shot him clean through the ear with an AW50 sniper rifle. The shot, of course, alerted the dragons inside and Leonardo's screaming stopped. We waited as I stood prepared to fight them on the front lawn. I called out to the dragons inside the chateau and began taunting them. Milos went around to the back and managed to climb undetected through a kitchen window and made it inside. The second dragon eagerly exited the house to challenge me on the lawn, his ego distracted him from the danger of his situation. Jean-Yves had a clear shot at the dragon and took him out.

Machine-gun fire erupted from inside the chateau and Milos was able to kill the third dragon before being disarmed and dragged outside by the remaining fourth dragon. As the dragon began to tear his left arm off his body, Milos dropped a live grenade on the ground with his free hand. The grenade went off and killed them both. My only solace is he died avenging his brother's death.

Jean-Yves and I entered the chateau and found Leonardo chained to a wall in the cellar. He was barely alive. The dragons had sadistically tortured him in the most brutal fashion. Most of Leonardo's human skin had been burned away by the dragons and he was in excruciating pain. You can't imagine the amount of fire needed to burn away a dragon's human skin in that manner. But thankfully, he is alive."

Valerian stopped and remained silent. It was clear that he did not want to continue the story.

"Valerian," Malcolm said, as the tears filled his eyes. "You need to tell me what they did to Trechus."

"We searched the chateau but did not immediately find him. Finally, after an hour of searching, Jean-Yves found Trechus in the kitchen's large freezer. By the time we got to him, he was already frozen."

Malcolm looked at Valerian. "So you're telling me he is not sleeping, but that he is dead?"

"No," Valerian said, standing up in defiance. "He is sleeping. I know he is sleeping."

Malcolm countered, "But you just said he was frozen alive."

"Siberian salamanders survive deep freezing only to revive in warm spring weather."

"Can Trechus survive in the same way?"

"There are legends that say it has happened."

"But it is possible he won't." Tears rolled down Malcolm's cheeks.

"Don't question me on this, it is not your place," Valerian warned with an uncharacteristically harsh tone.

"Where is he now?" Malcolm asked, trying to hold himself together.

"He is downstairs."

"Can I see him?"

Jean-Yves appeared at the door with a cup of tea and some biscuits on a tray.

"Here, drink your tea," Valerian instructed. "Jean-Yves will bring you clothes more appropriate for our winter climate. Suffice to say we are more masculine in our dress than you're used to on the streets of Paris."

CHAPTER XXXVIII

Jean-Yves entered the room soon after with a fresh set of clothes just as Malcolm was getting out of the bath. As he set the clothes on the bed for Malcolm he said, "Valerian likes to dress everyone when they are here and there is no use in protesting. He delights in dressing everyone as if they were performing in a Wagner opera at La Scala. A bit too costume for my taste. They will keep you warm as I am sure you realize, it is extremely cold here."

Malcolm was growing more comfortable with Jean-Yves tending to him, and he was thankful for the help as the clothes were decidedly Russian in style and reminiscent of a bygone era of different clothing with confusing layers that left Malcolm unsure of what to put on first. After Malcolm was dressed, Jean-Yves handed him a silver hairbrush and stood back watching Malcolm as he brushed his wet hair into place. Looking at him in the red tunic top layer he commented, "You do look quite handsome, monsieur."

Malcolm stood back from the mirror and studied his reflection. "I hardly recognize myself."

Suddenly, there was a loud cry of pain that emanated somewhere from the floor above.

"Excuse me, monsieur," Jean-Yves said as he hurried out of the room without explanation and ran up the wooden stairs to the floor above.

Unsure of the meaning of the noise, Malcolm was reminded of the uncertainty of his own situation. Malcolm sat on the edge of the bed and looked out the window at the barren white landscape and trying to fathom what his possible future might be. Chevalier got up from his resting spot in the corner of the room and walked over and rested his head on Malcolm's knee. There was another cry of pain from above, this time louder.

Valerian entered the room and, seeing the uncertainty in Malcolm's eyes, sought to console him. "Do not be sad. Be brave. It is certainly a better use of time. Now stand up for me and let me see how you look!"

Malcolm stood up for Valerian. "Now we have made a Russian out of you. Come, let us visit with Trechus."

Valerian led Malcolm through the small hallway of the Russian dacha down to the first floor. The house lacked the size and the opulence of Rodin's chateau but was full of interesting Russian objects that gave it a unique air of luxury. There were large portraits of all the great Russian Monarchs throughout the house and the tables were covered with personal photos of Tsar Nicholas II and his family. Valerian and the Nicholas appeared together in several of them indicating there had been some close personal relationship. The dacha's first floor was cold compared to the second floor. Valerian pulled back a heavy velvet curtain that covered a set of glass doors, and he led Malcolm into a dark room where Trechus' frozen body lay on a long table. Malcolm hesitated at the entrance to the room upon seeing the bluish corpse.

"It's all right," Valerian assured him in a soft tone. "He will be himself soon enough. The body should melt slowly and naturally so that when it thaws it will restore itself."

Malcolm approached Trechus and stared down at his face. Trechus' skin was a blueish white and his face looked pained in its frozen state. Malcolm lovingly touched his frozen cheek with his fingers. His cheek was ice cold and he did not feel familiar to him. It was the same feeling he had got when he had touched his mother's lifeless hand during her wake.

"He looks better today," Valerian said confidently, looking over Malcolm's shoulder. Yesterday he was almost all white. Today he is more blue. I think by tomorrow we will have him back."

"Can I stay with him for a while?" Malcolm asked.

"Of course. Just promise me you'll come and find me if he wakes."

Valerian left Malcolm alone with Trechus. Malcolm pulled up a chair from the corner and sat down next to the body. Valerian could be right. Certainly, he did not think Valerian would lie to him. There was no point.

A familiar voice from the doorway behind him said, "You need to know that he is not coming back."

Malcolm looked up to see Leonardo who was standing with one shoulder leaning against the doorway. In his other hand he held a cane. The hood of his cloak was pulled down so that Malcolm could barely make out his face in the dark shadow that the large hood cast across his face. What he could see of Leonardo's face was some black reptilian-looking skin with small patches of pale human skin with badly burned edges.

"Leonardo!" Malcolm leapt up and stepped toward him.

Leonardo held up his hand to keep him at bay as he said slowly, "I don't want you to touch me or even look at me. I just wanted to come down to tell you that Valerian has become sickened by his grief. He is out of his mind. Trechus is not some salamander that is going to come back to life."

Malcolm looked down at the body as he whispered, "It does seem somewhat impossible."

Jean-Yves appeared at the door behind Leonardo and chastised him. "Monsieur, you should not be out of bed."

"I am dying, Jean-Yves," Leonardo shouted in anger. "Trechus is dead and I am dying, and if I wish to spend my last couple of days on Earth walking around, then I only ask that you respect my wishes."

"Yes, monsieur! You have made your intentions clear."

Leonardo pushed Jean-Yves aside as he struggled with his cane to walk away.

"Monsieur, allow me to help you," Jean-Yves said, following behind him.

"Yes . . . you can help us both by gathering some wood and preparing to burn our bodies. For everyone's sake, stop pouring tea and pretending that everything is going to be fine. Snap out of the fantasy that Rodin is alive, that I will live, and that Trechus will rise from the dead." With that, Leonardo disappeared down the hallway.

The hope that Valerian had inspired in Malcolm quickly faded with Leonardo's words. Tears sprang to Malcolm's eyes as he realized the terrible suffering his friend, Leonardo, was enduring. He turned his attention back to Trechus who lay before him. All seemed lost now.

Jean-Yves returned to the room and handed his handkerchief to Malcolm who was looking down at Trechus.

"What do you think?" Malcolm asked.

"I cannot say if they will survive. Valerian believes they will both survive and this belief does give me hope. I am willing to accept that gift in my heart, even if my head wants to tell me otherwise."

"May I ask what your head tells you?" Malcolm asked quietly.

Jean-Yves started slowly. "I do believe that Rodin is still alive. Despite Leonardo's words, he himself is getting stronger each day and I believe he will recover over time." Looking down at Trechus' body, he paused.

Malcolm prompted him. "And Trechus?"

"I would rather not say, monsieur."

"I understand," Malcolm replied.

"Monsieur, if there is anything you need."

"I just need to be here, with him."

"I understand, monsieur. I should check on Leonardo." Jean-Yves turned and left the room.

Malcolm remained behind with Trechus, but he did not stay long. His head told him that Trechus was gone and his heart believed it too.

Before leaving, he kissed Trechus' frozen lips just as he had done with his mother and father years earlier, one last time.

DRAGONS WALK AMONG US
AND THE AUTHOR

To learn more about Jackson von Altek, the process of developing this story, and receive updates on the release of the second installment of the trilogy, *The Black Skies of Rome*, please go to www.dragonswalkamongus.com.

ACKNOWLEDGEMENTS

To transition from a storyteller to a novelist is not an easy task. Spoken words float out into the room and quickly dissipate, but the written word remains on the page indefinitely. As you can imagine, I was surrounded by a talented team of editors. As my line editor, Lucy skillfully polished my words and improved my work but always kept my voice on the page intact. Her knowledge of France and its customs was invaluable. My story editor, David, encouraged several character rewrites and constantly pushed me to do my best work in telling a quality story.

Every writer who is either partnered or married usually has an unpaid editor in their spouse. My partner Tim worked tirelessly reading every variation and has the claim of reading and editing the book eleven times before it was published. He continues to be my best friend and biggest supporter. This novel would not have been possible without him.

I would like to thank my friends, Frank, Jeff, Dennis, Fred, and Charles for reading the story and providing valuable and useful comments before the final edit.

My friends Pierre and Corrine took outstanding photos of the Eiffel Tower which allowed me to realize a book cover beyond my expectations. To my son, Jack, who worked hard to photograph our Great Pyrenees, Orleans, for the back cover on a very hot summer afternoon when the dog was less than cooperative.

Finally, I would like to thank everyone at Intelligentia for their continued support in publishing and promoting the novel and supporting the two novels in the trilogy to follow.